Echoes of Fire

(Book One in the Echoes Trilogy)
By Laurel McKinley

Laurel McKinley

Copyright 2013 by Laurel McKinley
ISBN: 978-0986069413

Emerald Dreams Publishing
Versailles, KY 40383
Author Photograph by Johnny Farris Photography
Cover design by Heather Plunkett

DEDICATION

This book is dedicated to the memory of my parents, Rick and Arlene McKinley, who sacrificed their lives to save mine, and is for my grandparents, Charles and Josephine McKinley, who sacrificed their lifestyle to become my parents. I also dedicate this to the memory of Carla Dills, librarian extraordinaire, who believed in this book before one word was ever written.

For my family – Amy, Drew, Calvin, Alex, Jared, and Karlie – I love you all.

CHAPTER ONE

I was cleaning the third floor bathroom – the one that the boys used – when the car pulled up. I heard it but didn't think too much about it since cars were always coming and going at the Franklin Group Home, and I was trying to hurry and finish. Kelly was supposed to be washing the window, but I knew she was watching the world go by. She squealed when she saw the car, but I still didn't think too much about it. Kelly was only twelve, and she squealed about everything. But when Kelly said it was a limo, I had to look for myself.

It was a long, shiny limousine with dark windows. I watched the driver – who was wearing a uniform with the hat and all – open the door for a man in a dark business suit and a woman who was wearing a crimson skirt suit. The man held an umbrella over the woman even though the sky was only partly overcast and it wasn't raining.

There was something spectacular about the woman. She was beautiful, but not in the usual way like a model or movie star. She had skin like porcelain, and her lips were as red as her obviously expensive suit. My first assumption was that she must have been one of those society women who donated money and held fundraisers so the Franklin Group Home could operate. Then she hesitated before walking up the steps of the porch.

The porch was a little rickety, and she wasn't the first to pause before stepping up onto it, but it wasn't worry that stopped her. She looked straight up at the window where Kelly and I were watching. Kelly ducked back with another of her squeals. I couldn't look away. There was something in the look that she gave me. Like she already knew who I was and hadn't yet decided if I was . . . I don't know. Good enough? Acceptable? Likeable? I wasn't sure what was being weighed in the balance, but, if it had to do with me, I knew I was likely to come up short. She stared for what seemed like an eternity but must have only been a moment before Mrs. Jenkins walked down and captured her attention. When they walked into the house, I sat down on the closed lid of the toilet.

Kelly was chattering on and on about all the things the lady could be here for, but I didn't respond. My heart was thundering in my chest, and I knew, although I didn't know how I knew, that she was here for me. I stood up and looked in the mirror to see if I could figure out what anyone would want from me. My reflection was even worse than usual. I was sweaty from cleaning. My face was flushed, giving it a splotchy appearance. My dark hair was piled into a sloppy bun on top of my head to keep it out of my way, but it was falling down in several places. My eyes seemed wider than usual and had that deer-in-the-headlights look. As bad as I looked, my clothes were even worse. I was wearing ratty sweat pants and a t-shirt that was two sizes too big. I smelled like bleach.

I cut off Kelly's ramblings. "If we quit now, no one will notice that we're only half done. You know, because of the guests downstairs."

She squealed and ran off down the hall. I heard her thumping down the backstairs, probably heading outside to tell some of the others what she'd seen.

I went down to the second floor bedroom that I was currently sharing with two other girls. I couldn't ignore whatever was pushing at me, but I didn't want to analyze it too closely. The luck that I had never known to work in my favor was finally with me because the room was empty. I pulled out my tiny suitcase from under the bottom bunk where I'd placed it when I'd arrived at the group home almost six months before. I unlocked it with the key I always wore around my neck. I pulled my notebooks out of my backpack and put them into the suitcase along with my battered but treasured books – *The Lion, the Witch, and the Wardrobe*, *The Hobbit*, and an old copy of *Grimm's Fairy Tales*. Not the sanitized versions where everybody lives happily ever after, but the darker, scarier ones where people die. I tucked them in with my favorite blue jeans, two t-shirts, my tennis shoes, pajamas, and underwear. I closed and locked the suitcase and pushed it back under the bed. I hoped I had enough time for a quick shower.

Ten minutes later, I was out of the shower with my teeth brushed and my hair combed but still wet. I gathered all the toiletries that I could call mine and carried them back to the bedroom with me. Unfortunately, my luck had run out. Gretchen was in the room. She saw what I was carrying.

Her voice was as biting as her glare. "Going somewhere, Bitsy?"

I ignored her use of the nickname she'd given me when she arrived at Franklin six weeks ago. I dropped the toiletries on my bed long enough to take my school books out of my backpack. The toiletries went into the backpack while Gretchen kept talking.

"Kelly told us about the limo. Some of the guys went around front to talk to the driver. I think they are hoping for a ride around the block. As if anyone would want them in their car. Maddy and LaShae went to the kitchen to try to hear what Mrs. Jenkins and her guests are saying. Aren't you curious, Bitsy? Or do you think you already know? Do you really think you're leaving here in that limo?"

I refused to even look at her. I went to the closet to find my only skirt, black cotton that came to my knee, and the yellow sweater set that had been my early birthday and farewell gift from my last foster family only a few months before. I put on the sleeveless part and put the cardigan beside my backpack. I was still on my knees, searching for my second flat, black dress shoe when Mrs. Jenkins knocked on the door. Gretchen looked up expectantly.

"Elisabeth, dear, I need you to come down to the office, please." I found the missing shoe and stood up. Mrs. Jenkins seemed grateful, if surprised, to see me dressed up for once.

"I'll be right behind you." I smiled at her. She headed back down the stairs, and I set my suitcase on the bed with the backpack.

Gretchen hissed at me. "They aren't going to take you. Why would they want you? You're nothing special, and I'm much prettier."

I kept ignoring her, but she was right. There wasn't any rational reason to believe I was going anywhere. There were other girls who were smarter and prettier than I was, with less legal trouble. One day I'd overheard my case worker talking to Mrs. Jenkins about the reason I was never adopted as a toddler or little girl. Somebody kept filing injunctions with the court regarding my orphan status, but every time the documents were backtracked, they only found missing files and more questions. Everyone believed I would stay at the group home until I turned eighteen and graduated high school.

It didn't matter. I picked up the sweater and went downstairs. I tried to wrap it around my shoulders in a casual way, but I couldn't get it to lay right. I settled for just carrying it.

I paused outside the living room-turned-office to take a breath and gather my courage. I felt sure I was leaving, but what if I was wrong? How would I ever be able to stand Gretchen's endless teasing?

While I was vacillating, I heard the lady say my name. Only my first name, but I knew she was talking to me, and there was something commanding, yet gentle in her voice. I didn't think; I just stepped inside.

She looked at me with the same searching intensity I had felt from the window, but this close I could see the brilliant green of her eyes. I waited and let her take a look at me without flinching from her piercing stare, and then, suddenly, she smiled. "Are you ready to leave, Elisabeth?"

I never took my eyes off her. "Yes, ma'am."

Mrs. Jenkins stood to protest. "She can't go now. We need to pack her things, and the other children will want to say good-bye."

I was afraid that the lady would change her mind if I didn't leave with her right away, but before I could say anything, she spoke again.

"Geoffrey, please go collect Elisabeth's things from the bedroom on the second floor. Her bags are sitting on the bed. We'll head out to the car."

The man in the dark suit snapped his briefcase shut and stood. He nodded to the lady as he stepped past her chair and walked off in the direction of the bedrooms.

Mrs. Jenkins dropped into her chair, still sputtering. "Ms. Mallory, I really must protest."

The lady stood and looked directly at Mrs. Jenkins. She spoke quietly but with complete assurance, as if she was used to having people do whatever she said. "There is nothing to protest. Geoffrey has given you all the necessary documentation. I am Elisabeth's guardian, and she will be leaving with me now."

She turned toward me. I had been leaning against the door frame but stood up straight when she looked at me. I realized how tall she was, close to six feet in her high heels at my best guess. She walked out past me, and before I turned to follow, I had one last look at Mrs. Jenkins. She was still sitting at her desk, her mouth hanging open, but her eyes had a glazed look to them.

Geoffrey was walking back down the stairs. The briefcase in one hand, so well-cared for and obviously expensive, was very different from my beat-up suitcase and tattered backpack in his other hand. The three of us were just about to step out of the front door when I realized that I had forgotten something.

"Just a minute!" I called out as I ran up the stairs to the nursery room that was blessedly empty most of the time. Sitting in the rocking chair was a small teddy bear with some of his butterscotch colored fur matted in clumps and his white satin ribbon faded and stained to a dingy yellow. He was sitting on top of a pale yellow baby blanket. I grabbed them both and ran back down the stairs, half afraid the lady would be gone. She was waiting patiently at the door, although Geoffrey had already taken my other things out. Her gaze settled on the bear and blanket, and for the first time I saw something other than her perfect sophistication. I thought she was horrified by the dirty bear and torn blanket, but then I realized her expression was caused by something else entirely. She recognized them.

Before I had a chance to ask her, she whisked me out the door and into the limousine. I had never ridden in one before and was distracted by the interior. Geoffrey did not sit in the back like he had on the drive to the group home, but sat up front with the driver. The privacy barrier was raised as soon as the engine started. I stared at all the controls for the BluRay player, iPod, and some game systems that I didn't recognize. I wondered idly if all these electronics were normal for limos.

The lady turned those brilliant green eyes on me again and spoke. "I know you have more questions than you have ever imagined, but I have a few of my own first if you don't mind, Elisabeth." She tilted her head to one side. "Do you prefer to be called Elisabeth?"

I nodded. "I never minded when a little kid couldn't pronounce my name, but I like Elisabeth better than any shorter forms."

She smiled. "I've never liked anyone to give me nicknames either." Something in her eyes changed. The emerald chips became softer, slightly unfocused. "With one exception." The softness disappeared so quickly I thought I might have imagined it. "Are you hungry?"

I shook my head.

"You must be thirsty then. Have a soda or a bottle of water." She pointed to the bar, and I took a bottled water to be polite. As I sipped it, we drove out of Franklin toward the interstate.

We sat in silence for a moment before she asked her next question. "Why did you have your things packed?"

I almost choked on my water. I swallowed hard and looked down at my lap. "It just seemed like something I should do. I just sort of knew." I was desperately hoping she wouldn't ask me to explain it any further because I couldn't. I didn't understand it myself.

When she spoke again it was with that same gentle, yet commanding tone she had used at the group home. "Look at me, Elisabeth."

I looked up reluctantly. Her bright eyes seemed mesmerizing, and suddenly I didn't want to look away.

"Never be ashamed to look someone in the eye, especially when you are being honest. I was hoping that you would know it was time to leave."

My eyes widened at her words, but before I had a chance to form a question, she was moving to a new topic.

"Do you know how you came to live at that . . . home?"

I shook my head as I answered. "My parents were killed in some kind of accident when I was a baby, but no one really ever said. I've been with at least ten foster families, but no one is ever allowed to keep me. Are you really my guardian? What should I call you?"

She laughed. It was a sound as elegant and refined as her appearance. I felt small and grubby.

"I thought perhaps you already knew the answers – the way you knew you would leave with me. My name is Julian Mallory, as I believe you heard Mrs. Jenkins say, but if you'd like you may call me Jules."

"But you don't like nicknames." I blurted it out before I could stop myself.

"My very best friend called me Jules." The softness returned to her eyes, and this time I knew I wasn't imagining things. "I think he might have liked it if his daughter carried on the tradition."

It was like lightning hitting the top of my head, racing through my body to my toes and then back up again. Every nerve ending twitched with anticipation. The amazing lady knew my father. She called him her best friend.

I tried to ask a dozen questions at once, but I was tongue-tangled and my mouth went dry. The only sound that I managed to get out sounded more like one of Kelly's squeals than a word. "How?"

Julian smiled, but this time I saw the tiny lines of sorrow that pulled at the corners of her mouth, tightening her lips so that the smile could never be more than an echo of what it once must have been.

"I knew your father from practically the moment we were born. His mother died in childbirth, and my mother became his surrogate. Your grandfather was . . . ." She paused, searching for words. I waited trying to be still so I wouldn't distract her from her memories.

"I remember him as a hard man, but all of the stories say he changed when his beloved wife died. Your father and I were best friends. We spent all our time together until we left boarding school for our separate colleges. Your grandfather had died by then, but your father refused to take on the . . . responsibilities of the . . . family business . . . until he had a chance to go to college and see the world. He met your mother on the Christmas break before his final semester."

Her voice grew softer. "Everyone we knew assumed we would get married, but I never loved your father like that, and he never loved me as more than a sister. He fell in love with your mother instantly. I don't know what kind of family your mother had, but when your parents eloped within two weeks of meeting, her family disowned her. As far as I know, she never had any contact with them again.

"I visited their off-campus apartment on my own spring break. I think your mother must have already been pregnant with you although she may not have known it." The wistful smile faded, and her voice gained a hard edge.

"I don't know everything that happened after that because I left as soon as I graduated. I was traveling in some remote sections of Asia. My mail was held for me in predetermined stops, but sometimes it was months old before I received it. I was in Ulaanbaatar when I heard about your birth and that was five months after it happened. When I reached Kathmandu, I was told your parents were dead. I rushed home, but it was already seven months from the day they died and you had gone missing."

I had tears in my eyes. I had just learned more about who I was and where I came from than I had ever known. But it was also information overload. The boarding schools and exotic trips, not to mention Julian's clothes and the limousine, all spoke of a level of wealth Julian was very casual about.

And there was something in her story that was . . . off. I couldn't put my finger on what it was, and I didn't think she was lying, but she definitely wasn't telling me everything.

"How did they die?" I hadn't meant to ask that question, but it came out of my mouth like a geyser erupting from deep within the earth.

"The three of you were traveling on a river boat, some kind of Mark Twain anniversary special steamboat. There was an accident, an explosion in part of the steam engine, and the boat sank. I don't know all the details of how you were rescued, but I am very grateful to have found you."

Her words led straight to my next question. "Why did it take so long to find me?"

She frowned. "I told you that your grandmother died giving birth to your father, and your grandfather died while your father was still a teenager."

I nodded without understanding.

"Your father had no siblings or other close relatives except his stepmother and her three children. There was some difficulty in contacting them initially, and, as I said, I was unreachable. You were put into emergency protective services. Later, there was a battle over who was your legal guardian. Your father's will had disappeared and the . . . family business was in . . . disarray. I had to fight legal battles each step of the way to obtain your medical records and your placement information. Someone gave the family documentation stating that you had died of injuries sustained in the river boat crash, but that was eventually shown to be some bureaucratic nonsense trying to cover up the fact that they had lost you. I hired Geoffrey to find you, and now, at last, you are found."

Dozens of questions flooded my brain, but before I could ask even one, the car stopped. I looked around stunned and saw that we were parked at the airport. I thought Franklin was much farther from the airport, but it didn't seem like we had been driving that long. The image of the limo driver traveling at excessive speeds floated through my mind, but I was too overwhelmed by everything Julian had told me to care.

When Geoffrey – I wondered if that was his first or last name – opened the door to help us out, I saw we were not in the commercial section of the airport. While the driver moved my worn bags onto a private jet, Geoffrey retrieved his briefcase. I followed him and Julian onboard the jet. I was too nervous to talk. I'd never flown anywhere before. Geoffrey made sure I was strapped in properly before getting to his own seat.

Julian pressed a button beside her chair. A voice came over the intercom.

"Yes, ma'am?"

"You may take off."

"Yes, ma'am," the voice repeated. Within minutes we were airborne.

I had to swallow several times to get my ears to pop and adjust to the cabin pressure, but it was an amazing feeling.

"Jules?"

Julian looked at me and smiled, probably at my obvious pleasure, but she wasn't laughing at me. "Yes, Elisabeth?"

"Can you tell me where we're going?"

She did laugh at that. "I'm so sorry. We are going to my apartment in Paris for a day or two. After we let Geoffrey out in New York, of course."

"Paris, France?" I squealed, sounding more like Kelly than I ever had before.

"Yes, Paris, France. I would like to take you to Milan to shop, but there isn't time. And you won't need much right now. I've enrolled you in the boarding school your father and I attended. You'll be wearing a uniform most of the time. Classes have just begun, but I'm certain you'll catch up quickly."

"I'm not staying with you?" I wished my voice hadn't sounded so little-girlish.

She shook her head. "Your father's step-family is still fighting his will which was finally found. He left everything to you and named me as your sole guardian. It's been very hard to search for you while trying to get control of your . . . family's resources and ensure you had an inheritance to return to."

"What does that have to do with sending me to boarding school?" The only picture I could conjure up in my in my mind was Harry Potter's Hogwarts.

"That school is the safest place for you. Your father and I had wonderful times there, and I think you'll like it. You are your father's daughter."

"Do I . . . ." I was almost afraid to ask, but Julian seemed to like talking about him. "Do I look much like my father?"

She sat back and looked me over thoroughly. "Not overly. You have your mother's lighter brown hair and her bone structure. Perhaps you have something of his coloring in your complexion and in your eyes, but . . . ." She broke off and shook her head gracefully. "Your father had a presence about him that was different from anyone else I've ever known. There is something about you that reminds me of him. In time you may have that same presence. But don't worry. I don't want you to be your father. I can see quite a bit of your mother in you as well, and she was a lovely young woman."

There were too many emotions swirling around inside me to be able to stop and sort them all out. My mind was jumping from one thought to the next without any discernable pattern to trace. I suddenly remembered a question I'd had before boarding the jet.

"Why did my father make you my guardian, and why didn't anyone else know about it?"

Julian nodded, her bright eyes approving. "Your parents asked me to be your godmother, in a letter of course. We were going to do a big christening when I got back. Your father was, well, estranged is the polite, if overly mild term, from his step-family. He had no reason to believe he would die so young and, therefore, no reason to announce his choice to them. They caused enough trouble as it was."

"I don't understand. Why did it take so many years to find me?"

"Even after gaining court orders to see your paperwork . . . To be honest, we're still investigating to find out how it happened, but you were . . ." For the first time Julian seemed to be at a real loss for words. She looked at Geoffrey who immediately spoke up.

His voice was as bland as his unemotional face. "I'm afraid that in the turmoil after your parents' deaths you were mislabeled."

"Mislabeled?" It sounded like what happened to books in the library or items on the grocery store shelves, not infants. "How does a baby get mislabeled?"

Julian's voice was hard, harder than I'd suspected it could sound. "I don't know, but when I do find out someone will pay dearly."

I was afraid to ask anything else, but I had to know. "What exactly does it mean that I was mislabeled?"

"Your name is not Elisabeth Sawyer."

Julian's voice was gentle again, but it didn't matter. It was like having my face ripped off. I didn't know who I was.

"Please don't panic. It's not as bad as you think. You are Elisabeth. That was always your name. Look." She pulled an old photograph out of the briefcase next to her. It was creased and worn, and the blue ink on the back was fading.

It was a baby laughing at whoever took the picture. The horrible thought that Julian was wrong squeezed my heart. I was nobody special. It was all a terrible mistake.

Then I looked closer and saw the yellow blanket the baby was sitting on and the brand new teddy bear at the edge of the photograph. I looked up at Julian who was smiling at me. She motioned for me to look at the back. I turned the picture over slowly and saw the faded script. It read "Elisabeth Julian, eight months" in large loops.

"They named me after you?" I asked.

"Me and your grandmother, your father's mother who died. Your last name is not Sawyer; it is Sinclair. It caused so much trouble, but, after the accident, there was a baby girl, Elisabeth Sawyer, who was apparently mixed up with you in the hospital."

"How did you know she was the wrong one?" I wondered about this other Elisabeth who had my name. Did they find her and take her away from a foster family only to dump her again when they found out she was the wrong one? Would I be dumped somewhere?

Julian sighed. "The other child was killed in a car accident when she was about two. I thought at first it was you. I couldn't make myself believe you were gone so, as your legal guardian, I insisted on a DNA comparison. That's when I realized you were, as Geoffrey put it, mislabeled."

"Will you need a DNA sample now? To prove who I am?" I wondered if it would hurt, but I was pretty sure they could do it from just a swab on the inside of my cheek.

"Unnecessary. I knew you the moment I saw you looking through the window, but Geoffrey knew before he brought me here."

Geoffrey spoke again when Julian looked at him. "I was able to obtain a sample covertly. There was no reason to upset any more lives if you were another wrong girl."

"I believe he used a hair sample combined with your medical records. They had your blood type and other genetic information listed with the agency. I have all that paperwork now." Julian pointed at the bear on the seat next to me. "Of course, none of the others had that. I wasn't sure you'd still have it."

"I've had my blanket and Ju-ju for as long as I can remember." I said the words automatically, then looked at the picture again and smiled sheepishly.

"Ju-ju?"

"That's her name. That's all I've ever called her."

"Maybe because I sent them to your parents before you were born. I ordered them from a store in New York after I found out they were expecting a child; I was already in Asia."

"I always thought of them as my only connection to my parents." It was strange because that wasn't true. I had another secret treasure that had been in my possession my entire life, but the wooden box didn't seem as personal. It wasn't something to snuggle up with or hide under when I was crying. Not like a bear or a blanket.

Julian seemed to understand my need for quiet, for time to think. We sat in comfortable silence until the plane landed in New York. I had so many odd questions. How did one baby get traded with another? What were the odds of two baby girls both named Elisabeth, being orphaned and then switched? It seemed pretty astronomical, but then I've never been any good at math, so calculating odds is outside my skill set.

In New York, Geoffrey left the plane, and it was refueled before our trans-Atlantic flight. While we waited, food was brought on board from Julian's favorite restaurant in the city. We were served by a waiter. The food was delicious, and I didn't have to help with any dishes or clean-up or anything.

I still had about a billion or so questions, but as we flew we headed away from the sun, and Julian darkened the lights in the cabin. She leaned back in her chair so I did the same and fell asleep far sooner than I would have believed was possible. The last thing I remembered in my fuzzy half-consciousness was Julian putting the old yellow baby blanket over my legs and her hand hovering above my cheek as if she wanted to touch me but was afraid to. That uncertainty was completely at odds with her confidence and elegant sophistication.

CHAPTER TWO

I was completely disoriented when I woke up. For a moment I thought I'd fallen asleep in one of the chairs in the group home. Then I saw Julian watching me.

"I was about to wake you. We've started our final approach into Paris, and I thought you might want to see it from the air."

I moved to look out the window closest to me and caught the dazzling view of Paris in the early morning sun. I checked my watch and was surprised to see that I had slept for most of the over seven-hour flight. "What time is it? My watch is still on Eastern Daylight Time."

Julian smiled. "It's almost eight a.m. here in Paris. What do you think of the city of lights?"

"It looks amazing. I can't believe you actually live here."

I could've watched out the window all day but suddenly there wasn't any more time. Julian made sure I was strapped in for the landing. My ears popped just like they did during the takeoff and landing when we left the States. Left the States. The phrase made me sound like a world traveler, or maybe it just made me sound like a poser. It was all so unreal to me.

Julian understood in that uncanny way she had of knowing what was going through my mind. "I thought we could pick up some croissants and coffee before we go to my apartment and talk."

I nodded my agreement and then realized what she had said. "I don't drink coffee."

She laughed at herself. "I'm just not used to having a fifteen year old around."

"I'm sixteen, Jules." My birthday had been a dismal affair not long after I'd arrived at the group home, but I remembered it clearly.

Julian shook her head and frowned. "No, you're still fifteen. Your birthday isn't until right before Christmas – December twentieth."

"My birthday was in June. I turned sixteen in June." A new wave of panic hit me as I realized I might not be the right Elisabeth even yet, in spite of the DNA tests.

Julian's voice was kind but held no room for argument. "Elisabeth Sawyer's birthday was in June. Your birthday, Elisabeth Sinclair's birthday, is in December."

I felt the blood rush out of my face, and my head seemed to swim. I leaned back in my chair as this new information filtered into my new identity. Wasn't there anything true about what I knew about myself? How could I be six months younger than I thought I was? I was still only fifteen! Did God hate me?

Julian unbuckled us both after the jet landed. "Get your things, Elisabeth." I slung my backpack over my shoulders and picked up my suitcase with one hand while the other clutched my bear and blanket. Suddenly, in a strange country with a stranger while holding my teddy bear and baby blanket, I felt much younger than fifteen. Julian smiled at me, reassuring me, and I followed her off the jet and into the cab.

I didn't see much of the city. Julian spoke in fluent French to the driver. I figured she had changed her mind about the coffee and croissant when we arrived at a large building. I thought it was a hotel. Julian spoke briefly to the uniformed doorman as we went in. She used a keycard to get the elevator to work, and again to open the door to her apartment on the top floor.

I stepped inside of the most beautiful room I'd ever seen. It was elegant and graceful like Julian. I was sure I was going to break something. For once Julian didn't seem to notice my discomfort. She was flipping through a small stack of letters and papers that had been on a table near the door. I stood waiting.

Julian finally turned and shook her head. "I've forgotten that this is new to you. I've spent so many days imagining you here, and your father was always so relaxed in my presence. Let me show you to your bedroom, and you can shower if you'd like."

I followed Julian to a storybook bedroom. It was pink, purple, and yellow with a large canopy bed in the center. There was a glass case filled with porcelain dolls and, best of all, a bookcase that stretched all the way to the ceiling filled with books. "This is for me?"

Julian smiled. "I bought a new doll for you on your birthday each year and kept them in the display case. The books are mixed. Some I bought new for you, some were mine, and a few were your father's. There's a bathrobe hanging in the closet and your bathroom is through that door." She pointed to the far side of the room as I gasped.

"I've never even had a bedroom to myself, let alone a bathroom too!"

"Don't get too used to it," Julian cautioned. "You'll be sharing again at the Academy soon enough. But this will always be here waiting for you."

"Do you live here all the time?" I still knew so little about my new guardian.

"Most of the time. It has been my refuge." Her voice trailed away, but then she shook herself out of whatever it was, and spoke again. "As long as you are at Saint Clare Academy, I'll live in the States so I can be close to you. Now go shower while I make a few phone calls."

I smiled at her and watched as she walked out of the room, closing the door behind her. I put my blanket and bear on the bed and set my suitcase on top of the dresser. I took my backpack with me into the bathroom. I shouldn't have bothered.

The vanity was lined with shampoos and body wash and lotions of all fragrances. I dumped everything I'd brought into the trash. I went back into the bedroom to get the robe. The closet was empty except for the selection of bathrobes in various sizes and colors. I found a dark red robe that was almost the same shade as Julian's suit. When I started the shower, I turned up the water as hot as I could bear to have it and let the steam fill the bathroom. I stayed in long enough to try three different shampoos and two kinds of body wash.

When I finished my shower and went back to the bedroom, Julian was knocking on the door. She walked into the room with a small woman following her.

"Elisabeth, I've called in a wonderful stylist to fit your clothes and do your hair. Go back into the bathroom with Anelle and let her cut your hair before it dries."

I obeyed Julian without thinking. Just over an hour later I was wearing a new school uniform and staring at a reflection I could barely recognize as myself. From the amount of hair that had landed on the bathroom floor I was expecting to see a short cut, but the length was only an inch or so shorter. Whatever Anelle had done to it, she had made it feel light and soft. The way she had styled it even changed the way my face looked. I was more grown up; my chubby baby cheeks were gone. I had cheekbones, and my eyes were huge and dark. Julian had taken Anelle out of the apartment and walked back while I was focused on the mirror.

"What do you think?"

I smiled at her. "I look so different, but somehow it's still me."

"That's what a good makeover does. It's still you, but enhanced. Come with me. You must be starving by now."

We went into the lovely dining area that was open to both the living room and the kitchen. Food was waiting.

"I wasn't sure what you would like so I ordered a variety," Julian explained. We ate quickly and quietly. I was awed by the way Julian ordered out for food and clothes and hairstylists. After we finished I carried the plates to the sink before sitting with Julian on her sofa.

"Thank you for being so patient with me, Elisabeth. I know you have many more questions about everything, and I'll try to answer as much as I can, but there are some things that I just can't tell you right away."

"Why? What can't you tell me?" I knew I was asking exactly what she had just said she couldn't say, but she seemed to understand that I wasn't trying to be difficult.

"Elisabeth, your father's family was very . . . powerful."

"You mean like the Kennedy family in politics?" I had just read a library book about the assassinations of John and

Robert Kennedy last month. I thought the librarian who recommended it may have been a conspiracy theory nut.

Julian smiled. "I suppose you might draw a parallel, but the family business is a little more complicated than that."

I had the sudden image of Al Capone flash in front of my eyes. Wealthy and powerful – could I be a mobster's daughter?

Again Julian seemed to know what I was thinking; I suddenly wondered if I was so easy to read. Did everyone know what I was thinking by the expressions on my face?

She laughed a little. "It's nothing illegal, but anytime there is that much money and power concentrated in one place it becomes dangerous. Your father knew how dangerous it could be but chose not to return immediately after graduation." Her brilliant green eyes were no longer smiling but seemed to look into the past, before I was born. "I suppose he was waiting until after you were born to take your mother back to his step-family. I wish I'd been closer. Since I was in Asia I'm not entirely positive of your father's rationales. It's become very difficult to ascertain all of his movements, but it seems he decided to travel with you and your mother before returning home. You were all three on a riverboat traveling down the Mississippi River."

My eyes widened. "The Mark Twain thing?"

Julian smiled again. "A nostalgia trip celebrating some kind of anniversary of something that your father found fascinating. He was always so eager to explore everything."

"And there was a boat accident?" I had always heard the word accident and assumed it meant car crash, but no one had really specified.

Julian's face was hard. "There was a malfunction with the steam engine that caused an explosion. Several people were thrown clear of the boat only to drown. Your parents were not the only casualties that night."

Then I realized the most obvious question that I hadn't asked. "If I'm not Elisabeth Sawyer, then my parents weren't Mike and Amanda Sawyer."

"My God, Elisabeth! I keep forgetting how much you don't know. Your mother's name was Carolyn, but your father always called her Carrie. I don't know what her maiden name was. She seemed to shut out her past as if she only began to live when she met and married your father."

I sat taking it in. Carolyn. Carrie. Mom. "You said she had dark hair like me?"

Julian smiled. "She was beautiful. She had dark hair that sparkled in the sunlight with red and gold. She was alive in the most vibrant sense, but when she was with your father – and they were rarely apart – there was a love in her that could have overshadowed the sun. I never saw her after you were born, but, later when I was remembering the week I spent with them, I think she may have guessed she was pregnant. I saw her twice, when she thought no one was looking, with her hand across her stomach and a ghost of a smile with an amazed look in her eyes. It was almost as if her only life's purpose was to love your father and their child. She would have loved you more with every day of her life. No matter what else happens in your life, Elisabeth, always remember that your mother loved you and wanted you and-"

Julian broke off suddenly and looked at me sharply.

"Please, Jules. Whatever you know, tell me."

Julian nodded slowly. "I'm not entirely sure you should know this, because you might be foolish enough to blame yourself when there is no blame. As your guardian I've had access to all the medical records and police reports. There is nothing definitive, but from the circumstantial evidence, it appears that your mother did not die in the first explosion. She was in the room with you and managed to get you both out. From what I understand you and your bear were wrapped in the blanket that I sent. The boat was on fire, and there was heavy smoke and lots of confusion, but somehow your mother found her way to one of the lifeboats that were more for show than use. She got it loose and put you in it, along with another woman and her child, and sent you to safety."

"She could have saved herself too?" I tried to imagine her putting her baby into a boat with another woman and staying behind to die.

"I don't think she meant to leave you. I think that once she knew you were safely off the boat she tried to find your father. He had not been in the cabin from what the other woman told the police at the scene."

"Did you talk to the other woman yourself? I mean, later, when you got back from Asia?" I couldn't imagine Julian simply reading a report if she could get information from the woman herself.

Julian shook her head again. "Apparently the woman had suffered some internal injuries that were not immediately evident to the police on the scene. When they went back to follow up with her, she had died at the hospital from internal bleeding. It was the same everywhere. Every witness who had come into immediate contact with either of your parents or you seemed to die. It was the most frustrating part of my search for you. No one seemed to know what had happened to the baby."

Her frustration was so palpable that I reached out my hand to touch her icy one. "You found me, Jules."

She seemed startled for a moment and looked at our hands touching. When she spoke again, she had tears in her eyes. "You are so like your father." She took a moment to gather herself before she finally began to tell me about him. "I was born forty-seven hours after the birth of Nicholas Augustin Merrick Sinclair. We grew up in the same . . . neighborhood, I guess would be the best way to describe it, but it was closer. Maybe more like a commune in that we all were a real community and, as children, just walked right into anyone's home. Nicholas and I were taught together and played together and fought together. We were the best of friends in every sense. When he left to go to college, I also left for my own college an hour away from his. It was the first time we had ever been so far apart. The first three summers, neither of us wanted to go home, so we spent them traveling together. We came here to Europe and spent the whole first summer exploring Paris and London and Rome. It was magical. The second summer we spent island hopping in the south Pacific."

Julian laughed as some memory popped into her head, and I waited as quietly as I could in case my presence would distract her from it. "Nicholas got it in his head to declare himself king of this little island. It was really more of a rock out in the water; there wouldn't have been room for three houses to be built on it. He got several natives from the nearby islands to take him over in their boats and they erected a pavilion of sorts from bamboo. I have no idea where he found the long pieces of silk they used to make the covering, but they were the deepest purple. The islanders wrapped bright red and yellow flowers around with the cloth. It was beautiful. We had a feast, and then the islanders' holy man crowned Nicholas with a crown made of vines with gorgeous red blossoms as big as my fist and delicate white ones that looked like tiny stars. There he was – King Nicholas. Somehow, no matter how improbable or ridiculous the whole thing seemed, I never doubted that if Nicholas wanted to be king of that rock, he would find a way to make it happen. That was just Nicholas."

She stopped talking and looked at me, almost surprised she wasn't alone.

"You really loved him." I wasn't asking. There was no doubt that he had loved her too since he had made her my godmother and guardian.

"He was an easy person to love. He was good and generous and funny. He liked to make his own adventures and experience new things. He was always learning, sometimes from books, but also from the people around him. He was my best friend, and when he married Carolyn, it was like he had found the piece of himself he'd never even known was missing. They were perfect together."

"What about his step-family? If his mother died when he was born, how long was it until his father remarried?"

Julian grimaced slightly. "In spite of how much he still mourned his wife, he remarried when Nicholas and I were about five. The new Madam Sinclair had been widowed herself not long before and had three children of her own. They were from outside of our community, and I think Nicholas's father thought the children would be good companions for Nicholas, but it didn't quite work out that way. Two of them were older, but the youngest, a boy, was our age. Maybe he was jealous of what Nicholas stood to inherit or maybe it was just his nature, but he was not our friend. Nicholas's father died when we were seventeen. The family business was left entirely to Nicholas, but his step-mother became the . . . trustee. Nicholas decided to leave to attend college, and I left as well. After Nicholas married your mother – during the week I visited them – I asked him what he planned to do after graduation. He told me he had told Carolyn all about the family business and that, with her by his side, he hoped he could make a difference in the world. He was very hesitant to go back to that life until he knew how his step-mother would react. There was no question that Nicholas had every legal right regarding how things were done, even to the house his step-family still lived in, but there were other provisions made for them. Nicholas didn't want to take your mother back there with them still in the house. I believe her pregnancy and your birth gave him the excuses he wanted to delay his return."

I thought about everything Julian had said for a while before I asked my next question. "Does his – or, I guess, my – step-family still live in the house? Do they still control the business?"

"I told you that I've had to fight for control of the business. There were legal arguments that since your father had never established his own possession of the business that my guardianship of you was still subject to his father's arrangements and Nicholas's step-mother should retain her role as trustee. But I have gained the upper hand, at last, and, when you are presented as your father's daughter and heir, then everything will be settled."

I felt the panic hit. "When I'm presented?"

Julian saw the fear in my eyes. "Don't worry, Elisabeth. I don't plan to present you until you've had at least one year of school. If at all possible, I'll wait until you're eighteen. I will not let circumstances push you too quickly."

I relaxed a little. Then I realized she had not answered my other question. "Do they still live in the house?"

Julian had that same sad, wistful look. "They do. I've brought out some of the more personal things that belonged to Nicholas, but the truth is the whole place was his and should be yours. When I think of where you should have been raised and that – that hole . . ." She broke off, unable to continue.

"It wasn't that bad, Jules. Besides, how can you miss things that you've never known?" I was trying to make her feel better, but it was also the truth.

"Elisabeth, you are a fifteen year old girl. I know that living in foster care has exposed you to things your parents would never have wanted you to know, but the worst part is how unnecessary it all has been."

I shook my head. "I won't pretend it hasn't been hard at times. But I've seen a lot of kids who had it worse than I did. Kids whose mothers were drug addicts and wouldn't take care of them but refused to give up their rights so the kids could be placed in a permanent home. At least I knew that my parents hadn't abandoned me."

Julian sat listening to me, and I was afraid something I'd said had offended her. When she did speak, her voice was shaky. "You sound so much like your father. Nicholas always believed he could change the world. He definitely changed mine, and here you are changing it again. Thank you for reminding me that there are others with more problems than we have. I'm sure you'll carry that same compassion with you to the Academy."

"What's it like? You said you and my father both were students there." I couldn't imagine it.

Julian relaxed. "It's beautiful. It's very private and secluded. There are mountains to the east and a lake to the west.

The lake is actually the western boundary of the property. It has over a hundred acres in all, but a lot of it is wooded. The main buildings include the instructional buildings, the three dormitories with their open study halls, the chapel, the cafeteria, and the stables. I'll make sure you have your own horse after you've had some instruction."

My eyeballs almost popped out of my head. "My own horse? Julian, how rich was my father?"

"I thought you understood. The Sinclair family was one of the wealthiest in the world. You'll be attending a very elite and secure school."

I stared at Julian, but her words weren't making sense. "If the Sinclair family's so rich, then why was it so hard to find me? Why haven't I ever heard about the missing heiress in the news or on-line?"

Julian frowned. "If the public knew you were missing, we would have had thousands of misguided people reporting well-meant but false sightings of the baby everyday. Thousands of false leads and wild goose chases. Who knows how long it would have taken for me to find you? Even beyond that, you are the last living person in the Sinclair line. Without you and the direct line of inheritance, the business might have been in more jeopardy than it already was."

I remembered a phrase I'd heard on one of the cable news channels. "Investor confidence levels would have been shaken?"

Julian gave me that half smile again. "Something like that. Do you have any more questions, or can we wait for later?"

"We can wait, except one thing."

"What one thing?"

I couldn't look her in the eye. "If my father was your best friend, do you have a picture of him that I could see?" I looked up at her face as I asked the last word and wished I hadn't. She winced as if I'd physically hurt her, not just the emotional sucker punch that I landed.

"I don't have any photographs in this apartment. The only one I carried with me was the one I showed to you on the jet. It's just not secure enough here. And your father hated to have his picture taken. There aren't very many good photos of him at all."

"I don't understand. If the Sinclairs were so rich, why-"

She interrupted me. "You forget that Nicholas's mother died when he was born. His father was always too busy to even think about photographs and his step-mother . . . Let's just say she wasn't interested in capturing Nicholas's childhood memories. And then there is the security issue. Someone has to print the images which means there could be unauthorized duplicates made. If no one knows what your child looks like, then no one can hire kidnappers with any real assurance of grabbing the right one."

"I hadn't thought of all that. The Sinclair family doesn't have paparazzi chasing it all the time?"

Julian laughed. "I'm sorry, Elisabeth. I just think it's funny how you refer to the Sinclair family as them when you're the only one left. But no, the Sinclair family was never one to flaunt their wealth. They kept it tied up in multiple layers of corporations so that it would be harder to trace them as the only shareholders. Just be grateful for the privacy. Nicholas was. It enabled him to go to the college of his choice and be treated like everyone else."

"Did they know at the Academy?"

Julian thought for a moment before answering. "When your grandfather was in charge, the Sinclair family always sent a group of neighborhood children. Your father and I were part of one attending via the Sinclair family money. Our group included your father's step-brother. Nicholas and I had a great time there."

I nodded and tried to look excited by the prospect, but I was terrified. Children of the rich and powerful. They would know that I was an interloper. I didn't have the proper upbringing or manners to fit in there. I hoped I wouldn't disappoint Julian or shame my father's memory, but I had my doubts.

CHAPTER THREE

We stayed in Paris for less than forty-eight hours before Julian was whisking me away on the jet again, back to the States where I would attend this mysterious Saint Clare Academy. I was beyond merely nervous, but I was looking forward to being able to read and study with the best teachers money could buy. Julian had let me pack up as many of the books as I wanted to take with me. They were in my new trunk packed away with my new school supplies. I didn't bring many new clothes aside from my uniforms, but I was allowed to bring several dressy outfits as well as jeans and things for when I was just in my room studying or goofing off. Julian said it might not seem like I'd have a lot of time to myself, but that she was sure I'd manage well enough.

I wasn't really sure where the Saint Clare Academy was, just some Midwestern state east of the Mississippi River. Julian told me not to worry and just enjoy my new school. I was half asleep when the jet touched down and then fell completely asleep on the long car ride to the campus. I wasn't sure if Julian planned it or if it was an accident of our travel schedule, but we arrived at the Academy just before dawn on a warm morning. It was September, but the weather didn't know it. The air was moist and heavy, promising to be muggy and humid in the heat of the day, with the threat of a thunder shower later. The sun was just beginning to spread its creeping tendrils of light over the mountains that lay to the east as we walked into the main offices. We were greeted by the headmaster and by the chairman of the board of trustees despite the early hour. Julian talked at some length with the chairman about some topic of debate the trustees were soon to meet over while Headmaster George Brindle asked me questions about my previous school.

Julian had sent all my records ahead, and Brindle wanted me to take a math test and write a composition for him to determine my placement. He assured me there would be time for that the next day or the day after that, when I'd had a chance to settle in. He gave me a map of the campus. It wasn't a plain outline map printed out on copy paper but a hand-drawn map on very fine paper that showed not only the buildings but also the landscaping. He explained that it was a product of the art class. I voiced my hope that I wouldn't have to take art since I had no talent for drawing or painting. He was very quick to reassure me that while all the students took art appreciation to learn about art history and the like, only students with a real interest or talent took the technical classes.

The trustee chairman had to leave, apparently being there for the sole purpose of greeting me and Julian. After he wished me well with my classes, he said his goodbyes, and Headmaster Brindle led us on a tour of the grounds. Julian made several comments about how little it had changed since she had attended. We walked through the courtyard with its bubbling fountain, raised flowerbeds, and bronze statue. Mr. Brindle told me Aleron St. Clare, the man the statue honored, had founded the Academy in the early 1800s as a branch of the European school his family had supported for generations.

Julian added her own memory. "During final exams, some of my classmates would bring small bouquets of flowers with a coin tied on a ribbon and toss them into the fountain. Then they'd rub the statue's left heel for good luck. If their bouquet would travel around the fountain five times before the coin dragged the flowers under the water, then they were assured of passing all their tests. The only person I ever saw who was successful was your father, and he would never tell anyone how he did it."

The headmaster smiled indulgently at Julian's story. "I believe Nicholas's academic success was a product of the time he spent studying rather than any flowers or statues."

It was no time at all before we arrived at the dormitory that would be my new home. I was to live in the same building that had housed Julian and my father in their schooldays, Kirkwynd Hall. Mr. Brindle left us at the hall's front doors with a Mrs. Bambridge, who had been the sponsor of Kirkwynd Hall in Julian's day as well.

Mrs. Bambridge remembered Julian fondly and seemed a little surprised at how grown up she was. She also remembered my father. She looked at me with watery eyes and said, "He was the kindest boy, Master Nicholas. Full of high spirits and mischief, but good-hearted. The trouble those two caused me – oh! I felt sure they would be the death of me with their antics." The way her eyes got crinkly told me she had loved every minute of their "antics" as much as she had loved both her troublemakers.

She was short, not even as tall as me, and plump all over, the way I'd always imagined a grandmother should be. Her eyes had permanent creases from her smiles, and she smelled like vanilla and cinnamon. I could tell she was more than ready to love me for my father's sake and Julian's, even before she could learn to love me for my own sake. She seemed to be the kind of woman that would never believe anything other than the best in anyone, and, even when presented with proof positive that someone had done something wrong, she would find a way to justify that behavior as long as they showed they were sorry.

"Let's see here, Miss Elisabeth." She looked at her clipboard sitting on the front desk. "I've put you up in the tower room. I do believe it's the same room that Miss Julian was in when she was here. How lucky we had a space there! Your things have already been taken up and put in the hallway, but I didn't want to disturb the girls who were sleeping."

Julian had nodded as if she had expected just that outcome. I hoped that the tower room was truly what it sounded like – a bedroom built into one of the Tudor-style turrets on the eastern side of the hall – but I only asked, "How many girls are in the tower room now?"

Mrs. Bambridge looked surprised by the question, as if it never occurred to her that I might not already know. "There are three others just now, although that room used to always have eight girls. We removed all the bunk-beds and replaced them about five years ago. If you'll follow me, I'll take you on a brief tour of the hall."

Julian smiled at being led around the hall she knew so well, but she was careful not to let Mrs. Bambridge see it. I could tell she didn't want to steal any of the sweet old lady's glory; Mrs. Bambridge was so evidently enjoying herself that it would have been a sin to disappoint her. She finally led us into a large rectangular room. There were doors on both sides of both fireplaces. The room itself had high ceilings with dark wood paneling on the walls. There were any number of cozy looking couches and chairs that seemed just right for curling up to read. There were also several tables where people could study or snack or play card or board games. Above the fireplace mantles hung identical banners of dark midnight blue and black. They had silver griffins and silver writing that I thought might be Latin. They were very beautiful. All the colors I'd seen at the school were the same blue, black, and silver with a little red thrown in. I guessed that the large room must serve as a common room for Kirkwynd Hall's residents, like Harry Potter's Hogwarts. I wished I had something else to compare it with, but at least I'd had the chance to read those books and had them for a reference.

"Are the other halls like this one?" I asked.

Mrs. Bambridge nodded, then shook her head. "They were all originally built on the same floor plan, but Wycliffe Hall was damaged in a fire, oh, I suppose it was ten, twelve years ago now. They all have large study halls like this one. Kirkwynd and Mandelton have the same overall structure, but Kirkwynd is the nicest."

Julian smiled at that. "You wouldn't be just a little prejudiced, would you, Mrs. Bambridge?"

I thought she might have been insulted, but Julian knew her better. Mrs. Bambridge just chuckled. "I might be if not for the fact that I know the students that live in Kirkwynd, and I've seen the students come and go from the other two. Kirkwynd is the best hall here at the Academy. We've got the best students, academically and personality-wise."

She led us through the door on the right side of the eastern fireplace and up the wide spiraling staircase. There was a landing for the second, third, and fourth floors followed by a door with a heavy chain and lock. The sign read "Roof access –

no admittance without authorization" but the staircase continued to curl its way upwards. When we reached the final landing, my trunk and suitcases were sitting outside a closed door. Across from a second door was a large bay window on the landing with an inviting looking window seat with blue pillows. Mrs. Bambridge was huffing and trying to catch her breath, so I took a moment to look out the window. It gave a view of the whole campus. With the sun coming up behind the tower, it cast strange shadows over everything. I saw a few people beginning to move around the campus below me. I put my hand up on the window sill and felt something strange.

I ran my fingers over the place and felt some grooves that seemed to have been filled in later. I leaned over to get a closer look. There was a faint carving in the wooden window frame. "N.S." and "J.M." I straightened back up and looked at Julian who was watching me with her sad little half-smile. She nodded at me, and I knew she and my father had left their mark on Kirkwynd Hall in physical as well as emotional ways.

Mrs. Bambridge had recovered from her trip up the stairs. She smiled at me reassuringly and knocked on the door. It was only a moment before the door opened a couple of inches and a girl's face appeared, haloed by silvery blond hair. She was very fair-skinned with large blue eyes that seemed to take up her whole face. She seemed startled to see Mrs. Bambridge standing outside her door.

"Yes, ma'am?" Her voice was sleepy but still light, like a soft flute playing low.

"Good morning, dear. I'm sorry to wake you, but we have a new roommate for you to meet."

At Mrs. Bambridge's announcement the door was pulled open violently, and I got my first look at my new roommates.

The three girls could not have been more different. The pale silvery girl who opened the door was wearing a long nightgown with an even longer robe over it, both in pale pink. The second girl, who had yanked the door all the way open and stood with her hand still on the handle, had fiery red-gold hair and bright turquoise eyes that were the same shade as her tank top and pajama pants. The third girl was standing close to the first one. She had short golden blond curls all over her head and dark blue eyes that were probably made darker by the navy blue satin pajamas she was wearing. They each had very different expressions on their faces, and yet they were all showing signs of their curiosity.

Mrs. Bambridge shook her head. "Charlotte Marie Deveraux! Will you ever learn to live in moderation?"

The bright eyed redhead grinned. "Sorry, Mrs. Bambridge. I heard you say new roommate and had to see for myself."

"What kind of impression are you making on Miss Elisabeth and Miss Julian? I'd be surprised if they didn't insist on a new room immediately."

But I'd already seen the glimmer in Mrs. Bambridge's eyes that was the same as when she was talking about the trouble my father and Julian had caused. If this Charlotte with the turquoise eyes could inspire that look, then I was staying here.

I spoke up. "Don't worry about a thing, Mrs. Bambridge. I have no intention of trading out this tower room for anywhere else that could be offered."

From somewhere outside, a bell rang deep and solemn. Mrs. Bambridge tugged on the long gold chain around her neck and drew up a watch. "Look at the time! I've got to get downstairs right away." She looked at Julian.

"Don't worry about a thing. I'll see Elisabeth settled and stop by to say goodbye before I leave," Julian reassured her.

"Thank you, thank you. Ladies, I hope you will all be very helpful to Miss Elisabeth and Miss Julian, but you are not to be tardy for any of your classes." With that final admonishment to my new roommates, she went back out the door to the staircase. We could hear the first few steps before the heavy door shut and blocked out the noise.

Julian picked up my suitcase and walked into the room. I followed her so I could see my new room. The walls were paneled in a medium oak and all four beds had tall canopies hung with heavy curtains in the same dark midnight blue as in the meeting room downstairs. Three of the beds were unmade, showing where my roommates had been sleeping. Julian set my suitcase down on the fourth. It was right beside a window, and the rising sun was shining a spotlight on it.

Red-haired Charlotte spoke again. "We all drew straws the first night to choose our beds. Sorry if you don't like it."

I turned quickly. "No. I love having the sun shine in at me."

Charlotte continued on. "I guess you're Elisabeth, then?" I nodded. "I'm Charlotte Deveraux, but everyone calls me Charly. That's Emma Bowen." She pointed to the navy-pajamaed girl with the golden curls. "And that's Lila Grace Trefford." She turned to the silvery blond in the pale pink.

"It's very nice to meet you, Elisabeth." Lila Grace said with her soft, musical voice.

"Thank you." I felt awkward.

Emma spoke for the first time. Her voice was not as quiet as Lila Grace's or as lively as Charly's. It was decisive, but not harsh. "I would love to stay and get acquainted, but I'm afraid I have a rather important test in my algebra class this morning, and I need to get ready."

Julian smiled at her. "Don't worry about anything. I'll get Elisabeth settled. This was my room when I was a student. We had bunk beds in here then. You must all be very thankful they're gone."

Emma smiled and nodded as she gathered her clothes and toiletries and left the room. Lila Grace followed her, waving a little goodbye as she walked out the door.

Charly had all her things gathered up, but just tossed them on the middle of what must have been her bed. "Would you like me to help you carry your trunk inside?"

Julian nodded to me, so Charly and I went to half pull, half drag it into the room and under the window. When it was in place, Charly sat on her bed and watched us for a moment as Julian unpacked my clothes and hung them in the small wardrobe that was next to my bed. Julian finally spoke to her.

"Do you have class this morning, Charly?"

"Yes, ma'am, but I was thinking Elisabeth might need some company when you leave." The turquoise eyes seemed even brighter than they had before.

"I have to admit that there have been some real improvements in these rooms since I was here, like the removal of the bunk beds, but the excuses for skipping classes don't seem to have changed at all." Julian smiled a little, and Charly responded with a huge smile of her own.

"Are you Elisabeth's mother? You don't look anything alike."

"I am Elisabeth's guardian. Do you ask everything that comes into your head?"

"Usually. If I don't ask, then I never find out anything. I'm too far out of the loop to hear the gossip, and Lila Grace wouldn't repeat anything if her very life depended on it. She's as sweet as they come, but a little dull. Emma is as much of a loner as she can be in a crowded atmosphere like this. She's brilliant and never minds helping anyone with their homework, but doesn't talk personal info. They're pretty good roommates. I just want to know what kind of girl you are."

I wasn't sure how to answer her. I had been an orphan, Elisabeth Sawyer, in foster care and group homes for so long. Nobody really wanted much to do with me then, since I had no money or family or even a permanent place to live. I'd only been Elisabeth Sinclair for a little while. I wasn't sure of who she was yet.

Julian answered for me. "Elisabeth is a wonderful girl. She's quiet and can keep to herself, but she knows how to keep up her end of a conversation when she needs to. And best of all, she's a good roommate. She knows how to clean up after herself and won't leave her things scattered all over the space and doesn't mind sharing."

"Well, I'm glad to hear all that, ma'am, but I want to know if Elisabeth will be the kind of girl that . . . that-"

Charly searched for her words, but in that moment I read something in her face that I understood very well. Charly was lonely in this school, even with Lila Grace and Emma around.

"I think we'll get along, Charly. I'm not as quiet as Lila Grace seems to be and, while I do love to read, I'm not brilliant when it comes to schoolwork." I stopped, not sure about how far I should go. Then I decided that no matter how insecure Elisabeth Sawyer had been in making her choices, Elisabeth

Sinclair would be bold. "I've never had a real, true friend before. I've always had to leave them or something. I hope we can be great friends."

Charly smiled at me, her turquoise eyes full of excitement and her red-gold hair alive with the energy that made her Charly. "I'm so glad you've come here, Elisabeth."

"Me, too."

Julian smiled at us both. "I'm glad you're both glad, but it is time you were getting ready for class, Charly. I won't be leaving before lunch, so you can take care of Elisabeth tonight."

"Yes, ma'am." Charly grabbed her things and practically danced out the door. I sat down on the end of my bed and looked around. Charly's bed was near mine, but in the only corner of the tower room, where it meet the landing. It was also the only truly dark spot in the room with the sunlight coming in the east window. Lila Grace had the bed closest to the door, which explained why she was the one to open it when Mrs. Bambridge knocked. Her bed, although covered with the same dark blue linens, was covered with stuffed animals, mostly white and pink cats, bears, and rabbits. It was very neat, even though she hadn't made the bed.

Emma's bed had been made. Sometime while she was getting her things ready, she had made her bed and had a satchel of books sitting on it. She had hung a poster on the wall near her bed. I couldn't make out exactly what it was so I walked over to get a closer look. I suppose I shouldn't have been surprised after what Charly said, but it was a poster showing the table of periodic elements like I'd seen in a chemistry class in my old junior high. I walked back over to my trunk just as the door opened. Emma and Lila Grace both walked back in carrying their nightclothes and toiletries, wearing their school uniforms. It was the first time I'd seen someone actually in them, other than my own reflection.

The outfits were identical. Knee-length black and blue plaid skirt, white Oxford-style shirts, dark blue sweater vests with a silver gryphon embroidered on the top left and knee socks, and red ties. Even though they were wearing the same thing, it looked completely different on them. Emma wore a dark blue head band, a black leather wristwatch, and brown loafers, while Lila Grace wore a gold bracelet, tiny diamond studs, and black MaryJanes. Emma seemed to have every pleat as sharp as possible and the folds of her tie were exact. Lila Grace, even though her pleats looked like Emma's, seemed softer. Her edges had all been blunted somehow. I decided that when everyone was wearing the same thing, the student's personality must shine through in spite of everything.

They put their things away, and Emma grabbed her satchel, waved lightly and left the room again. Lila Grace was quiet as she made her bed and put her stuffed animals in whatever order she had for them. She pulled out a light pink backpack from the bottom of her wardrobe. She hesitated at the door before she left.

"I'm very glad to meet you, Elisabeth. I hope you like it here. If you need anything, I'll be glad to help if I can."

"Thank you, Lila Grace. That's really nice of you." I watched as she left. A few moments later Charly came back into the room. She was wearing the same outfit, but she definitely looked different. Her shirttail was hanging out in the back and her skirt was twisted. She had her knee socks folded down to the top of her white tennis shoes. She tossed her things on her bed and had to get down on her knees to search under her bed for her backpack. Somehow when she pulled out the bright bag with the tie-dyed rainbow swirls, I was not surprised.

From the outside another bell rang. Charly looked at the clock hanging above Emma's poster. "Oh my gosh! Is it that late already? I'll catch up with you later, and you can tell me all about what you think of everything here! Bye!" She was out the door before she had finished talking, and I was left alone again with Julian.

I turned to find her watching me with an expression I couldn't read.

"Are you alright with this, Elisabeth?"

I was able to smile. "If you'd asked me that last night, I probably would have tried to fool you into thinking that I was, but now . . . I like Charly. Lila Grace seems sweet and Emma, well, she seems like she's glad I'm here to distract Charly. I'm so glad I'm here in this tower room by the window, where you slept when you were my age."

Julian smiled and was completely relaxed for the first time since I'd met her. "I wasn't sure it was the best thing to bring you here, but I had so many wonderful memories from my time here. Saint Clare Academy provides a very good education, and I know you'll be safe." Julian sat on my trunk. "Elisabeth, this school has a few secrets of its own. I don't know how many people know about this, but I want you to know. But promise me that you won't use it for the wrong reasons."

I've always thought it was unfair for someone to make you promise things when you didn't know what you were promising, but I promised.

"When this tower was built, they were afraid of having students trapped up here in the case of fire, but they didn't want students to have a back way out that was difficult to keep track of, so they put in secret passages. All the tower rooms in all the halls have them, although I don't know about Wycliffe since the fire. The passage is very narrow and has steep, winding steps. I don't know who knows about them these days, but I found out about them from your father. Nicholas would never tell me how he learned about them, but they are there. If you go to the corner . . ."

I walked over to Charly's bed. "How close to the corner?"

"The passage is right at the corner, but the trip switch to open it is about three feet over, by the floor."

I knelt down and began to feel along the baseboard. Just when I felt sure Julian was teasing me, I found a dip in the floor. It was as if a man had taken his thumb and pressed in wet clay. I put my finger in and felt something give. The wall suddenly developed a crack so that when I pushed on it a "door" swung open away from the room with hinges in the corner. I peered inside. The stairs I could see were stone.

"Is there some kind of light, Jules?"

"No. It was built without electric, but I used to keep a flashlight on both ends. I believe you'll find two packed inside your trunk." She stood and walked to the secret door while I moved back to my truck.

I found two heavy-duty flashlights packed inside and carried both of them over to her. Julian lead the way down the first three steps, and then we turned back to the secret door. She made sure it closed tightly and showed me the lever that opened it from the inside.

"The other end doesn't open to the outside. It actually leads to an underground passageway. There is a secret hatch into a storage closet just outside the study hall. I don't know where all the passages lead to, but your father did. I'm sure that you can get to each of the other buildings on the property through them, but I could never figure it out."

"Why not?" I was moving along slowly; the steps were very steep just as Julian had said.

"Some of the passages lead to dead ends or just stop. There may be other secret doors to get through them, but I never found out."

We finally got to the bottom of the stairs and had to go out another door. Julian shut off her flashlight and left it just inside the door. The passageway seemed to have its own light source, but I couldn't figure out what it was. I did know that the ground was made of paving stones, and some of them were wet. Julian showed me how to open the door and how to make sure it closed behind me seamlessly. She looked at the shut door.

"I marked this one, in case I ever got lost down here. There it is." She pointed to the small "J" on the upper corner of what would be the door. "I used to color it in with silver paint. The silver reflects best with the flashlight, but the paint would peel off in the damp."

"Why is it so wet here? And where is the light coming from?"

Julian smiled. "Can't you tell? Some of the water seeps in from the ground itself. If there's ever a lot of rain be extra careful of these tunnels. The rest of the water comes through the drains that are in various places around the buildings and in the courtyard, which is where the light comes in. Nicholas said there must be some kind of mineral in the stone facing that reflects the light, but I was never that good at geology."

"So, can people hear us now?"

"Not as long as we keep our voices down. Your father used to listen in on all kinds of conversations that were taking place right above his head. And I'm sure he knew how to get into the headmaster's office." Julian seemed to remember she was the adult and talking to me. "Of course, you have promised to only use this when necessary."

I hoped I looked sincere. "Of course."

I must have failed miserably because Julian sighed. "Let me show you how to get to the study hall."

I followed her to a place where there was a ladder attached to the wall. It reminded me of the ladders that are attached to the sides of swimming pools so you can climb out. There was a hatch right over the top of the ladder.

"Turn off your flashlight and put it on that little ledge." I swung the light to the place she indicated and saw that there was a small ledge carved roughly into the wall. I turned the light out and fit it onto the shelf.

"Did you and my father put that ledge there?" It looked rougher than the rest of the things she had shown me.

"Nicholas did. Now when I open the hatch you'll have to be very quiet or your voice will carry." I was quiet as she showed me how to open the hatch and went up into a broom closet located just outside the bathroom by the study hall. We closed the hatch back and made sure there was no trace of it before cracking the door open to peak out and see if the coast was clear. It was, so we stepped out and went into the study hall. It was deserted, but there were still remnants of the breakfast that had been left for Kirkwynd Hall's students.

"Do you know any more secrets about this place?" I hoped the answer might be yes, but Julian just shook her head.

"Nicholas knew all the secrets, and he didn't tell me everything. But even if I did, we don't have time for any more right now. We have to meet with the curriculum instructor and prepare your schedule."

I was only a little disappointed. I didn't mind the idea of finding out what classes I might have, but I wished I knew if my new roommates would be in any of them. I didn't even know what classes they had, other than Emma's morning algebra class, and I didn't mind not being in that one.

CHAPTER FOUR

Julian and I spent the remainder of the morning with the curriculum instructor, Miss Krancy, a fussy woman in her twenties who acted like she was an eighty-year-old. Actually that's not fair to eighty-year-olds; she was just deadly serious and dull. Miss Krancy told Julian that Headmaster Brindle had left instructions for me to take my placement test the next day after I had settled in, but Julian wouldn't hear of it. She told Miss Krancy that I wouldn't be able to settle in until after I'd started my classes.

Julian was right, of course, but it meant that I spent an hour with a math test that left me unsure if two plus two could possibly still equal four. The writing test was a little easier. The Franklin Group Home didn't have very many books, but someone had donated a series of old classic books from American and English literature, and I had read them all. The results of my placement tests had me in an advanced literature class and pre-algebra along with my other classes in science, history, geography, cultural appreciation, and physical education.

Miss Krancy explained that the cultural appreciation classes were mixed among the grades unlike the typical academic classes. She said it was also possible to add a foreign language to my schedule, although it was not unusual for the students to be multi-lingual before attending the Academy.

I suppose I had looked a little annoyed over the prospect of physical education because Miss Krancy immediately explained, "Here at Saint Clare Academy, we take great pride in exercising our students' bodies as well as their minds."

Julian put my dodge-ball fears to rest when she reminded me about the horse-riding lessons she had promised. "The physical education class also includes some martial arts training, fencing, swimming, archery, and whatever the administration has added these days. You'll be fine."

As soon as my schedule was entered on the computer and Miss Krancy had given us two copies – one for me and one for Julian – we left her office. Julian led me to the main dining hall where students could eat a full breakfast, lunch, and dinner five days a week. On the weekends they only served two meals, a midmorning brunch and a late afternoon dinner. Julian told me that unless things had changed a great deal since her schooldays, the weekday breakfast was the least attended meal. Girls, always being girls, tended to spend more time getting ready, and boys tended to sleep in longer. That was the main reason why the three dormitories had the muffins and fresh fruit and other simple breakfast foods in their study halls.

We arrived just before the campus bells rang. Before the sound had faded away, the students began pouring out of the other buildings and heading our direction. Headmaster Brindle was waiting for us just inside and guided us through the line and to a table before the students could crowd in. Julian and the headmaster carried on their conversation without my input. As I ate, I kept an eye out for the three faces that were slightly more familiar than the rest. I didn't need to worry.

There was no mistaking that fiery hair or lively nature of Charly. She must have been looking for me as well because even as she stood in line to get her food, she spotted me, waved, and walked over.

"Elisabeth! How do you like it so far?"

She sat down right next to me at the headmaster's table. I saw him frown, but before he had the chance to do anything, Julian had captured his attention.

"Charly, I'm so glad to see you. I got my class schedule and wondered if we had any together." I handed her the folded up copy, and she went over it quickly.

"We're in half our classes together. This is great. I'll be able to show you around and make sure you're caught up on notes and stuff."

I looked over the list again. "Which ones aren't you in?"

"I'm not in your phys ed class, English, and science. You've got chemistry and they won't let me take chemistry after the 'incident' last year."

I looked at her with widening eyes. "What kind of 'incident'?"

Charly helped herself to some of the potato chips on my plate. "I accidentally set fire to the science lab last year. I was mixing chemicals, and they didn't get along very well."

"Were you hurt?"

"I got a little singed, but luckily the chemicals were giving off some kind of reaction with smoke and Alexei noticed before it blew up. He put the beaker into the large sink and covered it over with his lab coat. Unfortunately, his lab coat actually caught fire, and it spread a little before Mr. Elendbein could put it out. Now, they're all afraid to let me back inside the lab."

Charly delivered her little speech with an I-don't-care attitude, but there was something in her eyes that made me wonder. "How did you end up mixing the wrong chemicals?"

"I was distracted."

I couldn't let it go at that. "What distracted you?"

Charly looked down at her suddenly very interesting fingernails. "It was Alexei. I wasn't used to being around him and he's – he's the best looking guy at the Academy."

I noticed that Julian was listening to our conversation while appearing to be completely involved in her own. I wanted to ask more about this Alexei. I hadn't had any exposure to the male student population and this dining hall was my first chance to see any of them up close. "What's he look like? And why weren't you used to being around him?"

"He's really smart. He came in new last spring but is a year ahead of us and in advanced science classes. He was acting as Mr. Elendbein's assistant in my class that day. What he looks like-" Charly paused and looked around the crowded dining hall. She was frowning when she spoke again. "I don't see him in here. He usually sits over with that crowd where Lila Grace is sitting, but he's not there."

"Are you sure? The table's really crowded." I gave Charly half my turkey sandwich and my apple.

She started to eat the food and then grinned at me. "Trust me. If Alexei was there, you'd know it. He's tall and drop-dead gorgeous. He's about six foot three with black hair and these piercing eyes that change colors, blue and green."

"Super smart and super good-looking. He must be a total jerk, huh?" All the really cute guys I'd ever known were so full of themselves they didn't have time for anyone else.

But Charly shook her head. "Not Alexei. He's the nicest guy. He tried to take the blame for the fire in the lab, but he's so smart no one would believe him when he said he must have given me the wrong chemicals. He tutors lots of younger kids and was really nice to the new kids last year, the ones who have never been away from home before."

"He sounds too good to be true." I tried not to let too much doubt show in my face, but Charly just laughed.

"Wait until you meet him. You'll see."

"What makes you think I'll meet him?" I asked her.

"It's a small school, Elisabeth, and we all live here together. Alexei is in Kirkwynd Hall like us. You're bound to run into him in the study hall from time to time." Charly gave me a huge grin. "Plus, we have two classes with him."

I rolled my eyes. The bells began to ring again, and the students started filtering out of the dining hall. Charly stood up and picked up my trash as well as Julian's.

"I'm heading out to the stables, so I guess I'll see you later tonight." She turned to Julian who was looking at her since the headmaster had just walked away. "It was a pleasure to meet you, Miss Julian. I'll keep Elisabeth out of trouble for you."

Julian's smile was as wry as her voice. "I'm sure I can sleep well with that comfort." Charly gave her another of the grins I was beginning to recognize as her most natural expression.

Julian and I walked back to Kirkwynd Hall in silence. When we were in my room, Julian opened the purse she had left inside my trunk. She pulled out a wooden box. For a moment I thought it was my secret box, but then I saw that the wood was lighter, maybe oak. She never noticed what had to be my guiltiest expression because she had been looking at her box the whole time. She took a small key out of her pocket that was almost identical to the one that hung around my neck, and she unlocked the box.

"I brought this here with me because I wanted you to have something after I leave you. These are letters your father wrote to me while we were in college and then when I was traveling in Asia. I know this is a difficult thing to ask, but I want you to promise that you will only read one at a time. I have them in chronological order."

I thought about her request for a moment and then put my hand out to touch the box. "I think I understand. If I was to try to read them all at once, I would be overwhelmed by them and they would just blur together in my mind. If I read one at a time and give myself the time to understand what we he was writing, maybe I'll have a chance to get to know my father."

Julian smiled at me. "You are the most amazing young woman I have ever met. You have wisdom beyond your years."

She closed the box and relocked it. She put it in my trunk and handed me the key. I slipped it into my pocket, vowing to slip it onto the chain next to the other at the first possible moment.

"That's not my only gift for you, Elisabeth. I had this sent to me here. While we were at lunch, the headmaster informed me that it had arrived and been delivered to your room." Julian picked up a small padded envelope that I had not noticed sitting on the window ledge. She opened the outer package and handed me the inner contents still wrapped in brown paper. It was about the size of a nice book, nothing too large, but it wasn't as heavy. I unwrapped it carefully to reveal the backside of a silver frame. I turned it over to see a photograph of two smiling people. I didn't need Julian to tell me they were my parents. I knew them from her description, but I also knew them from seeing my own face in the mirror. I didn't exactly look like either of them, but there was something in me that had both of them stamped there.

"I thought you deserved to have them with you, at least in some small way."

I knew I was crying, but I was also smiling. "Thank you, Julian. I can't say with words, but you know . . . ." I didn't have to finish the words.

"I know. I loved him, and they're your parents. It's almost time for me to leave, but I have one last thing I must discuss with you, Elisabeth, and it's very important."

I put the frame on the little shelf beside my bed and wiped the tears off my face. "You can tell me anything."

Julian smiled a little at that, and paused for a long moment before speaking. "I need to give you another warning about the hidden passageways that I showed you. I expected that they would show some signs of disuse, especially the one leading in and out of this tower room. It was clean, completely free of cobwebs or even the light layer of dust you might expect. Someone here definitely knows about them and uses them on a regular basis. That is all the more reason for you to be careful of them and stay out unless your life depends on it. Do you understand me?"

I nodded, but her warning seemed overly harsh to me. If she and my father had used them, wasn't there every chance that other students knew about them as well? Julian pulled her trick of seeming to read my thoughts again.

"It could be other students or it could be someone from outside living in the tunnels who doesn't belong here. I've told you about the dangers of kidnappings. You could be a target now, so there is no sense in making it easier for someone." I suppose my face showed her that I was taking her warning seriously because she moved on to her next topic. "I heard what Charly was telling you about this boy Alexei. I think you should stay away from him. Anyone who seems too good to be true . . . If he belongs to the . . . family that I think he does, based on that description, then he is not the right sort of company for you."

I was about to plead my case for not judging people on their families or apparent circumstances – wasn't I proof of that? – but Julian kept going.

"Elisabeth, you are in an incredibly difficult position. You know nothing of your family or step-family or the inheritance that the Sinclair name incurs. There may very well be others here who do know what it means and they may try to take advantage of you. I feel sure your father's step-mother has sent her . . . grandson here, although I haven't seen any sign of this. I'm asking you to be careful and wary of anyone who tries too hard to get close to you. Your roommates are fine. I've seen them for myself, but the other students . . ." She broke off with an elegant little shrug.

"I'll be careful. I promise." Julian looked at me with those brilliant green eyes, and I was a little surprised to see tears in them.

"It's time for me to go, and I'm finding it harder to leave you than I ever imagined it would be. Having you with me these last few days has been like having a part of your father back again and more than that, because I've grown to admire the young woman you are." She walked over to me and put her arms around me for a slightly awkward hug, as if she was out of practice. I heard her whisper "I love you" into my hair, and I whispered it back to her, trying to remember when I had ever heard someone say that to me before. When she let me go, she had regained control of her emotions and had that mask of elegant detachment back in place. She picked up her purse and walked to the door.

"If I can arrange everything, I'll see you at your Christmas break. Mrs. Bambridge has my address, so you may write to me as much as you want, but I hope you'll enjoy your time here as much as I did. By the way, I had the bed beside the window too."

I was smiling as she walked out the door. The very first thing I did when she was gone was to put the key to her box on the chain with the key to mine. I pulled the old teddy bear out of the trunk where it was waiting and carefully felt along the seam at the back of its neck. I pulled the loose strings until the seam was open enough to pull my box from its hiding place. I set it on the bed beside the other box.

The boxes looked identical, apart from the shade of the wood, but mine was shallower inside than hers. I'd realized a long time ago that my box must have some secondary opening, a false bottom or something, but I still didn't know how to open it, because Julian's didn't have that secret compartment. I wondered if I should have told her about the box and shown it to her. I put them in the top of my wardrobe on the small shelf above the clothes rod and placed a row of books in front of them so they would stay out of sight. I pulled out one of the books that had belonged to my father and went downstairs to wait in the study hall for my roommates to finish with their classes.

CHAPTER FIVE

I was curled up in one of the cozy chairs, completely engrossed in my father's copy of Milton's *Paradise Lost*. He had written in the margins, but I couldn't always make out what he had written. I quit reading the poem and started searching for more notes. At first, I thought they were notes for a paper or school project, but it was hard to figure out what they meant because they were just fragments.

I don't know how long the guy had been standing in front of my chair, waiting for me to notice him, but it couldn't have been for more than a few seconds. There was something about him that reminded me of the first time I'd seen Julian from the third floor window. He had a kind of presence that indicated command or leadership or some similar quality that made you notice him.

Plus he was gorgeous. Dark hair, amazing eyes. He had to be the Alexei that Charly had told me about. That Julian had warned me to stay away from. I suppose my look became a little frosty as I remembered Julian's warning because his smile faltered a little.

"You must be our new student, Elisabeth. I am Alexei Mikhailovich." His voice was a rich baritone with a British sounding pronunciation, but behind that was something more melodious that must have been his native tongue.

I was torn. I didn't want to get a reputation of being mean to the guy Charly described as the nicest guy at school, but I didn't want to disobey Julian. I nodded at him. I realized that I had sucked my lower lip in and was biting it and stopped immediately. It had always been a habit of mine when I was nervous, but I was trying not to show outward signs of my nerves. I was failing.

Alexei didn't act offended. "I hated to interrupt you while you were studying."

I smiled in spite of myself. "I wasn't actually studying. I was trying to decipher the notes my father wrote in the margins."

He sat down in the chair next to me. "Is his handwriting so difficult to read?"

"Not really, but . . ." I looked up at his face, into his eyes. They were startlingly blue. I thought Charly must be crazy to imagine that eyes so blue could ever look green.

"But what?" he prompted me.

"It's like half the words are missing. Or maybe it's just that I've never read *Paradise Lost*."

"May I?" He reached for the book, and I let him take it. He flipped through a couple of the pages. I saw a shadow cross his eyes, as if he was remembering some past sorrow. He looked back up at me, and I felt the same thing I'd felt when Julian had first looked at me, as if I was being weighed in the balance. Julian had found her missing goddaughter when she looked at me. I wondered what Alexei was searching for.

The moment seemed to last too long, but then he spoke, as if he had not been judging me at all. "Why do you not just ask your father what it says?"

I felt myself freeze and knew that Alexei was still judging me. "I can't ask my father anything. He is dead."

"Then your mother might know?"

"She died with him." My voice sounded brittle and high-pitched even to me.

"Then there is no one you can ask about your father and his book?"

His questions were too personal; I wondered if he was a spy for my father's step-mother or even her grandson. My voice turned cool. "I have a guardian. She warned me to stay away from boys like you."

The sorrowful look came back to his eyes. "I am sorry, Elisabeth. I was rude in my questions. I wish I could blame my poor English for my bad word choice, but I have been speaking the language far too long for that to be my excuse."

I knew Julian wouldn't want me to talk to him, but there was something about the pain in his eyes that made me listen to him. I'm not sure how I knew, but I was positive that Alexei was not a threat to me. And he knew more than he was saying.

"What aren't you telling me?"

"I know a little about your family. My father had many dealings with your grandfather."

I wanted to ask what he knew and demand he tell me everything, but his eyes were filled with real grief. I waited for him to continue.

"My family was killed when I was much younger. Not only my parents, but sisters as well. I was adopted by a very kind man who saved me, but he also died. He was the father that knew your family."

"I'm so sorry, Alexei. We have more in common than I ever could have guessed."

"And yet, we know very little about one another. I apologize again for my insult. I hope you will allow me the chance to make it right."

I reached across the short distance between the chairs and put my hand on his arm. "I don't think you have anything to apologize for."

He smiled at me, and I realized again how beautiful he was. "I really did not mean to talk about such things. I only wanted to introduce myself, and let you know that if there is anything I can do to help you, I am at your service. Perhaps we will become friends."

"Thank you."

He stood and looked at the book he still held before returning it to me. "Will you finish this?"

"The Milton or trying to decode my father's notes? I'll finish both."

"Perhaps we can talk about it when you are ready."

I smiled at him. "I'd like that."

He walked to the door on the other side of the fireplace from the door that led to my tower room. I was still watching him go when Charly threw herself into the chair he had just vacated.

"I should have known it wouldn't take long before you met Alexei. He's too nice a guy, and you're too pretty a girl." Her tone was teasing, but there was something more as well.

"He was nice, but he didn't tell me anything about himself. Is he Russian? He has that accent."

Lila Grace and Emma walked over in time to hear what I asked. Emma answered in her no-nonsense tone. "Alexei is Russian, but he was raised in England for most of his childhood, which explains the English accent that's blended with the Russian one. He is very smart. He's in my Latin class."

Charly shook her head. "How does he do that? He's the only student that I know of who is taking so many different grade levels."

Emma again had the answer. "He was tutored privately so some classes he needs and some he doesn't. He could outdo the professors in literature and science, but his math is awful. I think most of his history has been British and Russian. He's a little shaky on general European and knows very little of American history."

"What, are you his personal record keeper?" Charly's sarcasm seemed to hit its target with Emma, but Lila Grace spoke up.

"Charly, you should be ashamed. Emma has been helping Alexei with his math. Of course they talk about his other classes. And it's not like he isn't in your history and our geography."

Charly didn't look very ashamed, but I deflected the attention with a question of my own. "I'm sorry, but if he is so good at literature, then how can he not know much about history? Most of literature is dependent on knowing what was happening in the places at the time it was being written."

Charly shrugged, and Lila Grace looked surprised, but Emma gave me her full attention. "That's actually a really good point, Elisabeth. Alexei said that he was Russian and Russians could understand any piece of literature ever written based on their own history, but he would have to understand more of the cultures to truly understand the layers involved."

I thought that my comments gave Emma hope that I actually had some intelligence. I didn't want to keep talking about a boy Julian had asked me to avoid so I changed the subject slightly. I pulled my schedule out of the back of my father's book.

"Charly has already told me what classes I have with her. Why don't you two look at my schedule, and tell me if we have any?"

Emma took the page from my hand and whistled. "You've got advanced literature instead of the general English class. You must be really good."

I shrugged, unwilling to tell them about my time in foster care. "I read a lot."

Lila Grace read the list over Emma's shoulder. "We only have two together: geography and music. Actually we're all four in the same music class."

"You're in three of my classes, including music of course," Emma said. "We also have chemistry and the physical education rotation."

"I'm so glad. No one seemed to know what that rotation was doing right now."

Emma gave me an unreadable look. "We're doing riding classes. We've just started English saddle. Do you have a horse?"

I shook my head. I wished I had time to get some private lessons. "Julian has promised to buy me one, but I've never ridden before."

Lila Grace reassured me. "I hadn't before I came here, but you'll do fine. The school keeps some very gentle horses."

Charly nodded her head in agreement. "At least it's not baseball."

I grimaced slightly, remembering all the softball games the Franklin Group Home had sponsored as fundraisers over the summer. It had taken two concussions and someone else's broken nose to convince Mrs. Jenkins to let me sit out.

"Tell me about chemistry. I hear it involves a lot of math, but I'm not that good at math."

Emma was frowning slightly, still looking at my schedule. "I can't believe they would put you in chemistry when you're not even in algebra yet. The good news is that I don't have a lab partner, so I can definitely help you out. You're not going to blow anything up like Charly, are you?"

Charly started laughing before I registered the slight lilt to Emma's voice that meant she was teasing. I smiled along with Lila Grace.

"It's getting kind of late. We'd better take our bags upstairs and get ready for dinner," Lila Grace said. We all walked to the door and up the wide, curving stairs that led to our room. While they unpacked book bags and organized homework, I put the Milton book back in my trunk. I'd filled up the top of my wardrobe with a row of books, but I still had more than twenty packed inside my trunk. I wondered where I could put them. Maybe I could put up another shelf or something. I suppose Julian would send me one if I asked, but was I allowed to put one up?

As I was looking at the titles of the books I'd already unpacked, wondering if I should switch any out, I noticed that they'd been moved. I turned to my roommates.

"Have any of you been in here since lunch?" I hoped I didn't sound confrontational; I was more confused. Julian and I had been in here, and then I'd been downstairs the rest of the afternoon. I guess I could have been too wrapped up in my book, but wouldn't they have at least said hello if they'd come through?

Emma and Lila Grace looked at each other, and both shook their heads. Charly shook hers as well.

"Does Mrs. Bambridge or the cleaning staff come into the rooms?"

Emma answered me. "No, not unless they're called in or knock, like she did when she brought you up this morning. We're responsible for our own rooms."

Charly asked the question that they all must have been thinking. "Is something of yours missing?"

I shook my head and sat on my bed. I had barely put my weight on the mattress when I thought about my boxes. I got back up and moved a couple of books around until I could see that they were both still there. I sat back down, conscious of all three other girls watching my every move.

"Are you sure there's nothing missing?" Charly's turquoise eyes were sparkling.

"No. nothing's missing, but my books were definitely moved."

Emma looked at me with her head cocked to one side. "Not to sound like I'm doubting you, but are you sure? How do you know they've been moved?"

I gave her a wry smile. "It's a little embarrassing to admit, but I had all the books on my shelf alphabetized by the author's last name. I'm kinda OCD about it, I guess. I was trying to decide if I wanted to trade out some of the books I still have packed for the ones on the shelf when I noticed that *Jane Eyre* and *Wuthering Heights* were reversed."

Emma was nodding, but Charly looked at me like I'd grown a second head. Lila Grace sat down beside me and asked her own question, the soft musicality keeping her from sounding accusatory. "How do you know you didn't accidentally get the Brontes confused yourself? You have had a long day."

I smiled at her. "I understand you asking, but I distinctly remember questioning myself on if I wanted to put both of the Bronte sisters on my shelf and making sure I had them in the right order. Someone moved them."

Charly looked at the three of us. "Was I the only one who didn't know that they were books written by people with the same last name? Never mind. If you're sure they were moved, then I want to know why someone would be in here looking through Elisabeth's stuff."

Emma agreed. "If they were looking through Elisabeth's things, how do we know they haven't been through ours? I never considered the possibility so I've never paid any attention."

Lila Grace rubbed her arms like she was cold. "Maybe we should report it to Mrs. Bambridge. She should know if someone's going through other people's stuff."

Charly was shaking her head before Lila Grace was done talking. "Mrs. Bambridge wouldn't believe it. Nothing's missing, so she'd just write it off as Elisabeth's imagination or something because she's new and tired and maybe scared. She wouldn't take it seriously. Maybe not even if it was one of you two. She just wouldn't believe anyone in her building would mess around with anyone else's stuff."

Emma spoke again. "Charly's right about Mrs. Bambridge. I just wish I knew how someone else could get in.

Not counting the four of us, only Mrs. Bambridge has a key to this room, and the door was locked when we got here."

I felt my face flush as I remembered the other entrance, and Julian's warning that someone had been using it. Charly saw my blush.

"Don't be embarrassed, Elisabeth. We all believe you."

I shook my head. "It's not that, Charly. Julian told me something and made me promise to keep it a secret, but now I'm not sure."

Emma looked at me. "If you made a promise to your guardian, you should try to keep it if you can, but if it's something that could be dangerous, then I don't think Miss Julian would want you to let anyone get hurt." She and Charly sat on Charly's bed across from Lila Grace and me.

I nodded. "You all have to promise to keep this a secret from the other students. It's not anything that could hurt them, but if they found out it could make things more dangerous."

They all looked at each other and promised.

I stared straight into Charly's eyes. "I mean it, Charly. You can't let yourself be tempted to use this. Julian says it's not safe."

Charly looked back at me, and I guess she saw how worried I was. "I swear whatever you want me to, Elisabeth. I won't do anything to put any of us at risk."

I nodded. "You heard Julian say that when she was a student here, this was her room." They nodded and I continued. "She and my father were known for their pranks. My father found a system of underground tunnels that apparently link all the buildings. Julian told me that she didn't know where they all went, but she may have been saying that so I wouldn't ask her more. There is a secret passageway that leads in and out of this room."

Charly let out a low whistle, and Lila Grace looked scared, but Emma didn't look convinced. "Why would the Academy build secret passages into the rooms?"

"Julian said they were originally built as a secondary way out in case of fire, but that they'd been forgotten over time. She told me how she and my father had used them, but she also said that someone was using them now."

"How did she know?" Charly asked.

"She showed it to me and pointed out the lack of cobwebs or dust that should have been there after twenty or so years of neglect. She was right; the stairway that leads into this room was clear."

The ever practical Emma put it to the test. "Show us then. If there is a secret way in and out of the room I've been sleeping in for four years, I want to see it."

I understood her doubts. I got up off my bed and walked over to the corner by Charly's bed. I knelt down and found the switch in the floor and pressed. I didn't wait for any theatrical pause but pushed the door open while I was still kneeling. I heard the gasps from the other girls.

Charly walked over first. "This is amazing. All this time it's been right here beside my bed."

Lila Grace let out a tiny squeak. "Oh, don't, Charly! I'll never get to sleep now."

The same thought ran through all of us.

"There doesn't seem to be any way of blocking it from the inside and anything we did from the other side could just be undone from there as easily," Emma pointed out.

"What if we nailed a shelf or bar or something across it that was attached to the door and the wall?" Charly suggested.

I thought of something. "What if we had a latch? We could slow someone down, but if they were really determined to get in, they could. It would just take longer."

Lila Grace pointed out the flaw in our thinking. "We don't have any kind of latch and how would we get one? I mean, it's not the kind of thing we can ask Mrs. Bambridge to get for us."

"We can order one off the internet, some home improvement store or hardware manufacturer," Emma reasoned.

"But what will we do until it arrives?" Lila Grace was persistent in her quiet way.

Charly looked around the room. "We'll just have to rearrange some furniture. It might make for a tight squeeze on Elisabeth, but we can move my bed closer to hers and push my wardrobe in front of the door. That would slow someone down even more than a latch."

Emma looked at the wardrobe. "Can we even move it?"

The discussion was over. I reset the switch and shut the passageway door while Charly started pulling things out from under her bed. We each took a corner and moved the bed. Charly was right; it was a tight fit now between her bed and mine, but there was enough room to get through to the window where my trunk sat. Emma finished picking up the odds and ends that had been under Charly's bed while Lila Grace got the broom and dust pan from the closet in the hallway. I helped Charly move the clothes and other contents of her wardrobe on to her bed. The lighter we could make the it the better, but the wardrobe was a large piece of intricately carved solid oak.

It took a lot of pushing and pulling, and we ended up with some banged fingers and stepped on toes, but we moved it to the corner. Charly had just started to put her things back inside when the bells began ringing. She tossed the clothes back into the pile on her bed. "I'm not missing dinner for some stupid uniforms."

We all headed out to the stairs, but I watched Emma double check that the door was locked behind us.

CHAPTER SIX

I was surprised how fast the time flew by that evening. I remembered the long evenings at the Franklin Group Home with Gretchen and some other girls arguing with the boys over the television in the den. Even when I could escape into a book, the time seemed to pass so slowly. Here at the Academy, no TVs were allowed in the study hall, and most of the students didn't even have them in their rooms. If someone wanted to watch a show they would just catch it on-line. All of the students had their own laptops and tablets or whatever. It was a standard school supply for them. I was still figuring mine out.

Even though I didn't have any homework, I did spend some time going over Charly's notes for history and Emma's notes in chemistry and Latin. I wasn't too worried about geography, music, or physical education, but none of the girls were in my literature class, so I had no idea what to expect from it. The math class I just tried not to think about at all.

When we all finally went upstairs together, I wasn't the only one who held her breath waiting to see if the door was still locked and everything was still in place. It was locked and no one noticed anything odd, so Emma and Lila Grace went to the bathroom to get ready for bed while Charly and I waited our turn. It seemed safer to do it in pairs, not leaving the room empty, but not leaving anyone alone either. While they were gone, I showed Charly the box Julian had given me and its hiding place.

"Do you think whoever was messing with your books was looking for that?"

I shook my head. "I doubt it. It just has a bunch of old letters my dad wrote to Julian while they were in college. It was the first time they'd been apart for any real time since they were little kids."

Charly perked up with her interest. "Why did she give them to you?"

"Because my dad died when I was a baby, and she wanted me to be able to get to know him through the letters."

Charly nodded. "But why now? I mean, why didn't she let you read them before?"

I didn't want to go into the whole missing baby deal so I settled for only part of the truth. "She thought they would keep me from getting too homesick, or at least from missing her so much. Julian has 'homes' all over the world, but I guess your family does too."

It wasn't really a question, and I wasn't trying to pry, but Charly didn't seem to notice in any case. "We have a penthouse in New York, a house in the English countryside, and an island in the Caribbean. Of course, we never go anywhere together. If my mom's in New York, then my dad's in England. If she's on the island, he's in New York. And most of the time, I'm here. I guess it's the same for most of the kids who come here though. The Academy becomes more of a home than any of the places where you've ever lived that are supposed to be home."

I had never thought about the loneliness of growing up with too much money. I guess that's why rich kids go to boarding schools – so their families don't have to deal with them, and so they can have a place to belong. Maybe I had a lot more in common with my classmates than I'd ever believed.

While Charly watched, I unlocked the box, took out the top letter, and put the box back in the wardrobe, making sure it was well-hidden behind the books. I put the letter under my pillow and gathered my things to go change and brush my teeth and wash my face. When Emma and Lila Grace came back in the room, Charly and I left. The bathroom was the only other room in the tower, and it had a curved wall like our room. There were two shower stalls and two toilet stalls and a long vanity with three sinks. It looked more antique than I'd expected, but Charly assured me the hot water heater worked very well.

After we were all back in our room with the door carefully locked, we all went to bed. Emma set her alarm clock. Lila Grace put on her headphones and set her MP3 player to her playlist for sleeping. She said she had a hard time falling asleep if it was too quiet in the room and she could hear our breathing.

Charly laughed. "You mean Emma's snoring."

Emma gave Charly a look before retorting. "She means your snoring, Charly. It's like sleeping with a buzz-saw."

The light banter died out as each girl put out her own light and sank into sleep. I put out my light as well, but I had a small book-light that I had used at the group home that I turned on. I opened the envelope Julian had given me and unfolded the yellowing paper. The handwriting was bold, slashing across the page in black ink. It was as informal as Julian had said he was with her. There was a month and day in the upper right corner, and the letter was addressed simply "Jules". I supposed that was as far as he would go in concession of the rules of letter writing.

September 6

Jules,

    I hope you're adjusting to college life better than I am. I am terribly homesick for Kirkwynd Hall and dear Mrs. B. What I would give for one of her delectable chocolate chip cookies! My classes are fine, although they seem a little remedial after what we went through at the Academy. I can't wait for Christmas break to see you, but I don't want to go back home. Not with THAT woman living in my father's house. I know I'll have to return to claim what's mine and fulfill my familial obligations, but – not for a while still.

    I want us to travel together before we each graduate. I feel that it is very important for us to see the world before we have to return to . . . In any case, I propose we see the world during our summer vacations. SHE will be glad for me to stay away. Where would you like to start – Europe or the South Pacific? Maybe Australia would be nice, although it would be their winter on our summer break.

    I'll go now, Jules, but you must write back to me soon, or else I'll go mad in this not-so-homey dorm room. I miss you beyond words.

Love always,

Nick

I folded the letter and carefully put it back in its envelope. I turned off my book-light and tried to sleep, but I couldn't stop the tears. I wasn't making any noise; it was as if my eyes had sprung a leak, and I couldn't stop the waterworks. I knew everyone would notice my red eyes and assume I'd cried from being homesick, but I couldn't help what they'd think.

I'm not sure how long I huddled under my blanket, clutching my bear. I didn't remember falling asleep, but I immediately knew I was dreaming. Knowing it was a dream didn't seem to matter.

I was in my dorm room, and I got out of my bed. The other girls were still sleeping so I was very quiet. If I hadn't recognized it as a dream before, I'd have been certain when I noticed what I was wearing. I caught a glimpse of my reflection in Lila Grace's mirror. The nightgown was beautiful, ivory silk with antique lace tracing the sweetheart neckline, but it wasn't mine any more than the body inside it was. It was strange seeing my face attached to the well-endowed figure, but the oddness and creepiness disappeared as soon as I recognized the feelings. It was the same when I saw Charly's wardrobe back in its proper place, and the secret door standing ajar with a light coming from the stairwell; I knew that it would be foolish to go down there, but because it was a dream, I wasn't afraid. I pushed the door open so I could get through and then followed the flickering light to the bottom of the stairs. I wasn't surprised to see that the person holding the lantern was Alexei. He smiled at me and offered me his hand. I didn't hesitate. I smiled back and put my hand in his. It felt cool, but I knew that mine would feel hot to him. I could feel the heat in my face from blushing.

Dream Alexei spoke to me in the same polite tone the real Alexei had used when he'd introduced himself that afternoon. "I'm glad you came, Elisabeth. I thought that you might not after Julian's warning."

It didn't seem strange that he would know about Julian's warning. It also didn't seem strange that Alexei was wearing an old-fashioned tuxedo with tails while I was wearing someone else's body and lingerie.

"I don't understand why Julian wanted me to stay away from you. Charly, Emma, and Lila Grace think you're the nicest guy here."

He smiled but shook his head. "I don't want you to mistrust Julian. She was right to warn you, but not about me.

There are people who could be a threat to you, especially if they knew that you have the box."

Somehow I knew he didn't mean the box that Julian had given me. "But why? What does that box mean?"

Alexei looked at me, his summer sky blue eyes boring into my soul. "Didn't you ask Julian about the box? Didn't you trust her?"

I had to look away, ashamed that I hadn't trusted Julian enough to ask her about the box. Alexei put one finger under my chin and raised my head up until I was once again looking in his eyes. They were no longer that intense blue but the color of spring leaves, a pale green that sparkled with light.

"You can trust Julian, Elisabeth. She only wants what is best for you."

"I'm sorry. I should have told her I had the box. It must have been my father's. Julian gave me one that is very similar to it."

"Yes. They were both Sinclair treasures. Nicholas gave Julian hers, but even she does not know the secrets his box holds."

I noticed the way he said my father's name, as if he knew him, but I was curious about the rest of what he'd said. "Does it hold a secret?"

Alexei smiled, but it was the sad kind of smile I'd seen on his face earlier. "You know it does. You will know how to open it when the time comes. But, Elisabeth, you must keep it hidden. Keep it locked away where no one can see it. Hide it inside something if you can. If the box fell into the wrong hands, it would mean-"

He broke off abruptly and looked around. "We have lingered too long. Please trust me."

The look in his eyes was so full of emotion, pleading with me as if it were a matter of life and death. I nodded, but my voice came out as a whisper. "I trust you, Alexei."

He smiled again and pulled me into a tight hug. He bent toward me, and for a moment, I thought he was going to kiss me. My heart raced, and I remembered again that it was all just a dream. I felt his lips touch my forehead, and I closed my eyes.

When I opened them it was to find sunlight streaming through the window though everything else was the way it was when I'd fallen asleep. Emma was awake and getting out of bed. I felt the heat rush into my face as I thought about the nightgown and the way my heart raced when I thought Alexei was going to kiss me. This was one dream that I was not going to talk about; it would be bad enough seeing the real Alexei in class. I quickly got out of bed and gathered my things before heading to the shower.

CHAPTER SEVEN

Charly and I took our time getting ready. We didn't have a class in the earliest period of the day, but we did have history and then geography before lunch. I had my chemistry class with Emma that afternoon. I really like having different schedules everyday rather than the same classes at the same times like in my old high school. Unfortunately, the classes lasted later into the afternoons, and it was much harder to ditch. Not that I ever missed much school before, but sometimes you just have to take the day off.

Before Charly and I left the tower room, we checked carefully to make sure the door was locked. When we finally walked into the study hall, it was practically deserted. There were a few boys huddled around a computer watching something, but we didn't pay much attention to them. We walked through and were almost to the front door when Mrs. Bambridge called my name.

"Miss Elisabeth, dear, I'm so glad I caught you. The headmaster's office has sent your books over. You can just take what you need for right now, and I'll keep the rest here for you until you get a break."

"Thanks, Mrs. Bambridge. I appreciate it."

She clucked and hovered like a mother hen. "It's nothing at all. I'd take them up myself, but those stairs are getting to be just a little too much for me."

I quickly assured her that I didn't want her to put herself out on my account. "I'll have to come back anyway."

"They'll be right behind the desk here, in this box. You girls have a good day."

Charly gave Mrs. Bambridge one of her spectacular grins, and we headed out the door. I carried my new textbooks rather than taking the time to put them in my backpack. I didn't want to be late.

We walked across the campus, past the administration building to a large building with tall Corinthian columns at each corner. There was a second story balcony just above the main entrance. The plaque that hung by the front door said "H. R. Langford Building," but there was something else carved into the stonework above the balcony. It was very old and weather-worn and, from our angle, I couldn't make out what it said, but there were more letters than it would take to spell out "Langford". I started to ask Charly, but the bells began to ring, and we had to hurry inside. Our class was on the third floor. The building, while modernized with electricity and plumbing, still did not have elevators. I wondered how they could keep from doing that with the disabled accessibility laws, but I figured they had enough money coming in to the school to do whatever they needed to have done.

By the time we reached the third floor, I was just starting to sweat in my school uniform with its sweater vest. I figured my face was red, and I knew the wind outside hadn't done anything good for my hair. After the dream I'd had, I needed to look my best when I saw Alexei again. I knew I'd be nervous because he'd been in my dreams so I was hoping to counter my nerves by looking good. After the effects of the wind and the stairs, that wasn't an option anymore.

Charly and I walked into class as the instructor was checking his roll. He was a tall man in his fifties with some silver streaks in his brown hair and copper-framed glasses covering his eyes. He turned to look at us.

"Late again, Miss Deveraux. Are you trying for a new school record in detentions?" His voice, though serious, held a hint of humor.

Charly gave him her trademark grin before she spoke. "Sorry, Mr. Callahan. We were on our way, but then Elisabeth's books arrived, and we got held up."

Mr. Callahan turned his look from Charly to me, and I felt my face heat up as the eyes of my new classmates turned to me as well. "So you are Miss Sinclair? I suppose you would have to join Miss Deveraux in her detention, but in the spirit of fairness I'll let it go just this once. Perhaps you will be a good influence on her now that you know where this class meets."

I smiled at him, glad that I hadn't imagined that hint of humor. I looked around the room for a place to sit, but the seat next to Charly was already taken. Mr. Callahan noticed my discomfort and asked the boy sitting beside her to give up his spot for me. He moved to the back, and I took the now empty desk to Charly's right. It was also the desk immediately to Alexei's left. I hoped my blushes would be taken as simply embarrassment over being the new girl and being late to class.

When I dared to peek in his direction, Alexei gave me a friendly smile. I was relieved and then felt stupid. He hadn't been in my head; he couldn't know that I had seen him in my dream last night. I had to relax. Starting a new school was always tough and, with all the changes in my life, it was only natural that I'd be so worried about everything and end up having strange dreams. The class time actually went by quickly. Mr. Callahan was a good teacher, and his love for his subject came across in his lesson. Reading Charly's notes had helped. At least I knew what to expect from the topic. When we neared the end of class time, Mr. Callahan announced the homework.

"Today's lecture finishes this section so we will have a test the next time we meet. There will be twenty-five multiple choice questions, five short answer identifications, and one essay question. Miss Sinclair, you will, of course, be exempt from this test, but you will need to make it up when you've had a chance to catch up on the notes."

I nodded and looked at Charly. He dismissed the class but asked me to wait along with Alexei. Charly waited without being asked. Mr. Callahan gave her a look before he spoke.

"I appreciated that Miss Deveraux is helping you get acquainted with the campus and your classes, but . . . You might do better to get Alexei to help you with the notes. Miss Deveraux is rather notorious for her note-taking abilities among the faculty."

I was prepared to be offended on her behalf, but Charly just laughed. "Elisabeth has already looked over my notes, Mr. C. She knows how sketchy they are."

Mr. Callahan smiled at her, and I realized he really like having her as his student. Then he looked expectantly at Alexei.

"I would be glad to share my notes with Elisabeth, but . . ." Alexei gave me an apologetic smile.

"What's the problem?" Charly asked.

"They're in Russian. I tend to write my class notes in Cyrillic rather than with the Latin lettering that English uses."

"I definitely don't read Russian." I smiled as I said it.

Mr. Callahan smiled too. "Let me think about what other student may have good notes for you to study."

Alexei spoke again quickly. "Actually I wouldn't mind translating my notes for Elisabeth. It would help me review for the test and make sure I know the English spellings for the people and places we've covered."

Mr. Callahan nodded. "If you're sure, then it's settled. You'll have to excuse me; I have a meeting with the headmaster." He locked his desk and left the room.

I turned back to Alexei. "You don't have to go to any trouble for me."

He shook his head. "It is no trouble. I told you; it will help me study." He looked at Charly. "Do you need to show Elisabeth to her next class?"

Charly laughed. "Not a problem. She's with us."

Alexei smiled back at Charly. "Then allow me to escort you both across the hall."

He led the way from one classroom to an identical once across the hall. Both rooms were filled with student desks as well as a desk and podium for the instructor. The walls were painted the same gray and were covered with maps. Charly dropped her rainbow-dyed bag on one of the desks before taking a book out of it and putting it on the next desk. Alexei moved one desk over on Charly's other side and set his black backpack down.

"What's the book about?" I asked.

"Lila Grace is in this class, too, remember? I'm saving her a seat." Charly watched as I put my bag down on the desk between her and Alexei. I hoped he didn't notice my slight hesitation.

Alexei didn't seem to notice. "Do you have your class schedule with you? Maybe we have some other classes together."

I shook my head. "I left it in my room. I knew I would be with Charly, and we're heading back to the room after lunch. I have chemistry with Emma this afternoon."

"I am not taking chemistry. I suppose we will just have to be surprised."

We all sat down. Charly pulled out her notebook for class, but I saw her watching Alexei closely from the corner of her eye.

"Have you been reading more of *Paradise Lost*?"

I turned back to Alexei and shook my head. He was staring at me. I think I would have been frightened by his intensity if I hadn't been so captivated by his eyes. Yesterday afternoon I had thought Charly was crazy to imagine eyes so blue could ever be anything else, but in my dream they had changed color. Now, as I looked back at him, his eyes were the same pale green that I'd imagined in my dream. How could one person's eyes be so blue and then so green?

The moment seemed to last forever, but it wasn't more than a couple seconds. Charly cleared her throat, and Alexei looked away, breaking the eye contact and losing the force of his stare. The room began filling with students. They came in two or three at a time, and then they poured in like a flood just ahead of the instructor. Lila Grace was one of the last students in and gave Charly a grateful look for the saved seat.

The instructor was a woman with long white hair. Her face looked young so I thought that the hair was more blond than aged, but I'd never met an adult with such white blond hair. She read the roll in a firm voice, pausing only slightly over my name as her newest student. The class went by without any worries for me. They had only just started the chapter on Europe, after a review of basic geography and map skills. I had no trouble keeping up and even dared to raise my hand in response to a question. Knowing the right answer may have helped me gain the affections of Miss Elswick.

Before I knew it, the class was ending. Lila Grace said she was headed straight for the dining hall.

"We've got to go back to Kirkwynd. Mrs. B.'s got Elisabeth's books, and we don't want her to have to carry them up to the room." Charly's explanation caused Lila Grace to nod her head, understanding what wasn't mentioned.

"I'll save seats for you." We walked down to the first floor together with Alexei right behind us. I thought he might walk with us, but when we headed for the door he stopped.

"I have just remembered that I left my jacket in the history classroom." He turned and headed back to the stairs.

Charly shrugged her shoulders, grinning. "That boy's always forgetting something."

I didn't say anything. We walked out into the bright sunlight and across to Kirkwynd Hall. We retrieved my books and were only half-way across the study hall to our tower door when the door on the other side of the fireplace opened and Alexei stepped out.

"Where did you come from?" The words were out of my mouth before I could stop them.

Charly looked at me as though I'd lost my mind. "His room is up in that tower, Elisabeth. Don't be rude."

"I didn't mean to be rude-" I started, but Alexei cut me off.

"You were not rude at all. Think nothing of it."

"That's really sweet of you, Alexei. She's still new." Charly was smiling at him, but I was confused.

"May I help you with that box? It looks heavy." Alexei took the box from me, and I took my backpack from Charly who had been carrying it.

"Are you allowed to go up to our tower?" I asked, unsure of the rules.

"I am not supposed to in general, but Mrs. Bambridge has asked me to carry things up from time to time. I helped get your trunk and other bags up there yesterday."

"Oh! I'm sorry; I didn't realize. Thank you."

Charly stopped abruptly when we reached the door. "You don't need me anymore, so I can go on to lunch. I'm starving."

I couldn't help staring at her, but she seemed completely unaware that I might not want to be left alone with Alexei. There was nothing for me to do except nod in agreement unless I wanted to be rude again. I didn't want to offend Alexei, and I'd already been wondering if I would be able to carry the heavy box up all the stairs.

Charly left with a little wave, and I followed Alexei up the stairs. It was impossible to walk up the stairs behind him without appreciating the view. His long legs seemed to devour the steps, and I knew it was more than the long climb that left me breathless when we reached the top floor.

I carefully unlocked the door, making note that it had been shut tightly and checking to see if everything looked the same. Alexei stood in the doorway for a minute before he spoke.

"May I come in?"

"What? Oh, sorry, yeah. You can just put the box on top of my trunk, there under the window."

He carried it over to where I pointed, weaving through our new obstacle course. "Have you been redecorating?"

He was looking at Charly's wardrobe, so obviously out of place.

"We liked it better in the corner."

He smiled but didn't pry. I was glad because I had no idea how to explain it without telling him the truth.

"I guess we'd better get to lunch." I left my backpack on my bed.

"I am not really hungry right now. Are you?" Alexei walked over next to me.

I was nervous. My thoughts raced as I remembered Julian's warning, my roommates' descriptions of Alexei, and my own dream.

"Are you, Elisabeth?"

"Am I what?"

He smiled. "Are you hungry?"

"Oh, that. No, not really." My stomach was doing the kinds of tumbling movements that made food the last thing I wanted to think about.

"Can we have a talk? A real discussion without trying to hide everything from each other?"

"I don't know what you mean. I haven't been hiding anything."

He gave my arm a gentle tug so that I sat down on the bed beside him. He had a look on his face that said he didn't quite believe me. "I know who you are."

Now I was really confused. "I'm Elisabeth Sinclair. Everyone knows who I am; I'm the new kid."

"You are Elisabeth Julian Sinclair, only child of Nicholas Augustin Merrick Sinclair, the only child and heir of Augustin

Ruarc Etienne Sinclair, the last prince crowned of the Malhairer."

"The what of the what?" I stared at him in shock.

"You did not know? You really did not know?" A look of surprise that must have matched my own crossed his face before he became carefully blank. He stood up and paced back and forth in the small space between my bed and Emma's. "How could she just leave you here without telling you anything? Does she care? She cannot be so angry at Nicholas that she would risk you now."

He obviously wasn't talking to me, a fact made even clearer when he began muttering in Russian. I waited for him to stop on his own.

He finally stopped pacing and looked right at me. It was that same intense stare as before, but his eyes were flashing blue and green fire. I knew he was enraged, but I also realized his anger was not directed at me.

"Will you answer some of my questions now?"

Alexei stared at me for another moment before he found his voice. "I am afraid to. I have no idea what she has told you, and I could make things worse."

I nodded, not because I understood him, but because I was getting used to these cryptic responses. "Why don't we start with easy and work our way to complicated?"

He sat back down. "Ask away."

"The 'she' that you were cursing for not telling me anything, that was Julian right?"

"Yes, Julian."

"You know that she's my godmother?"

"I know. What I do not know is why it has taken her so long to find you." The anger started to build again. "You were out there unprotected-"

It was my turn to interrupt him. "You talk about Julian like you know her."

"Is that a question?" He sighed and seemed to be trying to let go of the fury that he felt. "Yes, I know Julian quite well."

"But she didn't recognize your name. Yesterday at lunch, Charly was talking about you, but it wasn't your name that got Julian's attention. It was your description."

Alexei smiled. "And she warned you to stay away from me. I understand now. I thought . . . it does not matter what I thought. When Julian and I knew each other I was going by a different name, and she had no reason to think that I would be here. She was warning you about someone else."

"Why were you going by a different name? Isn't Alexei your real name?"

"It is, but I am Russian." He seemed to believe that explained everything to me. I suppose the confusion on my face told him otherwise. "Russians have many names and nicknames. My Christian name is Aleksandr and sometimes I go by Alexei, but when Julian knew me I went by another nickname, Sasha."

"How is Sasha a nickname for Aleksandr?" I demanded.

Alexei laughed. "How is Bobby a nickname for Robert or Billy for William? It just is."

I stared for a moment, and then I laughed too. "I guess you're right. I'd never really thought about it." I let the smile leave my face. "So if Julian had heard the description of you linked with the name Sasha . . ."

Alexei's smile became a wry grin. "She still might have warned you to keep your distance, but she would have told you that I could be trusted. And she would have found a way to keep me from telling you too much, which I have done. So what did she tell you?"

"About what? You'll have to be more specific. When Julian found me, I thought I was the daughter of Mike and Amanda Sawyer, and six months older than I really am." I didn't try too hard to keep the bitterness from my voice.

Alexei was amazed. "You did not even know your name? But how could this have happened?"

"Apparently, I was 'mislabeled'."

Alexei stood up again. "This is insane! Julian cannot really believe this was all an accident!"

I felt the blood rush out of my head, and I was glad I was sitting because the room began to tilt. My voice was a harsh whisper, but in the quiet tower room, Alexei had no trouble hearing me. "Are you saying it was done on purpose?"

His eyes, once again that summer sky blue, were filled with the truth before he could even say it. "How could it have been otherwise?"

Hot tears fell from my eyes and my throat was burning and scratchy. I could barely get out the one word. "Why?"

"Do you not know? Your grandfather made a terrible mistake when he married that evil woman, his second wife. Thankfully, he was so in love with your grandmother that even after her death, he refused to give her title to another woman. It was bad enough that she gained temporary power when your grandfather died and your father was not yet to the age of maturity. Now, she has held her power for too long. She will not give it up easily."

Alexei wasn't telling me anything that Julian hadn't already, but it was easier to ask him the question that had been haunting me for days. "Do you think someone just took advantage of the confusion and chaos to hide me from Julian, or do you think my parents were . . ." Even without Julian's absolute love for my father staring at me, I couldn't make myself finish the awful thought.

I didn't have to. Alexei used the most gentle voice possible, but the words still grated like fingernails on a chalkboard. "I am certain they were killed. I am so sorry."

He opened his arms and held me tight against his chest while I cried tears I thought I'd used up already. I hadn't believed I could hurt anymore than I had before, but now I knew. Somehow my heart knew that Alexei was right; that Julian hadn't been able to say it, but that she had believed it too. My parents didn't just die in a freak accident. Someone set the fire deliberately to kill them without caring how many others were killed along the way. But they let me live, possibly knowing where I was all along, but not believing I was any kind of threat.

"Why, Alexei?" My tears had soaked the front of his Oxford shirt. "Why didn't they just kill me too?"

He held me close, one hand stroking my hair. "You have something they need. You are still in danger, Elisabeth. But you are not alone." I don't know how long we sat there, Alexei rocking me like I was a toddler, but the next thing I remember was Charly waking me up for dinner. Alexei was gone, but he left something behind. Sitting on the shelf, next to the picture of my parents, was a small box.

CHAPTER EIGHT

When I went to class the next morning, I took the small box with me, wrapped carefully in a silk scarf Julian had bought. All I could do was stare at the gift Alexei had left. There was no mistaking that he had left it for me. Although it was small, it had a beautiful bird painted on the top with my initials worked into the feathers. It was truly a work of art, so delicate and intricate. It sparkled in the light with its glossy finish. The other girls didn't realize it was new, since everything of mine was new to them anyway.

I was hoping to find a chance to talk to Alexei, so I took the box with me. I wanted answers. He knew so much more about me than I did, and he talked about Julian as though she was his equal when he was only a year or so older than me. Why did it seem like every time I got one answer, ten more questions came up?

I somehow managed to get through my first class of the day, and then I headed to the Langford Building, where I'd had history and geography the day before. I had a free period for studying, but something in me believed Alexei would be waiting. I was right. He was sitting in the study lounge on the second floor. With the beautiful weather outside, most students with free time were in the courtyard, near the fountain. We were left alone.

"How are you this morning, Elisabeth?" He seemed wary.

"Exhausted. Confused. Angry. Confused." I sat down in the chair across from him and pulled the scarf out of my backpack. "I know I fell apart on you yesterday. I'm sorry. I won't do it again, but I need answers that you have."

He was surprised. "You are apologizing for falling apart? I am the one who should be apologizing. I caught you completely off guard with everything, and you accepted it. Who would not fall apart after that?"

"Don't blame yourself. It's not your fault." I smiled. "You really are a nice guy."

He only frowned harder. "I am not nice, Elisabeth. The person your friends know, that is not me. Or at least not the entire me."

"Now, I'm not even allowed to say you're nice? If you're such a terrible person, why did you hold me while I cried? And why did you leave this for me?" I unwrapped the box and held it up.

"It is yours. It was made for you." Alexei had finally begun to relax but a dark look crossed his face. "I was beginning to believe I would never have the chance to give it to you."

"It's from you? Tell me about it. It's Russian?" I hoped that asking about the box instead of my parents would help him find a way to talk to me about everything.

"Yes, to both questions. The box is papier-mâché that is hand-painted and lacquered. They are made in villages in Russia and are very valuable collectibles, depending on how well they are painted. The best scenes represent images from Russian folklore or landscapes and are painted using magnifying lenses. This particular box with the firebird was commissioned in honor of your birth by my father. It was supposed to symbolize a sort of pact between our families, and I was supposed to give it to you when your father made you his heir, but that never happened."

I thought about everything he said and everything he was careful not to say. "The box is beautiful, but if I accept it . . . Does that endorse a pact that I know nothing about?"

Alexei's eyes held grief. "No. Not anymore. I told you, my family is gone. I am the last."

"I'm the last of my family."

He shook his head. "No. It is not the same. Your family has many more members of a distant nature. If the bloodlines were traced . . . I believe Julian would be your cousin several generations removed as it were."

"I don't understand that at all. Julian told me that everyone expected her to marry my father when they were adults."

Alexei smiled. "That is true, but think about history, Elisabeth. The royal houses of Europe were forever intermarrying with their own distant cousins. Our own Tsarina was a cousin to the British monarchy."

I searched my memory for what he meant. "Do you mean Alexandra, the one who was murdered with her family?"

"Yes, the Romanovs."

"But didn't that happen in the nineteen teens, like 1916 or 1917? You talk about it like it was personal."

"I am Russian. All of our history is personal." Alexei laughed. "I suppose talking like this makes me sound very strange."

It was my turn to smile at him. "It's just different for Americans, I guess. And maybe more so for me. America is such a young country that our own history seems very short when compared to Europe and Asia." I took a deep breath and then continued speaking, trying to sound casual as I revealed my newest source of insecurity. "The way I grew up, without even knowing my real name – I guess there's a lack of personal history that makes your identification with something that happened a hundred years ago seem very foreign to me."

Alexei looked at me, and for a moment it felt as though he was trying to peek inside my soul. "You feel it, do you not? You know there is something you are supposed to be connected to, like a piece of you is missing, and now that you know the truth about who you are, you need to know the rest so you can find the part of you that has been lost."

I sighed, feeling grateful. "You understand. I don't think Julian knew that. Does that mean that you'll give me answers – real answers?"

Alexei let out his breath slowly and heavily. "I have to. Understand me carefully, Elisabeth. I will give you answers, but I do not want to. There are things you must know and learn, but you will not thank me for being the one to do it. The truth can set you free, but it can also be hard and ugly."

I started with an easy one. "Tell me how you know Julian."

He shook his head. "That is not the place to begin. We need to discuss your family before we drag mine into it. What did Julian tell you about your father and grandfather?"

"Not as much as she left out apparently. My grandmother died when my father was born. I'm named after her and Julian. My grandfather was concerned that my father was neglected or something like that, so he married a widow with three children of her own who were to be my father's playmates. The older two never had much to do with him or Julian, but the youngest was close to their age, and they never got along. My grandfather died before my father was of age, so his wife was left in charge of the family business. My father went to college, and he and Julian stayed away from home, traveling the world on their school breaks. Then my father met and fell in love with my mother. They eloped during his senior year of college, and I came along the following Christmastime. Julian said he planned to return to the family, but he seemed to find excuses to put it off until after I was a year old. Then they died."

Alexei was staring off into space. "The family business, Jules?"

"Julian said no one except my father called her that!" I was surprised at how harsh I sounded.

"Sorry. I would never call her that to her face if it caused her pain. I suppose I picked up the habit." Before I had a chance to examine his words, he was distracting me again. "Julian never told you your grandfather's name?"

"No, the first time I heard it was when you . . . Didn't you say he was the prince of something?" That made no sense in my head at all.

"That is what I said. Augustin Ruarc Etienne Sinclair, last prince crowned of the Malhairer." He was watching me closely.

"I don't get it. What's the Mal-hor-ray thingy?"

"It is, well honestly, it is complicated. I suppose the easiest way to think about it would be to consider them a tribe or clan or – a principality, sort of like Monaco."

I think my jaw hit the floor. "You mean like an actual separate country kind of prince?" My voice came very close to a squeal.

"Like that. Except you will never find it on any maps or history books or the internet."

My eyes narrowed. "If you're messing with me-"

He shook his head quickly. "I am not. I swear I am not. It is just that the Malhairer are more of a shadow group. They have never had their own territory or nation, but they did have their prince. The prince is the ultimate leader and controls the wealth and resources of the Malhairer. Perhaps if you think of it like a Gypsy tribe from European history or a Bedouin tribe in the Arabian desert. They do not need a government to function within, and their home has changed over time."

"That sort of makes sense, but how could my grandfather be a prince? That's crazy."

Alexei seemed to understand that the concept of the Malhairer as an abstract was easier for me to accept than the idea that my family was some kind of royalty. "The Malhairer are ruled by a sovereign who falls into the direct line of inheritance. While the succession is based on primogeniture, it is not strictly patriarchal."

"So the first-born child, male or female, becomes the next in line?"

"Exactly. For several generations there has only been one heir to reach the age of maturity. When your grandmother died, your grandfather broke tradition. He married a woman who had other children rather than taking a younger wife who might produce further heirs. Then he compounded the issue by refusing his second wife the title "Princess" which had belonged to your grandmother. They say he adored his Elisabeth and refused to even sleep in the same room as his second wife."

"So he only married her to be a surrogate for my father."

"I think that is why he chose her, but the laws required the prince to marry again within five years. Your grandfather remarried on the eve of your father's fifth birthday. Nicholas was, of course, named as the blood heir."

I interrupted him. "The blood heir?"

Alexei smiled at my reaction. "It does seem a fairly barbaric term, does it not? They made it as simple as possible – the oldest child of the bloodline. There is a full ceremony, but with Nicholas still underage when Prince Augustin died, his wife became regent. I think Julian is still fighting to have you declared the blood heir, but the fact that your father was never crowned and that you were never named his blood heir in that ceremony gives the regent room to maneuver."

I recoiled as if he had hit me. He saw my reaction and just waited. We sat in silence for several minutes while the new thoughts filtered into my mind. They wanted to make me the blood heir and maybe their ruler. That's what Julian was fighting to make happen. And the regent didn't want to give up her power. If they named me, then Julian could become the regent until I was old enough. Then the thought that Alexei seemed to be waiting for finally registered in my sluggish brain.

"If the regent doesn't want to give up power to me or Julian, then she didn't want to give up power to my father. Did she have my father killed?"

Alexei took my hands in his. "It is very likely, but as far as I know there has never been the slightest evidence of that. But if she was behind it, or even one of her supporters, then you understand why your life is still in jeopardy?"

"What I don't understand is why I wasn't killed with them?" It was the thought that had haunted me for as long as I could remember. Why was I alive when my parents were dead? At least now, I knew it wasn't my fault they were dead.

"I have several theories about that, but they are no more than guesses. For now we should stick with facts. You are not entirely safe, but Julian was right. The Academy is the safest place for you. Did you know that this school's founder Aleron Saint Clare was one of your ancestors?"

"Really? Saint Clare, Sinclair. The headmaster said something about Aleron Saint Clare founding this as a sister school to the one in Europe."

"Yes. I believe the Malhairer moved from Europe to America at that time. Remember, Elisabeth, to think of Gypsies."

I took a deep breath to try to sort out the information. "If my family wanted to make a pact with your family, are you a prince?" That was so easy to imagine. Beautiful Alexei, with his amazing eyes, wearing the kind of uniform with ribbons that all the men of the European royal families wore, was the kind of prince people wrote fairy tales about.

Alexei maintained a wry smile, but nothing could disguise the heartbreak in his eyes. "My family is all gone. If I ever was a prince, now I am the prince of nothing."

"But you're Russian. Was your family like the . . . the Mal-hor-ay?" I enunciated each syllable carefully.

"I suppose you could say so. But it is not my first family that you mean. My Russian family was poor. It was my adoptive father that had the power and wealth. Now I have only part of the wealth."

Something about that bothered me, but I couldn't figure out what so I continued asking my questions. "What did my family gain from an alliance with yours?"

"An end to the wars that were depleting all our resources." He answered quickly and then seemed to rethink his answer because he immediately qualified it. "You know the kind of business wars that drain funds and such."

I nodded, but I didn't really understand. I didn't know much about business or any of what he'd been telling me.

"I am sure you have many more questions, Elisabeth, but we do have classes to attend. The most important thing for your protection is to act like you are unaware of any of this. You cannot miss classes, and you cannot tell anyone. I believe Julian was right in thinking that there could be someone here who-" He broke off, unsure of how much to say.

"Julian said that the regent may have a grandchild here. She checked the enrollment, but still thinks someone could be here that might view me as a threat." I tried not to think about it too much. I felt too small and insignificant to be a threat to anyone.

Alexei looked relieved to not have to explain. "It is a possibility. Names can be changed as I have demonstrated to you. For now, you need to be in class. Promise me you will not do anything to draw attention to yourself."

"I'll promise if you promise to keep telling me what you know." I knew I was begging, but it was worth it.

"I promise." Alexei's voice was so solemn and the look in his eyes was so grave, that for a moment, he seemed much older than seventeen years old. I blinked to clear my vision.

"You should probably get to class. Try to stay with your roommates as much as possible or at least in crowds of students."

I nodded and left the student lounge, reminding myself not to look back at him. I only had a little while before I needed to meet up with Emma and get ready for my first riding lesson. I needed to clear my head and focus. With my epic past failures at anything involving sports, I had to pay attention around the horses or I'd end up in the hospital without anyone else's help.

CHAPTER NINE

I had never seen a horse up close before. My first thought was how huge they were. The riding instructor, Ms. LeMaster, tried to be reassuring.

"Marigold is our gentlest horse. She's very patient with inexperienced riders. Just go over and say hello."

Marigold was in her stall with her head poked out over the half-door as if she was curious about what was going on. She was reddish-brown, but her mane and tail were dark brown, and she had a white patch on one shoulder. I put my hand out to touch her nose, and she bumped me in what Ms. LeMaster said was a playful gesture. When I actually touched Marigold, all my fear left. It was as if I could feel how gentle she truly was. As if I could see into her mind. I was able to push all my worries away and just focus on Marigold.

Ms. LeMaster showed me the halter and the lead rope she was carrying. When Marigold saw them, she held still. I felt her readiness to have them on and watched carefully as Ms. LeMaster demonstrated how to put them on, then removed them, and handed them to me. I didn't hesitate. It was like muscle memory where the body performs actions without consciously thinking about how to do it. Marigold was anticipating my movements, and I was synchronized with hers.

I led Marigold out of the barn and into a fenced-in practice ring. Ms. LeMaster walked with us a bit, letting me get a feel for how Marigold responded, before teaching me how to properly saddle and bridle a horse. When I led Marigold to the mounting block, I automatically checked the girth, as if I'd done it a hundred times. Ms. LeMaster adjusted the stirrups, and I urged Marigold to move, practicing the instructions I'd been given, but it felt as if Marigold knew what I was going to ask from her before I even thought it. It kind of made sense to me. She was probably the horse that they used to teach all the first timers and probably knew the routine so well that she could go through it even without the students.

Ms. LeMaster and Marigold walked me through a series of exercises that taught me how to control a horse. All too soon, I was off Marigold's back and leading her back to the barn. As Ms. LeMaster taught me how to properly remove the saddle and bridle and how to care for Marigold after her workout, she said I was a natural horsewoman. It may have been the first time I had ever called me a natural at anything.

As I rubbed Marigold's nose to say goodbye, I knew she was happy with me. She liked me as much as I liked her. I'd had fun. The idea of actually enjoying a physical activity was a little shocking. It might be great to have my own horse the way Julian had promised . . . as long as the horse was as sweet as Marigold.

After Emma and I changed our clothes, we walked to lunch together. I realized it was the first time I'd gotten to spend time with her outside of class without Charly around. I was a little awed by her. Aside from the fact that I knew how smart she was, she was also beautiful. I suppose some people might not think so if she was compared to Lila Grace's fragile, ethereal beauty or even Charly's bold, flashy looks, but Emma had her own beauty. Her golden curls gave her a sort of halo-like effect, like a Madonna in a painting, and her eyes were the darkest blue I'd ever seen.

"How are you feeling about your classes?"

"I'm behind in everything, but most of them seem like they're good classes."

"Don't worry too much, Elisabeth. We'll get you caught up in no time," Emma said.

I laughed a little. "That's beginning to sound like a theme in my life. I have so many things to catch up on; I feel like I'll never have a chance to catch my breath."

"It will happen quicker than you think. Most of the first month of school was just review and introduction."

I gave her a grateful look. "Thanks, Emma. I'm really lucky to have you as a roommate."

She shook her head. "I'm the lucky one. Charly used to drive me crazy with all her energy, but you seem to like it."

I smiled. "She's definitely got energy. I'm used to rooming with really bratty girls. They were more interested in boys and clothes than anything else." I spoke without really thinking about what I was saying.

"I thought this was your first boarding school." Emma's midnight blue eyes bored into mine.

"It is." I realized my mistake as soon as the words were out of my mouth. The rich, privileged daughters that attended the Academy only shared rooms at the elite boarding schools they attended. I clapped my hand over my mouth for a second before lowering it to speak. "I'm not supposed to talk about it, Emma."

Emma looked at me seriously and then nodded. "It's okay. We all have things we're not supposed to talk about,

Elisabeth. Just don't slip like that in front of Charly or everyone will know about it within the day. She means well, she just doesn't always know when to shut her mouth."

"Thanks." We walked into the crowded dining hall and got in line. As we waited, I looked around the room. I didn't see Charly or Alexei, but Lila Grace was sitting at a table with the same group of friends she sat with my first day. The headmaster and some of the teachers were again sitting at the table under the large midnight blue banner that had "Saint Clare Academy" stitched on it in silver thread.

A sudden thought went through my mind, and I turned to Emma. "Do you know much about the history of this Academy? About its founder?"

She looked at me and then around the dining hall. "Why don't we get sack lunches and enjoy them out in the sunlight? You never know how many days like this we have left so we might as well take advantage of it."

I nodded, and followed her through the serving line to pick out sandwiches, chips, fresh fruit, and bottled waters. Emma led the way outside and through the courtyard. She walked until she found a large clearing that was deserted. We sat down on the grass and opened our lunches. Emma looked around again before she spoke.

"Elisabeth, you have got to be very careful about the questions you ask and especially where you ask them. Most of the students here would never think to connect you and your Sinclair family with Aleron Saint Clare and this Academy, but if someone was listening for information about you, it could get dangerous."

"You know about my family? Does Julian know what you know?"

Emma shushed me. "I don't know if your guardian realizes what I know or not, but you can trust me. I did a research project on the Academy's history last year. I was able to trace the Sinclair family from Aleron Saint Clare's older brother, Etienne, down to Nicholas and now you."

"You found records about me? Where?"

"In the library. Apparently, your grandfather, Augustin, moved most of your family's records to the Academy when your father was a student and someone continued updating them, although the records are somewhat spotty."

"Can you show me? What do they say about my parents?"

Emma shook her head. "They're gone. I looked for them right after my test the morning Mrs. Bambridge brought you and Miss Julian up to our room. I was surprised to have Elisabeth Sinclair as a roommate when all the records had been so sketchy with information so I wanted to make sure I had the right name."

"But there was nothing there when you checked?" I asked.

"Right. Well, almost nothing. The older records were still there, but anything that mentioned you, your father, or your grandfather was gone. I thought maybe Miss Julian had taken them."

I shrugged. "Maybe, but I don't think she knew they were here. Do you remember what they said?"

"Some, but after someone was snooping in our room yesterday I went on my computer and re-read my paper. I deleted it from the hard drive, but I saved an encrypted file on a flash drive in case you ever wanted to see it."

"Where is it? How do I get it unencrypted?"

Emma laughed. "I can decrypt it for you, but it will have to wait a few days. I mailed it to myself. I didn't want the wrong person to find it."

"That sounds extreme."

"Some of what has happened to your family is extreme. And from the lack of information, I'd guess that a lot of what happened to you falls under that category."

I nodded. "Can you tell me what you remember? Anything the records said about my father or me?"

Emma's voice gentled. "There wasn't much. It had a record of your father's birth and his mother's death. Did you know her name was Elisabeth?"

"Julian told me I was named for my grandmother and my godmother."

"It had another date noted, but there wasn't really any kind of explanation with it. Just some sort of celebration or ceremony. The other dates listed were of your grandfather's death, your parents' wedding, and your birth. There was a notation about the accident that killed them, but it only stated that your mother's body was recovered, and you were missing. I remember searching through all the records, but I could never find anything that explained your disappearance."

I took a deep breath. "You must keep this secret, but I was truly lost after the accident. I was mistaken for another baby and raised in foster care. Julian has only just found me."

Emma gasped. "No wonder you're asking so many questions. You don't know anything about your own family."

I tried to smile at her, to reassure both of us that things were working out, but I don't think it was much of a smile at all.

"Does Miss Julian know how you were lost?"

"No, but it seems that my parents were killed and the accident was just a cover-up of their murders. Julian believes I may still be in danger."

"I think she may be right. Your family didn't just found the Academy; they run the trust that endows it. That's a substantial amount of money, Elisabeth, and it's only one tiny fraction of your family's wealth. You don't want to make it too easy for people to connect you to the Saint Clare family. There were many reasons your ancestors changed the spelling of your name."

"I'll be careful, but will you help me learn more about my family?"

I tried not to let too much of what I was feeling show on my face. With warnings from Julian, Alexei and now Emma, I wondered if someone was watching us even now.

"Of course I'll help you, but we have to be very careful about where and when we can discuss any of this."

We picked up our lunch trash before walking back to Kirkwynd. My mind was racing. Before we got too close to the building, I put my hand on her arm to stop her.

"Emma, what class was your project about the school's history for?"

Emma's dark eyes lit up. "I hadn't thought about that. It was a special project for my geography class with Miss Elswick. She wanted me to research the history of the school and write about how the geography influenced the architecture and resources. She kept talking about all the types of topology on the school grounds."

"Do you think she remembers what's in your paper?"

"I had to turn in two copies of my paper and copies of all my research notes, even if the research didn't become part of the paper. She said she was grading me as much for my research methods as writing and critical thinking skills." Emma explained.

"So she knows everything you told me? Do you think she was the one to pull the records?"

"Maybe, but . . . ." Emma leveled her dark gaze on me. "We can't jump to any conclusions. Just because someone may know something, doesn't automatically make them a bad person." Her expression softened. "And you need to try not to dwell on this. Spinning it all around in your mind all day, every day won't get you any answers any faster, but it will exhaust you and keep you on edge all the time. Miss Julian would not have left you here if she didn't believe you'd be safe. I know it's hard, but try to have some fun and just enjoy being at a great school with new friends and some seriously hot boys."

I giggled. "I think Charly believes that you stay so focused on your academics that you haven't even realized boys attend this school."

Emma laughed, a quiet but full sound. "Sometimes I let Charly believe I'm a little more involved in my classwork than I actually am. Before you arrived, it was easier." Emma shook her head. "Maybe I'm not as obsessed as Charly, but I would have to be dead, buried, and decomposed to not notice how hot Alexei is."

"Charly has a crush on him, doesn't she?" I felt a little guilty for the connection that drew Alexei's attention to me.

Emma snorted. "Half the student population has a crush on him; Charly is edging into stalker territory."

I knew Emma was teasing a little, but I had seen the way Charly had grown flustered just talking about him. Emma looked at me carefully.

"Don't worry about Charly's feelings too much, Elisabeth. In her heart she knows Alexei can never be hers. She's just caught up in the hormones."

CHAPTER TEN

I spent the rest of the afternoon and then the evening after dinner trying to catch up on all my schoolwork. The night passed quickly, and I felt better about my classes. I had kept an eye out for Alexei both at dinner and in the Kirkwynd study hall, but I never saw him.

Climbing the stairs with Emma, Charly, and Lila Grace, I felt disappointed. I hoped to learn more about my family and Alexei's strange connection to Julian. I didn't understand why he wouldn't just tell me everything. I had known Julian was editing everything she told me, but I couldn't imagine why Alexei felt like he had to hide things from me. Before I turned my light out for the night, I read another of my father's letters, hoping to find some clue in it. It was dated only two weeks after the first one.

Jules,

It's official then – Europe. I can't tell you what getting your letter meant to me. It was a breath of air when I didn't even realize I was drowning. The students here are average I suppose. They don't seem much different from most of the kids at the Academy. And no, none of the girls are worth looking at twice. They are nothing to get my blood boiling, even if I was old enough for it to boil. I wish I had more of a chance to be like them. They're all so innocent of the realities that wait for them after college.

Some are so idealistic, believing they can change the world. Is that what I'm doing here? Am I trying to change our world?

God, this letter is depressing. I should just tear it up and write you a different one — happy and full of fluff. But I can't. I need you too much to pretend with you. If it wasn't for you and your belief that spending this time in college will help me later . . . I'm not sure I could fight it. The pull is there all the time. I could just go back and give in, but I have to believe there's another way, a better way.

I'm sorry for my little trek into the darker side of life. I promise to be much more cheerful tomorrow. I suppose the full moon is bringing out the lunatic in me. Please write as often as you can.

Love,
Nick

The letter was so different in tone from the first one, but my father was just as cryptic as Julian. I realized it only seemed that way to me because I wasn't sure what he was really talking about while Julian undoubtedly had known. I guess the idea of being a royal heir would make anyone feel trapped at times. I could imagine my father wanting to have the same idealistic chance to plan for his future that his classmates had.

It was somehow comforting to know that my father had experienced his own moments of doubt and fear over his future, even after he'd grown up with the full knowledge of what was expected of him. I wondered what kind of pressures his step-mother must have been putting on him to keep him away or to push him into doing something he didn't want to do.

I fell asleep with his letter under my pillow and found myself dreaming again. It was like the dream two nights before. Charly's wardrobe was moved and the secret door was ajar with a flickering light coming from below. I was wearing another revealing nightgown over a body that was not mine only, instead of the ivory silk, this one was the exact shade of blue that I had first seen in Alexei's eyes.

I crept down the steps to find Alexei just like before in his tuxedo with an old-fashioned lantern. I was embarrassed that my nightgown was the same color as his eyes, but again the emotion faded with the knowledge that I was dreaming.

"I am glad you came, Elisabeth, but you should not be here. It is dangerous for you now."

"I don't understand. I'm so tired of everyone and their cryptic answers. I don't want any more secrets. I don't like the ones I already have." I knew I was whining, but I couldn't stop my true feelings from coming out.

"I warned you that you would not like the answers. I do not want you to hate me. I am running out of options, but you are not ready for all the truth. Not yet."

"Why not? What do I have to do to be ready?"

Alexei had the same sad smile as when he told me about losing his family. "I do not know if anyone is ever truly ready to hear what you must be told. Please, Elisabeth."

"Please what? I don't understand what everyone wants from me. I feel like everyone knows more about me than I do, and I'm not even allowed to ask or complain."

"I only want to protect you."

"I don't want to be protected. I want you to help me, to talk to me."

Alexei sighed. It was only when I felt his cool breath across my bare arm that I realized how close we had gotten. Close, but not touching. His breath smelled like peppermint and made my skin tingle. I looked up at him, so tall and so beautiful. Most of the time he seemed like the best looking guy I'd ever seen but here in my dream, somehow he was more.

He was beyond handsome. He was mesmerizing. It was partly the clothes. He looked better than any decent person had the right to look in the dressy outfit. But it was more than that. He seemed . . . more. I couldn't find the right words. Not more beautiful exactly. Not more interesting or more intense. Just more Alexei. It was the only thing that really seemed to fit for me. Somehow he seemed more himself. As if here in my dream, I was able to see more of the real Alexei, although that implied that I wasn't seeing the real him outside my dream, which was ridiculous.

I stared into his amazing eyes, watching as they seemed to shift from blue to green and back again every time he blinked. He was looking down at me, and the air became charged. It was as if every nerve ending in my body was suddenly at full attention. I realized for the first time how it would look if anyone could actually see inside my head, with me standing so close to him, wearing such revealing lingerie. It made me aware of how male he was.

Alexei noticed the change in the atmosphere too. I knew that I was hoping he would kiss me, even as I knew that the memory of this dream would make me blush the next time I saw the real Alexei. But it didn't matter. The dream Alexei treated me much like the real one did.

"We should not be here like this. You do not know what you are doing. I am not upset with you, and I will never hold it against you. I was the one who chose to play with fire, but I will not see you get burned. You need to go back to bed and sleep your nights without dreaming."

"Even my dreams are confusing and cryptic and full of warnings that don't make any sense. It's not fair. I need something real to hang onto, but I've lost everything I ever thought was real." I didn't say it out loud, but in that moment, I wished for the home I'd never had and the mother I couldn't remember. I wanted some place or memory of safety to be my refuge, my anchor, in the chaotic storm that was my new life.

"Elisabeth, please. This is not safe. Go back to your room."

"Why? If this is just a dream, and I know it is, then why can't I have one moment of peace? Why can't I just forget all the questions and confusion by losing myself in your eyes? They're so beautiful. I can't decide if I like them better when they're blue like the summer sky or green like spring leaves."

I was reaching up to touch his face when he grabbed my hands. He held both of them in one of his and pushed me against the stone wall, pinning them behind me. He was leaning against me, so tall and so masculine. My heart was thundering both from these newly awakened feelings and from fear. He was so much stronger than I would have guessed, and he looked so angry. He leaned down until his face was inches from mine, and he was staring me right in the eyes.

"I am not a distraction. I am not a way for you to forget who you are. I am not your path to peace of mind. I can never stop being who I am, and you can never take anything for granted. This is not a game. Not for me, and not for you."

It was more cryptic warnings, and I didn't think I could stand it any longer. In spite of the ferocity in his voice, I was hyper-aware of my bare skin and the well-endowed body I was wearing. I arched my neck so that my hair fell back, making my borrowed cleavage noticeable, knowing that it was like taunting a wild animal, and I wouldn't be able to control his reactions.

He took several deep, shaky breaths, never blinking, never taking his eyes from mine. I barely saw the movement when his tongue slid over his bottom lip, wetting it slightly. I held my breath waiting, waiting, waiting.

Then he let me go and walked a few steps away, muttering in Russian. I was pretty sure he was cursing me or himself or both. It was so real even though I knew I was still dreaming. I went to the door that led back to my tower room and hesitated. With several feet between us, he turned and looked back at me.

"I'm sorry, Alexei. I know you don't think of me that way, and I know this is just a dream, but-"

"Go to bed and sleep, Elisabeth. You have done nothing wrong so there is nothing to feel sorry for." He looked so sad that I felt tears spring up in my eyes, even as I reminded myself it was all a dream. I turned quickly so he wouldn't see me cry and slipped back up the stairs and into my bed.

When I woke up, the room was exactly the way it had been when I feel asleep with my father's letter still under my pillow. But my pillow was streaked with stains from tears I didn't remember crying except in my dream.

CHAPTER ELEVEN

It was Friday and a repeat of my first day, with a study period, history, and geography before lunch and chemistry after. I walked with Charly to the now familiar building where most of the classrooms were located. I'd made sure we left Kirkwynd Hall with plenty of time to spare before history. I didn't want to be late but, more than that, I didn't want to have to sit beside Alexei. He had avoided me yesterday, and my dream had done nothing to relieve the anxiety I was feeling.

We were almost the first to arrive. Mr. Callahan was sitting at his desk, deep in conversation with someone sitting on the other side of his desk and hidden from our view. We hesitated at the threshold, unsure if we were interrupting something important.

Mr. Callahan looked up and smiled. He motioned us into the room as he spoke. "Miss Sinclair, just the person we were discussing. We were going over the notes Mr. Mikhailovich has translated for you."

I had a moment of shock as Alexei stood on the other side of Mr. Callahan. Alexei stared at me while Mr. Callahan continued talking without really looking at either of us. "You're more than welcome to return to your room during today's test, or you can just wait for your next class in the student lounge. Do you know where it is?"

I tore my eyes away from Alexei and nodded.

"His notes are very thorough so you shouldn't have any trouble. Instead of making up this test, I've decided to let you write a paper summarizing what we covered. You can turn it in next week. I have the details typed out here for you."

He handed me a stack of papers, his one page assignment on top of Alexei's translated notes. I put them in my backpack and turned to walk out of the classroom. Charly dumped her backpack on her desk and quickly caught up with me in the hall.

"What was that about?"

I stared at her, unsure of what to say. "What do you mean?"

She shook her head. "Come on, Elisabeth. You couldn't take your eyes off Alexei. You turned three shades of red. And he was staring at you."

"I don't know why he was staring at me other than he probably thinks I've gone crazy, like you do."

She shook her head again, and the riot of red-gold hair flew everywhere. "I don't know 'bout crazy, but why were you looking at him like that?"

We had made it into the student lounge which I was relieved to find empty. "I had a dream last night, and he was in it."

Her turquoise eyes widened with understanding. "I know he's played the romantic lead in most of the female student population's dreams and probably a good number of the males, but it was just a dream. Was it good?"

I rolled my eyes at her. "It's embarrassing. I don't want to remember things like that, especially when he's been really nice."

"But was it good? Did you kiss?"

I started to shake my head 'no' and then remembered the intense moment when I was pushed against the wall and dream Alexei was so close. I must have shivered because Charly grinned.

"It was good. You lucky girl."

"No, not lucky," I corrected her. "Dreams like that make it hard to face the real guy, and he has no idea why I'm suddenly acting like a nutcase."

Charly shook her head at me, but she was still smiling. "I've got to get back to class. I'll meet you in here as soon as I'm done with the test."

"Okay. Good luck."

She waved as she sprinted back down the hallway. The noise of other students walking through the halls was very loud for a few minutes and then died out completely as classroom doors shut, muting the teachers' voices behind them. I started looking over the notes Alexei had copied out for me. They were written with the neatest penmanship I'd even seen from a boy's handwriting. I was alone for about fifteen minutes when I heard footsteps in the hall. I hoped it wouldn't be Alexei that soon, but I was terrified he'd find me in here alone.

The person stopped in the doorway, and I looked up. It wasn't Alexei. This new person was blond, although he was about as tall as Alexei. He was pale, more like Lila Grace's silvery blond than Emma's golden, but his skin was also pale. When I realized I was staring, I looked back down at my notes, but I couldn't seem to focus on them.

"Do you mind if I sit in here?"

I looked back up again. "I don't mind. Are you waiting for someone?"

He sat down at the table next to the couch where I was sitting. He put his backpack on the floor beside his chair. "I'm just waiting for my next class. I wasn't really ready to go all the way up three flights of steps."

"Are you okay?" I looked down quickly. "I'm sorry. That was rude. I just-"

He interrupted me. "It's okay. I've been ill, but I'm better now. I just don't have all my strength back yet. Are you the new student I've been hearing about?"

I gave him a wry look. "Elisabeth Sinclair, new girl."

He smiled back at me. "Nice to meet you, new girl. I'm Chase Elliot."

"Nice to meet you, Chase. What year are you?"

"Junior, although I should be a senior. I was sick and missed most of my last term at my old school, so my father transferred me here. I think he was hoping the weather here would be good for me, but . . . ."

I laughed. "Everyone keeps saying that it changes every other day, but all I've seen is sunshine and heat."

"How long have you been here, Elisabeth the new girl?"

"Just this week. I should be in class, but they're taking a test, and I'm behind."

"Lucky me, or else I may have had to wait weeks before meeting you."

I wasn't sure what to say to that so I just looked back down at my notes. He was handsome in spite of the pallor his illness had left him.

132

He seemed to be debating something before he spoke. "I'm heading on up now that I've caught my breath. I think this is the first time I've been glad that I was sick."

I looked back up at him with the question in my eyes.

"If I hadn't been sick and needed to stop to rest, I wouldn't have met you, and you wouldn't be sitting with me at lunch today."

"What makes you think I'm sitting with you at lunch?" I tried to sound aloof like I'd heard so many girls in my old school, but I couldn't help the little smile that slid out.

"Because you're curious about me, the same as I am you. Sit with me, you and your friends."

I smiled wider, but I wouldn't give in so easily. "We'll see."

He grinned, and my heart skipped a beat. "Yes, we will." It sounded like a promise that lingered even after he left the room. I looked down at the notes in my lap and knew it was useless trying to concentrate. I felt better than I had in weeks. The very handsome Chase Elliot was definitely flirting with me.

There was another sound at the door, and I thought that Chase had come back. I looked up to see Alexei hesitating in the doorway. I put my notes into my backpack as he walked over and sat on the other end of the couch from me.

"Elisabeth?" His voice was uncertain, and I knew it was my fault, so I smiled at him.

"Thanks so much for the notes, Alexei. They're great."

"You are welcome. I am sorry if I seemed to avoid you yesterday afternoon. I spent most of the evening in my room, translating."

"You shouldn't have gone to so much trouble. I'm sure Mr. Callahan would have waited."

"It was no trouble." He paused. "Elisabeth, I feel like I need to apologize."

I looked at him and saw that his eyes were blue today. "I'm not sure what you think you need to apologize for."

"Because I have not been able to tell you everything, and I know how frustrating it must be for you to have so many questions."

He looked really worried about me, so I pushed the remaining embarrassment of last night's dream out of my mind and tried to be honest.

"It is hard, but I think I understand why you have to be careful. I don't blame you if you don't want to have to deal with an overemotional girl who cries all over you and demands answers to things you aren't responsible for hiding from me. It's not your job to tell me. I'm grateful for everything you can tell me, but I shouldn't try to press any advantage or take out my frustrations on you."

He smiled at me. "I guess you needed a little time to yourself to work out how you feel."

"I guess I did. Thanks again for the notes, Alexei. It really was nice of you."

He checked his watch and picked up his bag. "It's almost time for geography. I guess we'd better go."

I nodded, picked up my own bag, and followed him out into the hall.

CHAPTER TWELVE

I had a hard time concentrating during geography. I knew that Charly thought it was because of my dream and Alexei, but I hadn't wanted to ask her about Chase in front of Alexei. It seemed tacky. Or maybe I was just remembering the times when some boy would strike up a conversation with me only to ask, within seconds, about Gretchen or some other girl. It wasn't that I'd had any delusions that Alexei or Chase was really interested in me. I just thought it was rude to get stupid over Chase in front of another boy.

So while I was supposed to be paying attention to Miss Elswick's lecture about the major industrial centers of Europe, I was replaying the conversation with Chase in the lounge. I thought about how handsome he was and realized I was comparing him to Alexei. They were both tall, over six feet, and they were both lean rather than bulky. I vaguely recalled Gretchen comparing the boys who were football players, basketball players, and baseball players. She'd said the footballers were bulky and big and would probably become fat when they left their teenage metabolism behind. The basketball guys were tall but lanky, all knees and elbows. Gretchen had pronounced the baseball player bodies the best because they were toned and muscled without being beefy. I'd never really understood what she meant before. Alexei and Chase were definitely muscled but not huge. Chase might have been bigger before he'd been sick, but he looked just about perfect right now. He was too pale, as if he'd spent the entire summer inside - which he probably had.

I was pale myself. Mrs. Jenkins had had to run me out of the house before I'd voluntarily go out. Even then, I'd sit in the shade under a tree and read. I'm sure it wasn't what she'd wanted, but at least I was outside.

Alexei, with his dark hair, should have reminded me of night, but his bright eyes – whether they were the summer sky blue or the spring leaf green – were all about the daylight. Chase, the blond, was nighttime. With his moonlight hair and hazel eyes that seemed to hold shadows, Chase seemed somehow darker than Alexei. Which was a very silly way to see it since Alexei was full of secrets and mystery while Chase was flirty and fun.

When the class finally ended, I turned to Alexei. "Are you going to lunch today?"

He shook his head. "I have to catch up on some reading, but I will talk to you in the study hall this evening."

I smiled. "Okay. See you then."

Charly watched me like I'd lost my mind and shook her head. As soon as Alexei was out of earshot, she pounced. "I guess you got over your embarrassment about your dream."

"What? Oh, yeah," I said. I pulled my backpack over my shoulder, and we started walking. "Actually, I was just surprised to see him this morning. It wasn't that big a deal."

"Yeah, right. That's why you turned as red as my hair this morning before history."

I looked down for a second, trying to figure out how to change the subject. "Actually, I'm really glad I missed class. I was sitting in the student lounge, and Chase Elliot came in."

"Chase Elliot! He's gorgeous! He's magnificent! I heard he was the fencing champion at his old school, and they were really mad when his dad sent him here. What was he like?" Her bright eyes were dancing as much as her feet, unable to hold the excitement inside her body.

"I guess you'll just have to see for yourself at lunch. He asked me – No, he told me and my friends to sit with him." I smiled remembering his cocky attitude. It was funny because in the past I'd always been irritated at boys with that kind of attitude. On Chase it was cute and kind of sweet.

"Ooh! You are so interested in him! I thought you had a thing for Alexei. Never mind. It figures; you haven't even been here a week yet, and you've got the two best looking guys in school falling all over you."

"Hardly." I gave her a skeptical look. "Alexei is just being nice because his family has known my family for ages or something, and Mr. Callahan asked him for the notes. Chase probably just wants to be nice to the other newbie."

"Chase was new for the first five minutes, and then he practically owned Wycliffe Hall. And Alexei is nice to everyone, but he doesn't go out of his way to do things for them." She shook her head. "It doesn't matter. I'm not jealous or anything. Well, not any more than any red-blooded girl would be."

I laughed, but I knew she wasn't being entirely honest, probably less with herself than with me. We walked into the cafeteria, feeling a little nervous. Charly was right about part of it. If I sat with Chase Elliot, who was apparently the other male item of adoration, after becoming friends with Alexei, it would definitely attract attention. That was one thing I didn't want to do. If Alexei and Julian were right, then there was a strong possibility that someone at this school wanted to hurt me.

Making myself the center of gossip was not the way to stay under the radar.

On the other hand, being the focus of so much attention might keep whoever it was that was out there away from me, scared of getting caught because someone was always watching. In the end, I knew I was just trying to justify my carelessness to myself in preparation for the explanation I would have to give to Alexei later. I had known from the moment Chase spoke, just as surely as he had, that I would be sitting with him at lunch.

He was waiting for me. He stood up and waved us over. Charly grinned at me, and we headed to the table. There were no empty places left, but when we approached with our trays, two younger students got up quickly and moved to another table. I looked at Chase questioningly.

"I told them I was saving a couple of seats. They just wanted to ask about something so they said they'd move when you got here."

We sat down, and two good-looking guys across the table immediately began asking Charly a thousand questions. She was laughing and grinning as usual, but I looked at Chase and caught his half-smile as he watched his friends. He saw me looking at him and shrugged his shoulders slightly.

"Did you put them up to that?" I hissed at him.

"What if I did? It obviously wasn't any hardship for them to be nice to her, and they seem really interested." He smiled at me, certain that I would see things his way.

"Why did you do it? Didn't you think my friend would be able to carry on a conversation without your help?"

The smile faltered. "No, that wasn't it at all. I just wanted them to distract her so I could focus on you and only you."

I wasn't sure how to respond to that. I knew I was supposed to be so flattered that I wouldn't be upset, but it seemed a little too manipulative. Kind of like insisting that I eat lunch with him in the first place.

"I heard you were really good at fencing."

He smiled, accepting the change of topic as evidence of my . . . acquiescence, if not necessarily forgiveness. "Have you been checking up on me, Elisabeth?"

I smiled back and shook my head. "No. That's what Charly said when I told her you'd 'invited' us to sit with you."

He laughed at my emphasis on the word invited. "I'm disappointed. I would have liked it if you were checking up on me. At least I can be comforted that you accepted my invitation." He gave it the same emphasis that I did.

"You were just lucky my social calendar was clear." I was amazed at the easy retorts flying from my mouth. I had never flirted with such easy banter. I had never flirted at all.

"I'd better take advantage of your clear calendar right now. Have lunch with me again tomorrow."

I laughed lightly and played with the straw in my drink. "That's too far ahead to plan."

"Then meet me tonight. We can take a walk before the curfew hits. Do you know where the arbor is on the side of the arts building?"

I shook my head, unable to remember it.

"It's the last building to the north, past Kirkwynd Hall and the little chapel."

"I think I know which one you're talking about, but I don't remember any arbor."

He nodded. "If you haven't been around that way, you'd never see it. It's on the north side of the building. There is a long trellis that is attached to the building and framed out with columns on the other side. It's covered in wisteria vines, and I bet it's spectacular in the spring. Even now when the sun is setting, the arbor is covered in shadows and fragrance."

"It sounds wonderful." Before I could stop myself, my brain had tiny images of holding Chase's hand under the cover of the wisteria, and then in the darkening shadows of sunset, he would lean over. His lips would come down to my –

The picture was interrupted by an image of Alexei waiting for me in Kirkwynd's study hall, ready to tell me more secrets about my family.

Chase was sure I'd accept. "I'll meet you there about fifteen minutes before sundown."

I shook my head. "I can't. I have other plans."

His shadowy eyes looked straight into mine. "Break them. Come with me, Elisabeth."

I really wanted to, and it was hard, harder than it should have been, to tell him no. Here was my ready-made distraction from the confusion and questions of my new reality, and I had to tell him no.

"I'm sorry, Chase. I can't put this off. I'm so far behind." It wasn't a lie, even applied to my personal life. I was behind. Everyone else knew more about my family than I did.

I was sure I had blown my chance with him but said, "Maybe we could do it earlier. I'd really like to see the arbor."

He smiled at me again. "You really do have to study? You're not just blowing me off?" I guess something in my face reassured him. "I'll meet you there around four-thirty."

I smiled back at him and finished my lunch. Charly's admirers were getting up to leave, and Chase stood with them.

"I'll talk to you later, Elisabeth. It was nice to meet you, Charly." He smiled at her and was given one of Charly's grins in return.

When Chase and his group had left, Charly and I suddenly had the table to ourselves. Even the two younger guys that had moved to the next table over left when Chase did.

"He has quite the entourage, doesn't he?" I asked.

Charly just laughed. "They're a lot of fun. Derek and Duncan kept asking me questions. I've gone to school with them for four years now, and this was the first time I've ever talked to either of them."

I knew what, or rather who, had prompted them to start talking, but maybe they were just too shy to have asked before. Maybe Chase's encouragement was only that, the encouragement they needed to start talking in the first place. Charly was really pretty with her bright eyes and fiery hair. And she was full of life and curiosity. That made her interesting to talk with. Maybe they had been too nervous before in the face of her natural exuberance.

We threw away our trash and headed back to our dorm room. I was hoping to catch Emma before she went to chemistry. I knew where the science building was, but I wasn't sure which room was the chem lab.

As my luck would have it, Emma was leaving Kirkwynd Hall as we arrived.

"Are you heading over to the chem lab?" I asked.

She nodded, her golden curls bouncing. "Are you coming to class?"

"Yeah. I was hoping to catch you and walk together, but I've still got to go up and trade out my books."

Charly waved a goodbye to both of us and went on in.

"I'm sorry," Emma said. "I promised to get there early and help set up for today's experiment. It's really easy to find though. You should probably braid your hair back before class."

I smiled at her. "Good idea. I'll see you there." I went inside and hurried through the study hall to get to the stairs leading up to my tower. Charly passed me on her way back down. I dumped my bag on my bed and grabbed my chemistry textbook along with a notebook, pencil, and calculator. I grabbed my brush and stood in front of Lila Grace's mirror. After I removed the worst of the tangles, I pulled my hair into a ponytail and then braided that. It wasn't as attractive as a French braid or even just a long, loose braid, but it was the fastest method, and I was running late.

I ran back down the stairs and out into the study hall and almost collided with Alexei. He put his hand on my waist to steady me and for a second I froze, my body reacting to the memory of him holding me in my dream.

"Are you alright?" he asked. His eyes were green but shadowed, making them look darker than I had ever seen them.

"Sorry. I'm fine. Just running late for chemistry."

He looked as if he were trying to make up his mind about something, then decided. "I know a short cut to the science building if you will trust me."

I'm sure a thousand questions poured out of my eyes as I looked at him, but I didn't want to be late and . . . Why wouldn't I trust Alexei? I nodded, and he grabbed my hand. He led me out of the study hall and to the storage closet that Julian had brought me out of the tunnels into.

"Are you talking about the tunnels?" I asked.

He pulled up short. "How did you know about them?"

"Julian showed me. A little anyway. She said she didn't know where they all go."

He seemed surprised. "I did not know that she knew that much about them." We walked into the storage closet, and opened the trapdoor. I hesitated before following him down the ladder.

"Julian said the tunnels were dangerous." I watched him pull a flashlight from his backpack.

"Not if you are with me. I guess it could be if you were on your own, but I know how to get into several buildings from here. And it is definitely faster."

I remembered the day he'd gotten back to the dorm after geography before Charly and I could get across campus. I climbed down. He took my hand again and led me through a confusing series of turns and forks. I had no idea where we were and just when I was sure it couldn't be a short cut, he pointed at another ladder leading up. We came up in another storage closet.

"How did you learn about all this?" I whispered as he checked to see if the coast was clear for us to leave the closet.

He pushed the door open and waited for me before shutting it tightly behind us.

"I have a map." He looked at me and stopped. "That is not precisely true, but it is too long a story for now. Would you like to meet here after class? We can go back to Kirkwynd via tunnels and talk without worrying who might be listening."

"You'll tell me the whole story then?"

He nodded. "I know it has been difficult for you, especially when I seem unwilling to tell you everything I know. I will tell you all about my family and the secrets of the tunnels after class. I promise."

His eyes were clear blue again, and it was very easy for me to believe him. I wanted to know the secrets that my father had known and how Alexei's family was connected to my own. I looked down and realized I was still holding on to the hand that had helped me up, out of the trap door. I gave it a squeeze, hoping the physical contact could express the gratitude and warmth I felt for him because I knew that no words ever could.

CHAPTER THIRTEEN

I barely remember the chemistry class that day. We were performing a lab, and Emma was my lab partner as she had predicted. The teacher was mid-sixties, or maybe even closer to retirement, and he had a brown and gray beard that was neatly trimmed. Other than his white lab coat, that was all I remembered of him and his class.

Emma noticed that I was distracted, and I heard her mumble something about hoping I didn't follow in Charly's footsteps. It wasn't until later that I remembered Charly had started a fire in the lab because she had also been distracted by Alexei.

The class ended early, and Emma told me to leave without her since she was staying to help put everything away the same way she helped get it set up. I left the class still tossing my books into my bag. I figured I would have to wait for Alexei, but he was already there, leaning against the wall beside the storage closet, waiting for me.

I smiled at him, and he smiled back, but it was the sad smile that he got when he started talking about his family or the past. I hated seeing the shadows on his face. Knowing the pain these memories were bringing to him was almost enough to make me say that he never had to tell me anything else. I reached my hand out to touch his face, but at the same time he straightened and moved to open the closet door. I only touched the air where he had just been.

We went down the trap door and into the tunnels in silence. He led the way through twists and turns and different forked paths until I had no idea where we were, but I knew we had not headed back in the direction of Kirkwynd Hall.

When Alexei finally stopped, I looked around in surprise. We were in what appeared to be a dead end. There were seats carved out of the rock wall and a ledge, similar to where Julian had hid the flashlight. It was very dark until Alexei lit the trio of fat candles that were stuck on the shelf with their own melted and hardened wax. He shut off his flashlight and dropped it into a mesh pocket on the outside of his backpack before setting it to the side. I waited.

He walked a couple of steps and then looked back at me. I was standing beside the ledge. He started to motion me to one of the stone benches but then moved to it himself. He took off the midnight blue sweater vest of his school uniform and folded it into a cushion. I murmured a tiny thanks and sat down, still waiting. He started pacing, pulled his tie loose, and undid his top button. After what seemed like forever, he finally stopped pacing, turned to me, and spoke.

"I have a great many things that I have to explain to you, Elisabeth, but they will be very painful for you to hear, and you may not even believe me. The problem is that I do not know exactly where to begin. There are so many things that will be disturbing and even frightening; I am unsure of what to tell you first."

His eyes were blue, bluer than I had ever seen them, in the candlelight. I glanced around at the odd shadows on the stone walls, and, despite the unseasonable late September heat, I felt a shiver along my spine.

"Just tell me something, anything. This is scaring me enough."

He was instantly repentant. He knelt down on the dirt floor in front of me. "I am sorry. If you cannot believe anything else that I tell you, please believe that I would never hurt you, not on purpose." His eyes were pleading with me. "Tell me you believe me, Elisabeth. Tell me."

"I believe you, Alexei. I get that this is as difficult for you to say as it probably will be for me to hear. I know that you're not trying to hurt me."

He seemed reassured by my words and stood again. He walked a little way away from me. I thought it was for my benefit more than his own. He seemed to believe that I would need that space.

"You asked me how I knew Julian and why I called her Jules when your father was the only one to call her that. The truth is, I heard him call her that."

My eyes narrowed as I tried to make sense of it. "Did they visit your family? That can't be right. Julian said she never saw my father after he was married except when she visited them at his college, and you can't be more than a year older than I am."

Alexei smiled. "Actually, I am. I am older than I look."

I looked at Alexei's face and tried to add years to it. The best I could do was eighteen; he couldn't be more than three years older than me.

He must have read my thoughts on my face because he smiled even wider. "I am quite a bit older than you are, Elisabeth. I was born in Russia in a place called Novgorod in the winter of 1552, just after our Tsar, Ivan, later called the Terrible, had defeated the Kazan Khans."

My first thought was that he was making fun of me. My second was that he was crazy. How was I supposed to react to the idea that the handsome teenage boy standing in front of me was claiming to have been born almost five centuries ago?

"It is alright, Elisabeth. I told you that you might not believe me, but humor me a little."

I nodded, thinking that if he was insane humoring was my best bet; I was lost inside the tunnels. He started pacing again as he spoke.

"Novgorod was an important city in Russian history, but during the first half of that century, it suffered so many attacks from the Kazans. Ivan was made Grand Duke of Muscovy when he was three, but when he was sixteen he was proclaimed the first Tsar, or emperor, of Russia. That was five years before I was born. My family was not important. My father was barely more than a slave. The first few years after I was born were more peaceful because of the Tsar's victory, but then came the famines and plagues. As if the plagues were not enough, the Tsar . . . ."

He looked at me to see if I was listening. I was. I didn't believe that he had been alive then, but the way he told the story – it was as if he could see it all in his mind. He gave me a rueful half-smile before continuing.

"History says the Tsar was half-mad. I have a slightly different interpretation, but that takes more explanation than you are ready for. In any event, in the year 1570, the Tsar led a private army of bodyguards called *oprichniki* into Novgorod and killed thousands. Records said he killed fifteen hundred Boyars –

nobility – and at least that many more 'little' people, including my family."

"Alexei, that's horrible. Why would the Tsar kill his own people?" I had gotten wrapped up in the story and ignored the fact that he thought he was talking about himself.

"Some historians believe he was mentally unstable, others believe it was a deep fear and distrust of the Boyars, and yet others believe it was some different cause lost to history in the fires of Moscow."

I tried to figure out how deep his own insanity went. "If you were alive in 1570, then how are you here now and why do you look eighteen instead of 500 years old?"

He knelt in front of me again. "I know you do not understand yet, but it is true."

"How?" The single word held so many emotions in it: anger, frustration, and fear were at the top of the list.

"In my home, in Novgorod, there were other things that came on the heels of famine and plague. Every place in history where there has been famine and plague and war and the deaths of hundreds and thousands in short times, there has been another . . . ." He searched for a word. "It is a plague of its own kind. It follows sickness. It follows hunger. It follows war."

An odd feeling of my flesh creeping crawled up my spine. I almost knew what he was going to say before the words came out of his mouth, yet I was still shocked to the very core of my soul.

He was staring straight at me, inches from my face. "It is the vampire."

In that moment, Alexei looked like a stranger to me; a remote alien, too beautiful to be human and too deadly to be alone with. I was trapped underground with no idea how to find my way back. The fear that I felt must have been all over my face because he bowed his head and covered it with his hands, but not before I saw the pain in his eyes. His beautiful blue eyes that were sometimes green. It was the pain that I had seen before when he spoke to me, so gentle and kind even as he told me his suspicions about my parents' deaths. The pain that had been there when he warned me that I would not like the truths he would tell me and that I might hate him for being the one to tell me. Did I believe him now? In that moment, in the dark tunnel, with the pain etched on his face, I could not believe anything else.

But he was still Alexei. I put a cautious hand on his shoulder, and his head jerked up so fast I thought he might give himself whiplash.

"Elisabeth?" His voice was full of wonder. I could see his surprise that I had touched him in spite of my obvious fear.

My voice was not as steady as I would have liked when I spoke. "You asked me to believe that you would never hurt me on purpose. I believe you."

I thought about all the myths and movies involving vampires and wondered at the humanity of the one kneeling in front of me. Tears slid down his face, but his eyes were full of relief. I reached out with one finger and caught a tear on his cheek. He seemed shocked that he was crying.

"Can you – if it isn't too painful – can you tell me about it? How you became one?"

He smiled his little half-smile. "I can hardly believe you are asking. Yes, I will tell you anything you want to know." He paused, gathering his thoughts. "When the Tsar came to Novgorod, he came to destroy the vampires that preyed upon his people. There were far more innocent people killed than vampires, but he did considerable damage to the group that was infesting Novgorod. Ivan was a religious man, and he knew that his guards, his warriors, would be afraid to fight the undead, the soulless creatures, so he did not tell them why they were killing Boyars. The vampires had gone after the nobility first – some to turn like they were, others to simply quench their thirst."

He gave me a quick look to see if I was afraid. I suppose whatever he saw in my eyes reassured him. He moved to the other stone bench, opposite me, and sat down.

"The Tsar slaughtered anyone he thought might have been infected, including my family. The vampires, I think afraid of being wiped out completely, fled, taking some people to feed upon during their journey. I was one. I watched as five people that I knew died, pint by pint. I do not know why they left me for last. I never knew why they changed their minds, but in the end they decided to make me like them rather than simply kill me."

He stopped, lost in the memories. I was afraid to press him, and yet I felt I had to encourage him to continue.

"How many were there?"

"Three. I suppose others escaped in their own ways, but the – the group – was splintered. Ivan the Terrible did the greatest service for humanity when he divided that collection of vampires and history remembers him as a bloodthirsty tyrant for it." He laughed a little at the thought before he went on. "There were two men and a woman. One man was very tall and had been injured by fire. I watched in fascinated horror as his skin regrew itself over the massive burns. It took weeks before it was really healed but, within the first twenty-four hours, it had lessened to minor burns instead of the raw meat that it resembled when they first made their escape. Out of the five people they killed, they gave him three. The woman had to subdue the first one and almost feed him because he was so weak, but he recovered quickly. It was the other man who – who changed me."

I found myself whispering to Alexei. "Did it hurt? Did you know what he was doing to you?"

He stared at me for a moment, eyes flashing both blue and green. "It was horrible and frightening and very painful. His teeth – his fangs – ripped into my neck. It was nothing like the movies, Elisabeth. It was not two little holes in my skin. It was a full set of teeth with four sharp fangs, two on the top and two on the bottom. His mouth was halfway around my throat and the force of his jaw was as powerful as a steel bear trap. He clamped onto my neck and held me there powerless simply by the strength of him. And the bite itself burned like acid pouring over my skin, but only for a moment. After a moment of pain like nothing else I have ever known, everything went blessedly numb. My body had gone into shock from the pain and the blood loss, but I was not permitted to slip into the sweet oblivion of death. With my blood pumping through the monster's body, animating him with my life, he took a knife and slit his wrist. It was my own blood rushing through him and then out of his veins, but it was now polluted, poisoned. He fed me on my own blood, and I was too weak to fight him. He never stopped sucking the blood out of my throat as he cut himself and poured my own blood back into me. It was a sick kind of transfusion, like a backward hemopurifier in a hospital that pumps the patient's own blood back into them. But it was changed as it traveled through the monster that made me what I am. And when my blood was changed, I changed. At some point all my blood had left my body, and the only life I had left was what I drank from his wrist. In the beginning it was his mouth at my throat that caused me to swallow, but then the taint took hold of me, and I began to drink. I drank to live. I drank and became strong, stronger than I had ever been before. In the hour of my death I felt more alive than any other time in my life."

I felt the tears rolling down my face and ached for the boy who had only wanted to live and for the man – his pain had aged him in my mind – that was speaking now. Alexei looked at me.

"Do you want me to stop? Do you want me to take you back to Kirkwynd?"

I shook my head. "I want to know how you survived. How you knew my father."

Alexei stood and walked to my bench. "The rest is very simple. The ones who made me were killed within days of my creation. I was still so new that they had left me behind while they went out to hunt. After the first burst of strength, gained from my own blood, I was weak and helpless. They had to feed me as the woman had done for the injured man. I found out much later that vampires gain more from their own blood than any other. If my family had been close by, I would have slaughtered them in my initial bloodlust. Without my family to feed upon and after my own blood faded in my dead body, I had to feed as often as a newborn child, but I was without the strength to hunt. It is one of the ways that makes it hard for a new vampire to survive. After the ones who made me disappeared, I was found by a strange family of vampires. They were different. They did not kill when they fed. They had powers and could compel humans to forget their existence and leave them dazed but alive. They did not require as much blood and were not opposed to using animal blood instead of human. They took me in when I was still new and helped me through my first days of bloodlust and violence. They believed I could be rehabilitated. They had chosen a different path and made me a part of their family."

"Is this the family you were talking about when you said they wanted a treaty with mine?" I was wondering why my family knew about vampires and would make treaties with them.

"Yes, they were my family for over four hundred years. Over time we structured ourselves into a royal family to match the people we were dealing with. Your family and mine had fought some rather bloody wars over our feeding habits." Alexei smiled, a real smile. "I am sorry I lied to you about that. I spoke before I thought. It was not finances, but survival, that caused our families to fight. Your family objected to my family's use of compulsion to make human victims forget they were ever attacked. Your family insisted on full informed consent, even when there was no death involved, or else a strict adherence to animal blood. I was to be the representative of my family, but my father decided not to send me to deal with Prince Augustin, your grandfather. He decided to deal with him in person and sent me, disguised as a teenager, to school at the Academy."

"You were a student here before?" I couldn't keep from being shocked now. He was beyond talking about the abstract histories of Russia or my family. "You were here with my father and Julian!" I said it more like an accusation than I really meant.

"I was, but I was enrolled as Sasha Beloi at that time. That is why Julian would not know Alexei Mikhailovich."

"Why are you Alexei Mikhailovich now?"

"Beloi comes from the word for white. I was enrolled under a name your father's family would recognize. The white or pale ones, vampires. Mikhailovich is my real name."

"The name of your family that was killed?"

"Yes. My father, Misha, my mother, Nadezhda, and my two sisters, Sofya and Yelena." His eyes became unfocused, and I wondered if he could still picture their faces clearly. We sat quietly for a moment.

"What made you return here as a student again? Charly said you were here last spring."

"I knew that Julian had been hunting for you. You and your father's secret box. I was certain that she was getting closer and that she would send you here for your own safety. I also believed that there was the outside chance that Nicholas had returned here to hide his box since Julian was not having any luck finding it."

"Tell me about him."

The harsh lines on Alexei's face softened. "Nicholas was an amazing person and a very good friend. He and Julian were like opposite sides of the same coin. I think sometimes they only had one heartbeat and when Nicholas died, Julian's heart stopped. Do not misunderstand me; I do not doubt that he was completely in love with your mother, but she was outside our world. Nick was the heir and his stepmother was and is a hard woman. Julian loved Nick, but they were more like siblings and best friends than anything else. Nick's marriage was one thing his stepmother could not anticipate. It broke the rules to a large extent. And then there was you. When I heard of your birth, I commissioned the box with the firebird for you. I was going to present it to you on the day Nicholas was crowned prince and you were named his heir, but he was killed. The truce we wanted was never acknowledged by his stepmother, and she used the false pretense of negotiating a new one to lure my family onto her territory. She slaughtered them all under a flag of truce."

"How did you escape?"

"I was never there. I was so heartsick over Nick and his young bride that my father sent me to join the search for you, hoping that helping would ease my grief. It only compounded it." His voice held a hard edge.

"Alexei? I'm not trying to be stupid here, and I know that one person cannot replace another, but couldn't you have – Why didn't you just-"

He smiled faintly, understanding the question I didn't know how to ask. "Make more family?" I nodded. "It was forbidden. The family that took me in never made another vampire. Just as we refuse to end life to feed, we refuse to end a life to damn another person to our existence."

"Is it such a terrible thing to live as long as you? To gain strength and eternal youth?" My questions were simple and straightforward.

"You are not seeing all of my existence. My face will not age, but it will also never see the sun. I know these underground tunnels because I dug many of them out so that I would have shelter to pretend to be human and attend classes with your father. I do not eat food for nourishment, I drink the blood of a living being. No, I do not kill humans, but I still crave the taste. I can control the bloodlust, but I can never make it go away. I am a monster."

I shook my head so fast my braided ponytail hit me in the face. "You're Alexei. You're a good person, and you're my friend."

He sighed. "You are wrong, Elisabeth. Not about me being your friend, but I cannot be a good person. I am not even a person at all."

I looked up at him, suddenly exhausted. "Maybe we can talk about that later. I'm sure you're far more than a regular person, but you're definitely not a monster. I won't argue though, because I need to sleep." I must have been really tired because that was the only explanation for the next words out of my mouth. "God, I hope I don't dream tonight."

Alexei suddenly looked very guilty. He pulled a long leather cord out of his pants pocket. There was some kind of symbol on it, but I couldn't see what it was. "This will keep you from dreaming, at least from the kinds of dreams that are too real."

A dawning horror rose in my face. My voice was scratchy and barely audible. "Was it real?"

He didn't answer, but he wouldn't meet my eyes either. How could my dreams have been real? I remembered what he said about his family's ability to compel their victims.

"Did you use vampire tricks on me to get into my dreams?"

"No!" His denial was too quick. "Not exactly. Your family has some 'tricks' of its own. How else would they be enough of a threat to mine that we would negotiate? I invited myself into your dreams, but you always had the power to make me leave, you were just unaware."

I couldn't speak as the memory of those dreams rushed through my head, leaving me mortified. But no matter how embarrassed I was or how hot my face burned, I couldn't pull my eyes away from his. He didn't seem embarrassed about my dream, but he was ashamed of something.

He moved closer and dropped the leather cord over my head. I felt the weight of whatever was on it hit my chest, but I still couldn't look away. "It will keep your dreams private until you learn how to guard them for yourself. I am sorry I was not honest with you before, but . . . ." He took my hand and held it lightly in his own. "Please, Elisabeth, think about this. If I had told you the dream was real on the first night, you would not have believed me, not while you were dreaming. And if I had told you it was real the next day, you would hate me, as you do now."

I shook my head slowly. "I don't hate you, Alexei. I told you that you're my friend and I meant it. I don't understand, and I can't help but feel embarrassed by the way I looked and acted. I wouldn't act like that if I thought it was real."

He smiled a little at me. "I know that. I knew that inside your dream. If you had been aware of your abilities and the truth of the dream, you could have chosen your appearance as easily as your behavior. I never held any of that against you. I blamed myself for deceiving you. I took advantage of your innocence."

I felt the blush creeping back into my face. "God, Alexei, you make it sound like some kind of crime. I understand why it was hard for you to be honest, but I don't understand how I could change my appearance."

Alexei sighed and sat down on the bench, pulling me down beside him. "This is going to take some time."

"I'm listening," I answered.

"You are also missing dinner," he said.

I knew he was trying to give me a chance to postpone this discussion, but I was finally getting answers, and I was afraid to stop. It didn't really matter that the answers I was hearing sounded crazy. Maybe when I was back in my dorm room or out in the sunshine, I would question my sanity, but in the cool, dark tunnels with the flickering candlelight, everything Alexei said seemed plausible.

"I'm not hungry. I just wanted to understand."

He nodded, as if that was the answer he was expecting to hear. "I told you that my kind can compel our victims. Your family has abilities of its own. You can use a similar kind of persuasion to influence people.

"Not me," I said quickly, remembering the way I could never get Gretchen to do anything back at the group home.

"You have the ability, Elisabeth, but not the training. I am certain Julian will be training you, perhaps during your school break, but she has a lot of ground to cover in your family history. Until she finds a way to tell you the truth, she will continue to ignore your training in an attempt to keep you safe and give you time to adjust."

I made a sound that Alexei took as disbelief. He looked at me hard.

"She is trying her best. How would you have felt if, ten minutes after she found you, she told you that vampires were real, and your family had connections to them, and you have some unconventional abilities of your own. You would have thought she was crazy and run away the first chance you had. Then you would never have been safe."

"Am I safe now? I know I'm safe with you, but my father was killed by his own family, and they probably want me dead as well."

I was feeling sorry for myself again, but I was also truly afraid. If the people that killed my father shared my family's abilities, especially the ability to persuade someone to do something for them, then I was in danger even hidden away at the Academy.

Alexei left his bench and knelt on the stone floor in front of me again. "Elisabeth, I stood at your parents' graves, and I swore an oath to Nicholas that I would find you and guard you no matter what the cost. I swore it then for his sake alone, but now that I know you, I swear it again to you. I will not let anything happen to you."

The chill that had been creeping along my spine, a chill that had nothing to do with temperature, was warmed by his words. "I believe you, Alexei."

He smiled that dazzling smile that sent Charly to her own private fantasyland. The moment I thought of Charly, a dozen new questions entered my mind. "Did you use your mind-powers on Charly?"

He frowned. "I have kept to the treaty I made with your father. I only use my compulsion to protect my secret. If someone started asking questions about why they never see me outside, it could get tricky maintaining my cover as a student. Are you angry?"

I shook my head slowly, but I was biting my bottom lip. "You've never made her – I mean, she is completely flustered by you."

Alexei nodded as understanding came. "She is entranced. I have tried to enter her dreams and present myself as a regular teenage boy with nothing special to attract her attention, but she is strong-willed. I am not sure I could compel her to forget the truth if she found out."

"You mean her crush is a real crush?"

"Yes and no. I am afraid that she is more susceptible to a different vampire effect."

"The fact that you are so beautiful? Weren't you always?"

Alexei shrugged his shoulders. "I do not know. My family was poor. The only reflection I ever saw was in the river, and it was always moving. I think of it more as a pheromone, rather than just looks. It is intoxicating, and you are not supposed to be able to fight it. I have tried to keep the students from being over-exposed, but the day in the science lab, with the fire . . . ." He shrugged again.

"I suppose that kind of makes sense, but I'm not science girl. Why aren't you worried about me? Does my family have some kind of anti-vampire ability?" Then I thought about the vampire shows I'd seen in reruns. "I'm not supposed to be some kind of slayer, am I?"

Alexei actually laughed. It was a deep, rich sound that echoed in the tunnels. "You are definitely not a 'Buffy.' I did watch that show, but there is no such thing as a slayer. It was make-believe. Just like vampires turning into ash, garlic and crosses as weapons, churches as a holy sanctuary that vampires cannot enter, and most importantly, sleeping in coffins. You can tell for yourself that I have no difficulty staying awake during daylight hours."

I laughed at his exasperated tone. Then I thought of something else. "I guess the whole sunlight thing is real though."

Alexei winced. "That was one of the things that 'Buffy' got right, mostly. Direct sunlight burns. If I was left in direct sunlight long enough, it would kill me. I can do indirect sunlight though. As long as there is something between me and the sun, I am safe. It can be clothing, tree cover, whatever. It is not the most comfortable feeling though, like having a constant heat rash."

I thought about it for a second. "You use your compulsion on the P. E. teachers so you don't actually have to be outside."

He nodded, looking slightly guilty. "I have them give me B's. I would not feel right about receiving the highest grade, but I did not want it to be too different from my other grades."

"Do you actually go to your other classes?" I knew I'd seen him in my classes, but I wasn't sure about the rest.

"I cannot take too many chances and risk exposing myself. I like most of the teachers and the subjects that I study."

"Are there any more secrets?"

"Oh, yes, Elisabeth, but not now. You need time to adjust and think about the things I have told you. And in truth, I need some time myself."

"Why do you need time?"

His eyes were bright. "I truly believed that after I had told you what I really am, you would never want to speak to me again. That you still call me friend, it is a gift beyond anything I had imagined."

I smiled at him and stood up. I handed him his vest that had served as my cushion before picking up my backpack. He pulled it from me lightly.

"I think we both know I can handle the weight of your books better than you can."

I took the small teasing as a good sign. He turned the flashlight back on before blowing out the candles. Then, he took my hand and led me back through the twisting turns to the corridor where we would climb up into the storage closet. I cast a look over to the door that led up to my own room.

"Were you the one in my room? The first day when my books were moved, was that you?"

He winced. "Yet another thing for which I must apologize. I was looking for your father's box. When I saw two, I knew that Julian had given you hers as well. I am sorry for trespassing, but I needed to see if you had the box. I believe it holds the key to your father's legacy."

I realized I was more relieved than upset. "Do you know how to open it? Does Julian?"

"No, neither of us does, as far as I am aware. I do not understand why you never told Julian that you have it." He wasn't accusing me of anything, so I answered him as honestly as I could.

"I'm not completely sure. I think it was partly because I wanted to be wanted on my own merits, not because of my father. But it was also because I was afraid of what you just said. If the box really does contain my father's legacy, then Julian's battles with my father's stepmother can end, and I have no more choices. To be honest, Alexei, I don't want to be a princess."

The sad smile was back. I realized how terrible my words must sound to a man who had lost his choice violently in an attack that left him feeling like a monster.

"I'm sorry, Alexei, I didn't mean it like-"

He interrupted me. "There is no need to apologize. Not to me. I understand what it means to struggle against your identity and your destiny. And even if I could not understand it on my own, I had several conversations with your father during our treks in these tunnels. And, as far as the door to your room is concerned, you may move the wardrobe back to its normal place. I will show you how to set a gentle compulsion on it so no one wants to use it."

My eyes grew wider. "I can do that? Is it like magic?"

He laughed. "It is not magic, only your natural ability, and you will not be able to do it until you have practiced a great deal. If we go up that way now, I will fix it for you."

"But we can't get in," I reminded him.

He laughed again. "I can get in quite easily. That wardrobe might be impossible to move without making noise if you are simply human. For me, it is child's play."

I followed him up the dark staircase to my tower room's secret door. He listened closely for the sounds that would reveal the other girls' presence inside. Hearing nothing, he tripped the switch, and the door swung toward us. He quietly and carefully lifted the wardrobe out of his way and entered my room. I followed him and shut the trapdoor behind us, thinking that the required invitation for a vampire was another myth that Alexei had just burst.

CHAPTER FOURTEEN

We were standing in my room, and I was suddenly very conscious of his presence again. It was hard to define, even in my mind, but one moment everything was normal and the next, I was hyper-aware of him. Part of it was physical; I would have to be dead to not notice how amazing he looked, which was sort of funny because technically he was undead. Maybe that – his unnatural existence – was part of what drove my awareness. Maybe it was more of those vampire pheromones playing havoc with my senses.

Alexei had said my family had some sort of natural resistance to vampire abilities, so I guess I couldn't really blame it on the pheromones. I wasn't sure how to act anymore. The comfort level we had found in the tunnels seemed to fade away in the bright dorm room.

I turned to look up at his now green eyes. "Would you like to see the box?"

"I would like to see it sometime, but I do not know how to open it."

I was biting my lower lip again. I turned away and opened the wardrobe, moved the books, and carefully removed the box. "Do you know what kind of wood this is made of?"

I held it out to him. He took it and ran his long fingers along the grain lines showing on the side. "Nicholas never told me much about the box. I suppose he never told anyone much about it since he used it to hold his most precious treasures."

Alexei returned the box to me, and I returned it to the shelf, hiding it once again behind a row of books. Alexei stepped close behind me. I saw him leaning over out of the corner of my eye. He was reading the book spines. I wondered what he thought of my books.

He noticed me watching him and straightened up. "I recognize some of your father's books, like the Milton you were reading the day we met."

I smiled a little. "Books have always been my refuge."

"I understand. Until I met Nicholas, I did not have any friends outside of my family. Within my family, I was treated differently. After my attackers were killed, and I almost died for the second time, when the thirst had become unbearable, I was found by the head of my new family. Many of them considered me to be a pet of his, and they were jealous and resentful. The family might have splintered on its own had the Duchess not slaughtered them."

"They resented you for five hundred years and hadn't splintered yet?" I barely managed the whisper.

Alexei laughed a bitter, angry bark. "Not for five hundred years. I told you it was only later that my family reorganized itself as a monarchy more like the others we were dealing with. It was only forty years or so before the end that we imitated your family. My father named me his heir less than two years before he died."

"I'm confused," I said, feeling the creases furrowing my forehead. "Why would your father wait so long to do that and what changed that made him finally act?"

"Insightful questions. There were only a few who dared ask. The answer to both questions is you. It was only after your birth that my father decided to name an heir."

I frowned harder. "What did I have to do with anything?"

Alexei looked sorry that he'd said anything. "Elisabeth, please do not ask me any more questions tonight. I am not certain either of us can handle more truth, and I do not wish to lie."

I took a deep breath to try to corral my thoughts. Alexei had been painfully honest with me and had answered so many questions already. It couldn't have been easy for him to talk about the attack or his family's deaths. "One last question."

He nodded and waited for me to ask.

"Do you think I should find a way to let Julian know that I have the box?"

He thought about it and shook his head. "I know she is looking for it and that may work to your advantage right now. As long as the other people searching for the box see Julian searching, they might stay away from you. If they knew you had the box, it might make you more of a target. If you were able to send Julian a message, it might be intercepted. I do not know who is watching her or how aware she is of the surveillance she is under. It is probably safer to wait until you can tell her in person."

I sat down on my bed. Alexei moved Charly's bed and wardrobe back to their original positions. I watched him in awe. It was hard just to accept the idea that Alexei was a vampire while I was sitting in my room with the last of the day's sunlight filtering through my window. But what else could possibly explain how he was able to single-handedly move the heavy wardrobe that had taken all four of us girls to move? His casual strength was both amazing and terrifying. If he could do that to such a massive piece of furniture, what could he do to a human?

He turned back toward me, and the slight smile he'd had died on his lips. "You are not comfortable seeing me moving things like that, are you?"

"Not completely," I answered. Then I gave him a little half-smile of my own. "At least I know who to call on moving day."

He tried to smile back and then sat down on the bed beside me.

I gave him what I hoped was my most winsome smile. "I was wrong. I have another question."

"Somehow I knew you would not be held to just one more question. Go ahead and ask."

I did quickly, in case he changed his mind. I spoke so fast he had to make me repeat myself. "I just want to know what I'm supposed to do now."

"The same thing you do almost everyday. You go to your classes, you eat your meals, you do your homework and study, you read and re-read your books, and you spend time with your friends."

I knew Alexei meant Charly, Emma, and Lila Grace, but when he said the word "friends" I realized that I had left Chase waiting at the lilac arbor. And it was too late to get my face washed and the dusty cobwebs and awful braid out of my hair, let alone change my clothes, with any real hope of catching him. I guess Alexei saw something in my eyes because he asked what I'd remembered. How are you supposed to tell one guy that you can't help being attracted to that you just realized you stood another guy up because you were with him? You aren't. I knew that any normal girl with any normal guy wouldn't say anything, but Alexei is not exactly normal. If I didn't just tell him, would he be able to get inside my head and figure it out? Or did my family's anti-vampire abilities protect my mind from his eavesdropping? Maybe I was just over-complicating everything.

I looked at him for a second, and then became incredibly occupied with removing the imaginary dirt from the side of my shoe. "I just remembered that I was supposed to meet someone, and I can't now."

He was instantly apologetic. "I should never have distracted you the way I did. You probably needed to catch up on some study time, and now I have interfered."

I felt even guiltier. "It wasn't any big deal. I wasn't planning to study; just talk and maybe take a walk or something. Like a tour of the grounds, I guess."

I chanced a quick glance up at his face. He was frowning.

"You are lying to me. Not an outright lie, but you are definitely hiding something." He sounded disappointed.

"What makes you think I'm lying? I thought you said your vampire tricks don't work on me."

"That reaction proves you are hiding something. My so-called tricks are not affecting you, but I am not deaf. I can hear your heartbeat racing, and your breath is uneven. You are hiding something." The disappointment in his voice changed to something even sadder. "I thought you trusted me, Elisabeth."

Like an idiot, I looked up into his eyes and they seemed, for once, to be cloudy rather than the clear summer sky blue they usually were. Guilt on top of guilt.

"I do trust you, Alexei. It's just awkward. Before you told me the truth about who you are, I thought that maybe your interest in me was – well, a little more personal. I'm not complaining; I was just confused. And this morning I met a guy who wanted me to meet him for a walk this afternoon. I just didn't know how to say that without sounding stupid and girly."

Alexei was very quiet for a moment that seemed to last for ages. "The last thing I would want to do would be to interfere with your . . . ." He seemed to be searching for the right words. "I do not want to get in the way of your friends, but I will not allow some teenage boy to hurt you."

"I appreciate how you want to protect me, Alexei, but you need to save it for the real dangers, not my social life."

The fierce look in his eyes reminded me that he was a predator by nature. "You are too young and naïve to understand the full impact of your heritage, Elisabeth. But there are boys here at this school that can understand the power your family holds, if not the full knowledge of your family secrets. I will not let them treat you casually."

"I'm not a child!" I knew that yelling in his face was not the most mature reaction.

He stood up so that he towered over me. "You are fifteen years old. That is a child, even when it is considered within a normal human lifespan. Compared to my centuries, you are an infant."

I stood up to face him. "Great! Play the vampire card with all the centuries of experience that make you so much better than I am! That's real fair."

Alexei's eyes flashed from blue to green as his temper blazed. His deep voice, usually so peaceful and melodic, snarled at me. "You want fair, Elisabeth? Life is not fair. Death is not fair. And living beyond death, living with a thirst that drives me to steal the heartblood from a living creature to make my dead heart beat again, that is nowhere close to fair. You stand there in your foolish innocence and demand your right to play schoolgirl when there are armies searching for the box that lies hidden behind your books. When there are creatures more vile than anything you can imagine plotting your death. When I stand here, inches from your unprotected throat, and I can hear your heart pounding the blood through your veins, and I can smell the fear and desire you have tried so hard to keep hidden. It would be so easy for me to take you back into my tunnels where no one would ever hear your scream. You would only scream once. After that you would not have the strength to push the sound around my teeth piercing your skin. I could feed on you for a few days, drawing out the torture, or I could just snap your pretty neck with the flick of my wrist. And there is nothing you could do to stop me. Does that sound fair to you?"

He had pulled both of my wrists behind my back and held them with one of his hands, forcing my back to arch up and baring my neck. His other hand was wrapped around my neck so that I could feel how powerful he was and how easy it would be for him to do just what he said. My heart was hammering inside my chest, and I could feel the rush of adrenaline that came with the fight or flight survival instinct. But it was the look in Alexei's eyes that bothered me the most.

He was afraid of what he could do to me.

And seeing his fear, I was reassured. I knew he didn't want to hurt me. I knew that he would rather die himself than let me get hurt. I stared back into his eyes as they flashed green and blue, and tried not to blink, so I could show him the truth that I knew.

I whispered my apology because I was afraid my voice would crack if I said it out loud. "I'm sorry, Alexei. I was acting like a child. I know life isn't fair, and I was way out of line with what I said."

He looked horrified as he released me. I thought that he might want to leave, and I grabbed his arm before he was out of reach.

"Let me go, Elisabeth."

"We're not done talking yet."

He wouldn't look at me, but he didn't pull away. "I could force you to let go, but I do not want to hurt you."

"I know you don't want to hurt me. I think maybe I know it better than you do."

I was still holding on, and he finally turned back to me.

His voice was a harsh whisper. I wondered if he was as afraid of losing control as I was and if our reasons were anything close to the same. "You have no idea how hard it is."

"Tell me." I sat back on the bed, drawing him down beside me. "Make me understand."

"I do not think I can. It is like a starving man or an addict but to a degree that was unimaginable when I was human. My family was poor. There were times in my childhood – I remember the famines when there was no food. I remember the hunger and then the pain of eating when we did receive bread. Even after all these centuries I can remember the taste of my own blood. It was more addicting than anything I could describe. In all the time that I fed on blood, I never killed, but I always wanted to."

"Why? What would killing gain you?" I surprised myself by being truly curious, not repulsed by his confession.

He wouldn't look me in the eyes, but he took one of my hands and held it between both of his and kept his eyes locked on them. "The last of the blood to pass through the heart before it stops beating, the heartblood – it is the most potent drug and the source of amazing power. All you have to do to get it is kill a living creature."

"Any living creature?"

He did look at me when I asked that. "All living creatures have a potency to their heartblood, but the closer to your own form, the more potent. Mammals more so than, say, reptiles or birds. And larger mammals more so than smaller ones. But there is nothing that moves on the face of the earth that matches the taste of human blood."

"And you still crave it despite your belief that killing is wrong."

His grip tightened for a split second before he relaxed again. "Always."

I looked down at my hand, so small and fragile inside his. I forced myself to look back into his face, knowing that if I could ask the question I needed to see his face to truly know the answer. "Do you crave my blood?"

His eyes widened for a moment, but he was shaking his head before the words could escape his lips. "I am afraid of your blood. I do not know what would happen to me if I even tasted someone of your family, and especially of your purest bloodline."

"Because of my family's abilities? You think it might make a difference?"

"It could. I would not want to mix the cocktail, so to speak. Either of us could have unforeseen reactions. I would never want to do that to you in any case."

I looked into his green eyes and touched his face with my free hand. "I know you have no interest in hurting me. I didn't want my presence to hurt you."

He kissed the top of my head, and I leaned against him, grateful that I had someone who really did care about me.

The door opened. My three roommates walked in and gasped. Emma recovered first.

"Elisabeth! Where have you been? And Alexei is not supposed to be up here."

Before I could react, Lila Grace noticed the room's rearrangement. "Who moved the wardrobe away from the wall?"

"I did. Well, with Alexei's help of course. It's okay. I found out who was maintaining the tunnels."

Emma turned her navy glance on Alexei. It seemed she had some sort of immunity to his vampire looks and pheromones. "You're the one who snuck into our room while we were gone and snooped through Elisabeth's things."

"Yes. She has forgiven me, and I promise to stay out of your room unless I am with one of you or perhaps retrieving something for one of you."

"Boys are not allowed in the girls' rooms," Lila Grace said.

"Don't be dense, Lila Grace," Emma chided. "He'll come up through the hidden door, and no one will ever know he was here. I believe you, Alexei. But no one can ever know about that door, or I will find a way to seal it up."

"I will help you myself should it become necessary."

He stood to leave through that hidden passage when Charly finally managed to say something. "Chase was looking for you, Elisabeth. He said you were supposed to meet him, but you never showed up, and he was worried."

Before I had the chance to ask her anything else, Alexei had turned to me. "Chase? Chase Elliot? That is who you were worried about not meeting?"

I nodded, mute, unsure what Alexei was feeling, or why I cared so much about his reaction.

But Alexei seemed thoughtful. "I have not met him personally. We never seem to be in the same area at the same time. I hope you remember what Julian told you about the other students who might be here."

I understood his reference, but it didn't track. Chase didn't know anything about me or my family. He was just a new kid like me, and a very cute one at that.

"I haven't forgotten, but you can't forget that Julian's suspicions tend to run wild. In fact, I believe they were even extended to you."

He made a face at me while the other girls stared. "And Julian was not completely wrong about me. Besides, I have heard a few rumors about Chase Elliot. I did not like what I heard."

"I'll be careful and if you hear anything that's more than just a rumor, I trust you'll tell me." I arched an eyebrow at him, waiting for a response.

He smiled at me with that sweet sad smile. "You may count on that. Good night, ladies. Good night, Elisabeth."

"Good night," I answered and heard my voice echoed by Emma, Lila Grace, and Charly.

Part of me wished I was going down the stairs to the underground tunnels with him. Because I knew that the moment the trapdoor was reset, my roommates would turn on me and begin an interrogation that would make the Spanish Inquisition seem like a picnic on the beach. The door disappeared into the wall with a soft click, and I was confronted by three sets of blue eyes: dark navy, bright turquoise, and palest azure.

CHAPTER FIFTEEN

I sat down on my bed and took a deep breath to prepare for their questions. Charly spoke first.

"Elisabeth Sinclair, are you trying to date Alexei and Chase Elliot at the same time?" The outrage in her voice reminded me of how entranced she was by Alexei.

"It's not like that at all, Charly."

"What is it like?" Lila Grace asked. "Because you were alone in this room with one boy while another boy was waiting for you. That looks like you're trying to string them both along."

Emma snorted. "Well if she was, she's not now. Alexei did not like the idea of Elisabeth spending time with Chase."

I sighed, knowing this was not going to be a fun conversation. "Alexei and I are just friends. Our families have known each other since long before I was born. It's almost like he's a cousin or something."

Charly made a derisive noise. "There is no way that any female who was the least bit attracted to the male species could think of Alexei Mikhailovich as nothing more than a cousin. And if your families are such old friends, why didn't Julian recognize his name?"

"Because Julian has been out of touch since my parents were killed, and Alexei's surname is not the one his family was known by a generation ago." I hated to use Charly's weakness against her, but I'd always heard that the best defense is a good offense. "Besides, Charly, just because you can't think when Alexei's in the room, it doesn't mean the rest of us are incapable of being just friends."

Charly's turquoise eyes flashed with anger and embarrassment, but Lila Grace was quick to defend her.

"If you're not interested in Alexei, then why were you sitting in this room, alone, on your bed, holding hands. I saw him kiss you."

"On the forehead, Lila Grace, like you would a family member. He was holding my hand to offer comfort. We were talking about my parents and his family members who have died. It was about being friends." I was getting frustrated. I wished that I had some training in those abilities that Alexei said I possessed so I could get Charly and Lila Grace to let go of their obsession. As soon as I thought the word obsession, I wondered if Lila Grace was as susceptible to Alexei as Charly was.

Emma changed the topic slightly. "So, are you interested in Chase Elliot?"

I must have blushed because she didn't give me any time to answer.

"You are. If you're so interested in Chase, what were you doing up here with Alexei?"

I had to think quickly because the truth was not something I could get anywhere close to. I walked over to my shelf, and I saw the shiny black lacquer box that Alexei had given me. I pulled it down and showed it to the three girls. "Alexei gave this to me. When I was born, his family commissioned it to be made. Do you see the way my initials are painted into the feathers of the firebird?"

"It's beautiful." Lila Grace held it in her hands, looking at the amazing artistry involved in the painting.

Emma was still looking for answers. "Why didn't they give it to you before?"

I took a deep breath and gave my new friends a little of the truth, hoping it would be enough of a cover for them to accept my strange relationship with Alexei from then on. "Before I tell you, you've all got to swear not to breathe a word of this to anyone, not even to your own parents."

Charly nodded immediately. It seemed that the more time that passed, the less affected she was by Alexei's memory.

Emma thought about it for a moment. "I'll agree as long as you promise that it's nothing that will hurt any of us."

I smiled tightly. "As long as no one says anything, then no one will get hurt. The only danger is if this information becomes general knowledge."

"Then I agree." Emma turned to Lila Grace, who was biting her perfect nails.

"I don't know. This all seems so . . . sordid." Her musical voice was soft and quivering with something less than fear, something closer to disapproval.

"Pull yourself together, Lila Grace. If Elisabeth needs secrecy, then we have to give it or stop asking questions that aren't really any of our business." Emma's no-nonsense approach was as good as throwing a bucket of cold water over Lila Grace.

"Fine. I agree."

I motioned for the three of them to sit with me on my bed, close. I kept my voice to a whisper as I spoke. "When I was about a year old, my parents were killed. It was made to look like an accident, but they were murdered, and I was kidnapped.

Julian, my godmother and guardian, has been searching for me for almost fifteen years. She found me tucked away in foster care under an assumed name, but she still can't prove who killed my parents or kidnapped me in the first place. She told me that the Academy was the safest place for me, but that I shouldn't trust anyone. Alexei's family was close to my family, and he had heard about my parents' murders and my kidnapping. Actually, Alexei is the one who confirmed my suspicions about my parents. Julian couldn't quite bring herself to say that they were actually murdered."

"Oh my God!" Lila Grace was shocked. Emma seemed horrified, but Charly didn't look surprised.

"I knew there were some odd things about you. You've been far too easy to get along with. I knew you didn't grow up with the kind of money that we all take for granted, more or less."

I looked at her in surprise. "You never said anything."

Charly grinned at me for the first time that night. "I was just glad you weren't a spoiled brat. How does Alexei fit into your story?"

I smiled back at her. "He knows all the stories about my family that I should have heard growing up. And he doesn't mind telling them to me. That's what we were doing today, and the time just got away from me. I guess I forgot about Chase until it was too late."

"So you really don't want to date Alexei?" Charly asked.

"It would seem very strange to date Alexei," I answered with complete honesty.

"I wonder why he was so upset at the idea of you meeting Chase." Emma's thinking out loud was a little too insightful, but she found an answer for herself before I could come up with anything. "He's probably concerned with someone finding out where you are. You're probably not safe enough, even here, if rumors about you started spreading outside the campus."

"I think you're right," I agreed quickly. "Alexei seemed more concerned about me in general than worried about Chase specifically."

"Why didn't you just tell Alexei about Chase yourself?" Lila Grace asked.

"Honestly, at first I forgot. I was so excited about hearing some stories about my family that I just wasn't thinking about the present. And after that, it seemed a little rude. I mean, after all, Alexei is still a guy."

"Do you think he has feelings for you?" Charly asked.

I smiled. "Only the feelings he might have for some long-lost relative. We're friends, only friends. End of discussion." Then I thought about the overwhelming feelings Charly experienced around Alexei. And the effect he seemed to have on Lila Grace as well. "I think he has a girlfriend either back in Britain or in Russia. I'm not sure which. I know he's spent a lot of time in both places when he's not here at school."

Lila Grace looked devastated, and I made a mental note to tell Alexei to check out her dreams. Maybe she would be easier to persuade to forget him than Charly.

Charly stared at me closely. "Maybe he does have a girlfriend elsewhere, but I wouldn't be too sure that he's not interested in you. There's something else going on, besides just filling you in on old family stories."

I rubbed my neck, wishing Alexei had been wrong when he described Charly as stubborn and strong-willed. As I rubbed my neck my hair twisted on the leather cord and pulled. I reached around the front of my sweater vest and pulled it out, looking at it for the first time since Alexei had slipped it around my neck. The silver pendant that hung on the cord was some sort of griffin or eagle. It looked very mythical, but I couldn't quite place it.

Charly grabbed my hand and held it up to her face. "Did he give you this too? It's just like on your box."

I realized Charly was right and felt like an idiot. It was a firebird. I nodded to Charly. "He said it was a good luck charm to keep me from having nightmares."

"Good," Emma said. "You've been having some noisy dreams the past couple of nights." Then her look softened. "Although, I guess with everything you've been through it's not too surprising. I hope it helps, Elisabeth."

"Thanks." As if by some unspoken command, we all got up and started getting ready for bed.

While we were walking back from brushing our teeth, Charly asked me a question I had been wondering about myself. "What are you going to tell Chase when you see him?"

"I have no idea."

We went into our room where Emma and Lila Grace were already in their beds. The lamp next to my bed was on, so I turned out the overhead light before crossing the room. As soon as Charly and I were both in our beds, I turned out the lamp. The darkness was welcoming and, though I wasn't the first to fall asleep, I wasn't the last either. I was relieved to find it was a deep sleep without dreams.

CHAPTER SIXTEEN

I didn't see Chase for the next week. I didn't see much of Alexei either. I spent most of my time catching up on my schoolwork. I was about to begin my third week at the Academy and was finally getting into a normal routine. I suddenly had more free time than I was used to having. Even on Sunday afternoons at the group home, I always had chores to do, homework to finish, or younger kids to babysit. With my schoolwork under control, I felt lost. I tried reading, but not even my old favorites could work their magic on me. My mind kept traveling an endless circuit between thoughts of my family, Alexei and his vampire 'family,' and Chase.

I wondered if Alexei had said something to him, some kind of warning to stay away. Or if he was just ticked off at me because I'd stood him up that night at the arbor. Either way there didn't seem to be much I could do about it, but it still stayed in the front of my mind.

The afternoon sun was hiding behind dark storm clouds that refused to let go of their raindrops. It left everything gray and dingy, but I knew that Alexei was probably outside taking advantage of the indirect light. It was harder to accept his story outside the dark tunnels where time seemed almost meaningless and back in the real world. But I'd seen him move the heavy wardrobe without effect, and I'd seen the effect he had on both Charly and Lila Grace. It still seemed impossible, and it was hard to make myself think the word 'vampire,' but there was no other explanation. I wished I could understand how my family connected to the vampires in the first place. I wished Alexei would tell me more about my family's special abilities that made vampires have to negotiate with us rather than simply destroy us. I wished I could talk to Julian about everything I'd heard from Alexei.

I had to get out of the Kirkwynd study hall. I decided to explore the campus. I was tempted to go into the tunnels, but after my promise to Julian it didn't feel right. Plus, when I had been with Alexei, I realized it wouldn't be hard to get completely lost. I walked out near the fountain and the statue of Aleron Saint Clare. It was deserted in the gloomy weather, and I found it peaceful.

But there was something decidedly un-peaceful in my heart, so I started walking again. I headed past the main buildings, back toward Kirkwynd Hall, then farther east. When the front hit the mountains so high in the atmosphere, it allowed the precipitation to fall which could cause massive snows in the winter and flash floods with rain. I knew that scientifically from one of my classes, but the way the air was charged, it seemed as if the mountains were stirring up the storm all on their own and were pushing it back to the Academy.

I knew it was my own imagination, spurred into overdrive by Alexei's vampires. If one strange nightmare was true, what kept them all from being true? Maybe there were werewolves living in the mountains. Or maybe the mountains weren't really mountains at all but giants, frozen to stone under a curse, and the storm was them trying to break free. Or there could be ghosts haunting the valleys where white settlers trespassed on sacred Indian grounds and were killed. Maybe some hideous, monstrous creature, brought to unnatural life by a scientist or cast out of society at birth, lurked in the shadows and caves. Or possibly –

Lightning sliced through the sky, followed almost immediately by the loud clap of thunder. I jumped and probably squealed like a scared little girl. I was relieved that I was alone with no one to witness my childish behavior. A second burst of lightning lit the sky in an odd blue-yellow light for a split second. The echoing thunder was accompanied by fat drops of hot rain. I looked around for shelter and saw the wisteria arbor attached to the closest building. I ran to it, grateful that I was wearing my blue jeans and tennis shoes and not my uniform skirt. Although I covered the short distance quickly, I was still soaked by the time I reached the arbor.

Most of it was open, the fragile blossoms falling beneath the powerful rain, but one end had a section of closed lattice. I was only a few feet away when I realized there was already someone there. I kept walking to get out of the most direct rain, but it wasn't until I was directly behind him that Chase seemed to hear me and turn around.

"Elisabeth." His voice was flat, without emotion. He turned back to stand leaning against the wall, watching the storm just beyond.

"Chase." I tried to keep my voice as neutral as his. I still had no idea what to say to him. We stood in silence as the storm gained strength around us. The wind shifted, and the rain began to blow sideways, hitting us under the half-roof.

Chase looked at me and shook his head. "We can't stay out here in this. The arts building might be unlocked." He grabbed my hand and led me around to the side of the building with a small door. He twisted the doorknob a couple of times, and I thought it was locked, but then he twisted once more, hard, and it opened. He pushed me inside in front of him, and then shut the door behind him. It was dark inside until a flash of lightning momentarily allowed me to see the art studio with various easels and supplies. Chase moved away from me to the wall.

"The lights are out. The storm must have knocked out the power. The dorms and the cafeteria have backup generators, but most of the other buildings . . . ." He shrugged.

"Is there a flashlight or candle or anything?" I asked.

"I don't see anything. Be still, and I'll check the teacher's desk." He moved carefully through the room, and I heard him rummaging through the drawers. "I can't find anything. Oh, wait. I found a lighter. It's not much, but we can use it to find a place to sit and maybe something to dry off with." He flicked the switch on the small black cigarette lighter and walked back toward me. The dark skies and streaking lightning outside combined with the odd flickers of light from the tiny flame to cast eerie shadows on his too pale face.

He took my hand, and we headed out into the hallway. There was a supply room next to the studio, and we found towels there. We grabbed a few and headed on before the lighter ran out of whatever liquid it was burning. The smell was making me a little lightheaded. A few doors further up the hall, we found a teachers lounge. It was smaller than the student lounge in the Langford classroom building, but it was dry and had a couch to sit on. There was another door on the other side of the room but no windows. It was darker than even the hallway had been.

Chase let go of my hand just inside the door. "Wait here, and I'll see if I can find a candle or something." He walked to the cabinets on one wall and began searching. A few seconds later he gave a little shout of victory and turned back toward me with a thick candle that had three wicks in it. He set it on the table and lit one of the wicks. It was brighter than the lighter had been, and the light reflected off the white walls.

I handed Chase one of the towels I was carrying and then wiped off my bare arms before rubbing my long, wet hair. Chase pulled off his soaked t-shirt and laid it across the back of one of the chairs to dry, and then he took off his tennis shoes and socks.

I took off my socks and shoes as well. The building was cooler than it had been out in the rain, and I was already getting chilled. I rubbed at my hair harder.

"Stop that before you pull all your hair out." Chase was standing beside me, and before I could say anything, he had taken the towel out of my hands and began gently drying the tangled mess.

I stood there unsure of what I should say or do. It seemed so strange to just let him take care of me, but I didn't want to seem ungrateful after he had gotten us out of the storm and found us a dry place to wait. After a minute or so, he stopped.

"I think it's dry enough now that it won't drip all over you." He smiled at me, and I smiled back.

"Thanks." I started to say something else, but a violent shudder passed through my body as I reacted to the colder temperature.

"You're freezing." He looked around. "Come here." He walked to the couch and, when I followed, pulled me down to sit very close to him. He put his arms around me from behind trying to warm me with his own body which was as cold as mine. "I'm sorry there's not a blanket or anything."

"It's okay. Thank you for everything. I'd have never thought to come in here."

"What were you doing out in this weather in the first place?"

I wished I could see him, to try to read some meaning from his hazel eyes. "I just couldn't stay inside. What were you doing out?"

He laughed. "I like storms." The laughter left his voice. "I wasn't expecting to see the lightning quite so close. I wasn't expecting to see you either."

"I wanted to apologize for the other day. I didn't mean to leave you waiting."

I felt him take a deep breath. "It's okay, Elisabeth. I was really disappointed, but someone told me they saw you take off with Alexei Mikhailovich out of the science building."

"It's not what you think. Alexei is just a friend. We have history class together, and Mr. Callahan asked him to give me some notes, so he was explaining them. I was back in my room, and I realized I'd lost all track of time."

"You're not interested in dating Alexei? I haven't met him, but most of the girls in Wycliffe Hall seem to think he's the hottest thing to hit the Academy since it was built." Chase's voice stayed even, but his arms tightened slightly around me. I didn't think he'd realized it.

"That's funny. Most of the girls in Kirkwynd think Alexei is yesterday's news; they want to know more about Chase Elliot."

Chase leaned closer until he was whispering in my ear. "I don't care what most of the girls in Kirkwynd think. I just want to know what one girl in particular thinks."

My heart picked up its pace, but I tried to sound nonchalant. "What's her name, and I'll try to find out."

"Her name is Elisabeth Sinclair, and she shouldn't be too hard to find because she's the new girl." Chase's lips were brushing over my ear as he whispered the words.

"The new girl? I'm pretty sure she only thinks of Alexei as a friend. I heard she was interested in Chase Elliot."

My pulse thumped in time with the thunder outside. Chase dropped his head so that his lips were moving down my neck. Suddenly, he pulled me backward, into his lap, and before I knew what he was doing, his lips were on mine, and we were kissing. I wasn't sure if the pounding was my heart or the storm outside. Chase pulled back from the kiss and stared at me. I could finally see his hazel eyes, but they were full of questions.

"How old are you, Elisabeth?"

I managed to remember the correct age before I answered him. "Fifteen."

"Have you ever been kissed before?"

I ducked my head to keep from having to admit the truth, but he put his hands on the sides of my face and gently forced me to look at him.

"It's okay if you haven't. I kind of like the idea that I'm the first one to kiss you."

"Really? You're not annoyed that I'm not very good at it?" My voice was quiet, and I wasn't sure I truly wanted an answer.

He laughed softly. "Don't ever worry about that, Elisabeth. You did just fine, and everyone can get better with practice. I like that you are more innocent. I don't like the girls who throw themselves at guys."

He leaned forward, still holding my face in his hands, and kissed me again, lightly. I slid my arms around his neck and let my fingers tangle themselves in his pale blond hair. It was still damp and trying to curl.

He moved so that there was a couple of inches between our faces. "I really like you, Elisabeth. I don't want you to get scared or uncomfortable with anything I do, so if there's something that you don't like, I need you to tell me. Will you do that? Will you tell me if I do something you don't like?"

The look in his hazel eyes was so sincere that I immediately assured him of what he wanted. "If I get scared, I'll tell you."

He smiled at me, and his hands slid down from my face to my shoulders and then my back. "I want to kiss you again. May I?" I couldn't speak so I just nodded. His mouth hovered over mine for a moment before he pressed against it. The kiss was still gentle, but it was more intense this time. He nibbled at my lips, sucking the bottom one between his own until a small sigh escaped from me. He pressed his advantage to deepen the kiss.

I felt his tongue skim lightly over my lip and move to touch mine. I wasn't sure that I was ready for that kind of kiss but, before I had the chance to protest, Chase was pulling back. He held me close to his chest, and I could hear his heart beating loudly. He rubbed his hand up and down my arm. As his hand moved in perfect rhythm with his heartbeat, I relaxed. He seemed to feel even the slightest change in my body language. When I relaxed, he slid his hand up my arm to my face. Tilting my chin up to face him, he leaned over and began kissing my face with soft, short kisses like he was tracing a pattern, starting at my temple and moving around until he ended back at my lips.

He rained the feathery kisses around the edge of my mouth. I was determined to keep my lips firmly together this time, so I wouldn't give him the wrong idea. And suddenly he was kissing me again. His lips were so soft and gentle on mine. He wasn't pushing me to do anything more than what we'd started out doing. I was the one who was stubborn and unyielding. It seemed as if the room was spinning, and my head was buzzing, and I couldn't breathe. I heard his voice, but I knew that it had to be in my head, because he was still kissing me. The voice in my head was telling me to relax and open myself up to him. Chase continued kissing me, still very gently, but his voice was making my head buzz, and it grew louder and more intense.

I pulled away suddenly. Chase looked at me, and I could see the concern in his hazel eyes. "Did I do something?" he asked.

I shook my head quickly, drawing in a shaky breath. "My head was spinning."

Chase smiled. "That's what it's supposed to feel like. Just relax and let yourself feel. It's okay, whatever you feel. No one can make you feel something that you don't feel. Don't you like kissing me?" He sounded so unsure, so different from the cocky boy who'd told me that I would eat lunch with him only days earlier. It was sweet. I wondered if he was still worried about my relationship with Alexei, no matter what he had claimed.

I smiled, hoping that it was at least a little seductive in spite of my certainty that I looked like a drowned rat. "Of course I like kissing you, Chase. I just didn't want you to be disappointed with me."

"Never," he vowed. "Even if I never got the chance to kiss you again. As long as I know I can be your friend."

I was nervous, but I thought he must be too, so I decided to take a risk. "I hope we're more than just friends." I was relieved that my voice didn't shake. The husky whisper sounded sexy rather than scared.

He smiled at me. It was a spectacular smile that made me glad I'd risked getting laughed at or rejected. "I'm glad we both want the same thing."

He leaned down to kiss me again. This kiss was intense. My head started buzzing like before, and I heard his voice demanding 'more.' I didn't fight it. I let my lips part, and the kiss progressed. Instead of the tentative searching of his earlier kiss, he took possession of my mouth, confident that I would accept him. I was lost. The voice in my head chanted 'more' over and over until it became an echo of my racing heart. The unfamiliar sensations his mouth was producing in me were intoxicating. My entire consciousness was focused in the kiss that had our lips fused together.

Before I could process what was happening, my body responded to him. Our tongues were moving in a furious half-dance, half-war. It wasn't until I felt his hand sliding across the skin of my back that I even realized he had slipped it under my soaked t-shirt. There was something enticing about the feel of his strong hand on my flesh. It seemed like his kiss had acted like a drug on me. My brain was slow to react as if it was wrapped in cotton. Before the thought that Chase shouldn't have his hand under my shirt, even in the back, could register through the haze clouding my mind, my body had betrayed me. The feel of his warm hand across my chilled skin caused me to shiver, and he pulled me closer to him.

He ripped his mouth away from mine but, rather than giving me a chance to think and clear my head, he kissed his way to my jaw and down my neck. The scooped neck of my t-shirt allowed easy access to the hollow of my throat. His hand was no longer moving on my back, but held me in place as his lips traced across the prominent lines of my clavicle, exposed on one side with a gentle tug on the top of my shirt. I'm not sure if he would have tried to take it any farther, but his voice was still echoing through my foggy brain, demanding more and more.

A sudden boom of thunder startled me, and I jumped, almost falling off his lap completely. He caught me, but the spell was broken. The noise acted as an alarm, clearing the cobwebs out of my head and silencing the voice. I stood up and moved away from him quickly.

"Elisabeth?" He sounded wary.

"I'm sorry, Chase. The thunder scared me."

He stood up and took a step closer to me. "Come back and sit down. It's not over yet."

I wasn't entirely sure he meant the storm, but I chose to answer him that way. "Charly and the other girls will be really worried about me if I don't get back. I can just run back to Kirkwynd, and then I can get some dry clothes."

He took another step. "I don't know if that's such a good idea. If the thunder is that loud, then the lightning must be really close. I'd never forgive myself if I let you go out in this storm and something happened to you."

I shook my head. "Nothing's going to happen to me. But I really do have to go. I can't stay in here. We shouldn't have been in here like this."

His hazel eyes narrowed slightly. "Are you trying to say that I made you do something you didn't want to do? Because you wanted that kiss. You kissed me back. And you promised you'd stop me if you didn't like what we were doing, but you didn't stop me."

He sounded like he had been betrayed. I hurried to reassure him. "That's not what I meant at all, Chase." I couldn't look him in the eyes when I said the next thing. My gaze dropped down to our bare feet. "I guess I just got a little scared."

"I knew it! I've ruined everything."

He was so upset that I moved back to touch his arm. "It wasn't like that, Chase. I wasn't afraid of you. I guess . . . maybe I was just . . . ." I had to pull my eyes away from him again. Then I finally got it all out in a rush. "I was just scared because I'd never felt that way before."

He rested his arm on my shoulder while his hand played with my hair. "What way?"

I still couldn't look up, but I could feel how close he was to me. "You know." My voice was a broken crackle.

"I know how I feel, Elisabeth, but unless you tell me I have no idea what you're feeling. You have to say the words."

I knew my face had turned deep red with the blush that was burning in my cheeks. I couldn't manage anything more than a whisper. "I didn't want you to stop kissing me. I didn't care if the storm never stopped as long as you could go on kissing me."

His hand moved out of my hair and under my chin, lifting my head to meet his eyes. "I didn't want to stop kissing you either, but I guess we got a little carried away. It's my fault. I should know better-"

I had to interrupt him. "No! It's not your fault, at least not more than mine. We both got carried away."

He smiled at me. "That's sweet of you to say, but I know I have more experience than you, and I should be able to control myself better. It's just that you make me forget everything except kissing you."

I didn't think it was possible, but I blushed harder. I felt so much more sophisticated and powerful, hearing that I had made him lose control when no one else did.

"I'm not blaming you or mad at you or anything, Chase, but I do think it's time I got back to my dorm."

He let go of my face and moved slightly in a way that put plenty of space between us. I picked up my wet socks and shoes, holding them in one hand and turned to go out into the hallway when he stopped me.

"Take the candle, Elisabeth. I don't want you to get hurt trying to get out of the building."

"What about you?" I asked.

He smiled and pointed to the lighter on the table. "I've still got that."

I nodded and carefully picked up the fat candle with my free hand. Just as I got to the door, he spoke again.

"Elisabeth?"

I turned back to look at him, waiting.

"Will you have lunch with me tomorrow?" It was definitely a request this time, unlike the commanded appearance of the first day we met. His voice was soft, but strong. He had told me he wanted to be more than friends, and not even my awkward inexperience could change his mind about me. I nodded my answer.

He smiled at me, that slightly cocky grin. I walked out into the hallway and made my way back to the door we'd come in. The storm was lessening, and the sky was already brighter. I blew out the candle, leaving it near the door. I noticed the broken doorknob on my way outside and thought that it must have been the reason Chase'd had so much trouble getting it opened in the first place.

With my socks stuffed inside my shoes and a firm grasp on them, I took off across the school grounds back to Kirkwynd Hall.

CHAPTER SEVENTEEN

I was afraid the study hall in Kirkwynd would be packed because of the stormy weather, so I let myself into the tunnels using the janitor's closet. The tunnel floor was wet, and I remembered Julian telling me how some of the drains emptied into it. The air was full of moisture but colder than the temperatures outside had been. It occurred to me then that Alexei might return to his room using these tunnels. Of all the people I didn't want to encounter, Alexei was at the top of that list.

I found the door that led up the stairs to my room. I eased it open and then closed as I slipped through as carefully as I could. I knew I was being silly. If Alexei could hear my heartbeat, then he would definitely hear my footsteps and the sound of the doors. But I didn't want to take any extra chances.

I was still carrying my wet socks and shoes, and my hair was once again soaked. The drips from my hair and clothes, combined with my already wet feet, made the stone steps more precarious than usual. I was so busy concentrating on not slipping that I hadn't noticed how close I was to the top until I turned the final corner and came face to knee with Alexei. He was sitting on the top step but, when I jerked back in surprise, and lost my balance, he was standing beside me with a steadying hand on my arm before I could blink.

"Elisabeth? Are you alright?" His deep voice was filled with concern.

"You surprised me, that's all."

He frowned. "I realize that. I meant . . . Why are you wet?"

I looked up at his eyes, a shadowy green in the dim beam of my flashlight. "I was outside when it started raining."

"That is obvious. I was trying to figure out why you stayed outside after it started raining." He started to say more, but I interrupted him by sneezing. He opened the door to let me into my room, calling out, "It is Elisabeth and me, Alexei. May I come in?" He pushed me through the door while he was still speaking.

I saw Emma at her desk, and Charly jumped up off her bed.

"Where have you been? We were so worried when it started storming." Charly got a good look at me and grabbed my robe along with a towel.

Emma answered Alexei. "It's okay to come in, Alexei. Lila Grace is downstairs in the study hall, keeping watch for Elisabeth. I guess I'll let her know you're back." Emma walked out of the room while Alexei walked into it.

"She is too cold, Charly. Take her to the bath and get her in a warm shower," Alexei said.

I knew he was only trying to help because he was concerned about me, but I didn't like being treated like a child. Before I had the chance to say anything, Charly was nodding and agreeing.

"You're right, Alexei. She does need to be warmed up. Come on, Elisabeth." She grabbed my arm and pulled me out the door, but stopped in the doorway. She looked back at Alexei. "Will you still be here when we get back?"

He smiled and nodded. "As long as that is what you wish."

Charly grinned and nodded, but I was glaring at him. He arched a dark eyebrow at me, letting me know that he understood I hadn't liked his heavy-handedness or his manipulation of Charly. I might have argued about it right then, but I was shivering, and I sneezed again.

The warm shower was perfect, and I washed my hair, using lots of conditioner on the tangles. Maybe Emma was smarter, keeping her curls cut short. I ran my hands across the wet mass of hair and knew I really liked the cut Julian had arranged for me in Paris. The thought of Julian and Paris brought a sudden wave of emotion that I had trouble identifying for a moment. I realized I was homesick for her and the place I identified with her. So much had happened since I'd seen her. I was rocked by Alexei's revelations and the secrets about my own family, and I was confused by Chase and my new feelings about him. I was suddenly aware that I was wanting to talk to Julian the way any other girl would want to talk to her mother.

Julian, the elegant but reserved woman who always looked perfect. It was hard to imagine her as a mom that would make peanut butter and jelly sandwiches or patch up skinned knees. It wasn't so hard to picture her in court or a boardroom, doing battle with my step-grandmother to save my future. But I wanted her here now. I needed to talk to her about the past and the future, but more than either of those, the present.

Charly came back into the bathroom. "Elisabeth? I brought you some clothes. I thought you might like a sweater to wear over a t-shirt."

"Thanks, Charly." There was something in her voice that made me wait for whatever it was she really wanted to say.

"Are you about done? Alexei is waiting to talk to you. He said he wanted to make sure you were okay."

The tentative tone in her voice was at odds with the way she normally spoke about Alexei. I shut the water off and wrapped myself and my hair in a couple of towels before opening the curtain. I looked through the steamy room at her worried face.

"What's wrong?" I asked.

"I don't know." She was searching for a way to explain what she was feeling. "I don't know what happened today between you and Alexei, but if you're avoiding him, I can just tell him to go away." I knew, better than she did herself, how hard it was for her to concentrate with Alexei around, so I was surprised at the offer.

"I wasn't with Alexei today. He was waiting for me at the top of the staircase. I guess he figured that I wouldn't want to go through the study hall after being caught in the rain."

"But – if you weren't with him, then why has he been so agitated waiting for you?" She was twisting her hands together like she would tighten them on a baseball bat.

I wondered if Alexei's agitation was spilling over to Charly. I'd never seen her get the least bit ruffled over anything except him. I thought about what she said. "Maybe he was just worried because I was caught out in the storm. I told you that he knows all about what happened to my parents, at least as much as anybody knows."

"Do you want me to make him leave?"

"No. I'll talk to him." I bit my bottom lip, then realized I was doing it, and wondered if I would ever break that habit. "I might need to talk to him alone. He might not like it if he knew that I told you all about my family."

Charly nodded. "Emma is still downstairs with Lila Grace. I'll tell Alexei that you'll be right out, and then I'll head down and keep them there until you let me know otherwise."

"Thanks, Charly. You're a great friend." I hoped my eyes would tell her how much I meant what I said.

Charly grinned at me, the wonderfully familiar grin that made me feel normal. "Just remember to tell your 'great friend' all the gory details later. I'm dying to know what has Alexei so riled up." She left the room, and I hurried to dry off and dress.

Even though the shower had warmed me up – the steam was still hanging in the bathroom so thick that the mirrors remained foggy – I was grateful Charly had brought the thick sweater. I pulled it over my head and wiped off a section of the mirror so I could comb my hair. I didn't bother with a blow dryer or any kind of styling. It was all I could do to pull the comb through, and Alexei was waiting.

Finally I was dressed, and my hair was de-tangled and dry enough that it didn't drip. I couldn't avoid him forever. I walked back into my room and hung my towel and robe on a hook by the window to dry. I turned around to look at Alexei. He seemed paler than I had ever seen him, and his eyes, usually so bright, were full of shadows.

"Tell me what happened, Elisabeth. Start from the time you decided to go outside and tell me everything."

For a moment I was just in shock. Then the anger kicked in. "Who do you think you are, demanding to know everything I've done?"

He was shaking his head before I finished. "I am not demanding, at least not for the reasons you think. Something has happened, and I have to figure out why and how much damage has been done." He moved across the room before I could blink, and he was holding my hands in his. He wasn't demanding at all; he was begging. "Please, Elisabeth. Your life could be in danger this very moment. You have to tell me."

My heart was racing as I saw that Alexei absolutely believed what he was saying. What could have happened that would put me in such immediate danger?

"Is Julian . . . ." I couldn't finish the thought, let alone say it out loud.

"No. It is not Julian. As far as I know, nothing has happened to Julian. The problem is here at the Academy. If you tell me where you have been, who you have been with, then I will tell you everything I know."

"Everything? About my family?"

He hesitated. "I am not sure if you would believe everything, but I may not have any other choice. Please, Elisabeth."

I nodded. I took a deep breath, then decided I didn't want to talk about it standing up. I tugged on Alexei's hands and walked to my bed. I sat down, and he let go of one hand to sit beside me. There was something comforting about sitting close to Alexei. He seemed full of warmth.

"Aren't vampires supposed to be cold? You feel so warm."

He smiled slightly. "Someone made that up. Something about comparing vampires to reptiles, cold-blooded. The truth is that I do not feel the hot or the cold, but I can regulate my body temperature to match a normal human's."

"I don't get it. How can you make your body feel as warm as a normal human's. I mean, aren't you technically dead?" I bit my bottom lip, hoping the question wasn't overly rude.

"I died, but I am not dead. Dead people do not walk and talk, do they? I am other. I cannot explain it for you other than to say that vampires do not follow human biology. If we did, we would not exist. My heart beats like yours and moves blood through my veins. The difference is that it is not my blood. There are a good many mysteries in this world, Elisabeth. Perhaps if we allowed certain scientific minds to study us, we would know more, but that option is not so appealing."

"Because they would keep you caged like some kind of freak or . . . or-"

His eyes were sad as he finished my sentence. "Or monster. I told you that is what I am. Now, enough of your stalling. Tell me where you went when you left Kirkwynd Hall today. Why did you go out in the first place?"

I looked down at Alexei's hand holding mine, and I mumbled the truth that I knew. "You're not a monster." Before he could argue or try to refocus me, I went on to answer some of what he'd asked. "I'm not sure why I went out. I felt so, I guess it was restless, but more than that. It was like I was trapped in these walls, and I had to get out. I knew there was a storm coming, and I could feel it." I broke off, positive that I sounded like an idiot.

Alexei nodded. "You could feel the storm building inside you, like it was inside your blood, and if you did not move, did not go, then it would rip you apart from the inside."

I stared at him in awe. "How did you know? That's exactly how it felt."

He gave me his little half-smile. "Have you ever felt like that before? Think carefully."

I started to just shake my head, but I realized I had. "Mrs. Jenkins used to say that the only time she ever saw me outside without being pushed into it was when a storm was coming. But it was never as bad as it was today."

"You are getting older, and your family traits are beginning to manifest. I have seen your father take off before a thunderstorm and not return until it was over. He told me how it felt, but I never saw it in him. Maybe that is not the best way to say it. No matter how restless he was feeling, he never let anyone see any difference in him. Julian felt it too, in a lesser degree. Nicholas would take Julian out running in the mountains before the storm would hit, but he made sure she was back before the rain fell. He said that physical activity helped, moving would displace the anxious, jittery feeling."

"Why didn't she tell me? She could have warned me or something."

He gave me a wry look. "Warned you how? Besides, Julian was probably not expecting this to bother you yet. Nicholas told me that Julian and most of the people in your extended family did not suffer from the effects until they were closer to twenty. Julian was never bothered by the weather until the last semester before she graduated. Nicholas, with his purer bloodline, felt it from his mid-teens. I suppose you are on schedule with your father, even with your mother's genetics."

"What exactly was I feeling? I don't get it."

"It is tied to the gifts that make your family more than the average human. Even if you had been raised knowing all about your heritage, some of this would still be guesswork because of your mother's DNA."

There was something that he said that caught me by surprise, and I didn't think he'd realized that he'd said it. "Are you telling me that my family, my father's family, is not completely human?"

He was shocked. "That is not what I said!"

The guilt in his face and voice confirmed it. "If we're not completely human, what are we?"

"I never said anything like that, Elisabeth. Technically, your family is genetically superior to the average human, more perfect than the average."

"You're splitting hairs," I accused.

"Perhaps, but you are still trying to avoid the real issue. When you left, where did you go and who did you see?"

A thousand angry retorts flashed through my brain, but I pushed them back and swallowed my anger. He was right. I was trying to avoid the subject.

When I spoke again, my voice was quieter. "I was exploring the grounds. I've been spending so much time trying to catch up in my class work I felt like I hadn't really taken the time to see the school. I went over by the fountain and the statue. It felt very peaceful there, but I didn't want to feel peaceful. My brain was racing, and I felt like I was on fire inside."

I glanced at him to see if he was really listening. He was tracing the blue-green veins in the back of my hand with one finger. I wondered if he was trying to distract himself or just unable to stop the fascination.

"I went north and east toward the mountains. I knew the storm was coming, and I knew the mountains were acting as a meteorological boundary. I do pay a little attention in my classes." I caught his faint smile. "What I didn't know was how far I was getting from the other campus buildings. It didn't start with a sprinkle or a few warning drops to let you know it was coming. The storm broke all at once, and it was pouring. I just ran for the closest building. I didn't even think to try the doors. I went straight to the arbor on the side of the building, trying to find shelter."

"Who did you meet there?" If his voice hadn't been so full of worry, real worry, I would have gotten angry at his insistence.

"I wasn't planning to meet anyone, Alexei. I didn't even realize he was there until I was a few feet away from him." I sounded defensive even to my own ears.

"Just tell me, Elisabeth. I am not angry with you. None of this is your fault."

"None of what? If you'd just tell me what was going on, maybe I'd know what you're trying to get me to say."

"The only thing I want you to say is who you found under the arbor. And what happened after you found him."

"It was Chase, Chase Elliot."

Alexei smiled bitterly. "Of course, it was. Then what happened?"

"The wind shifted, and the rain began blowing sideways. The arbor wasn't giving us any kind of shelter. Chase suggested we try the building. At first the door wouldn't budge, but then he managed to get in. I noticed, on my way out, that the door was broken. I figured that's why it was so hard to open. The storm had knocked the power out, but Chase found a cigarette lighter in the art teacher's desk. We found some paint towels in the supply closet and used them to dry off. We found a candle in the teachers' lounge and sat in there waiting for the storm to let up before we headed back out."

"You have to tell me, Elisabeth. What did he do to you?" Alexei was holding my hand and seemed so earnest that I was confused.

"He kissed me."

A dark rage welled up in Alexei's eyes. "And then he tried to hurt you? Did he – are you alright?"

I realized with a start that Alexei thought Chase had tried to make me do something I didn't want to do. That he had tried to force himself on me or something.

"It wasn't like that, Alexei. I swear. He just kissed me." My face flushed as I thought of the kisses and the warm touch of Chase's hand on my back. I knew my heart was racing, but I hoped Alexei would attribute it to a crush rather than a lie. I really didn't want to go through every detail with him.

Alexei seemed stunned. "You are certain? There was nothing frightening or threatening?"

I thought carefully for a moment. "I guess I was a little scared, but not of Chase. I was afraid I wasn't-" I broke off, unable to admit to Alexei that I was so inexperienced that I was afraid of doing something wrong.

Somehow Alexei seemed to understand. "It was your first kiss. I am a fool."

The last bit sunk through my embarrassment. I turned so that I was finding Alexei. "How are you a fool?" His tone was dry when he spoke. "In a million ways. I overreacted. I thought you were in danger, that you were afraid. I did not understand enough to realize that you were nervous about yourself, not afraid of someone else."

"How did you know at all?" If the danger that Alexei was so worried about was something he had picked up from me, how was that even possible?

He looked sheepish. "Would you believe me if I said I was not completely sure?"

"I'd believe you, but only because you promised not to lie to me. If you're not totally sure, then what are you sure about?"

He sighed. "Yes, please, use my own guilt against me. I have heard of something similar to this happening before, but only twice and never exactly like this, so, please, bear with me." I nodded, so he continued. "Do you remember how I told you about the compulsions my family put on humans to make them forget they ever knew anything about us at all? We had another related talent that worked between us. We could use it to communicate, but only short bursts of emotion. It most often served as a warning system when a group was out hunting together."

A shudder ran through my body as I imagined seven or eight vampires working together to hunt humans.

Again Alexei seemed to read my thoughts. "It was my second family, Elisabeth. We only hunted wild animals, large game."

I nodded as I remembered, but the picture refused to fade from my mind.

"Twice in all the history that my family could remember, and that goes back over many centuries, only twice in all that time, has there been a joining of minds that goes beyond the quick flash of feeling. In both of these cases, they were ones who had lived together in close contact for centuries. They had so many shared experiences and knew how the other would react in each case. Slowly, over a century or two, their flashes increased and the thought behind them filtered through the emotion until, in the end, their minds were linked."

I knew I was staring at him with a dumb look on my face. "Linked? Like in a chain?"

Alexei frowned and shook his head. "I do not think so. Both of the pairs died before I was found, so all my knowledge comes from secondary sources. From what I understood, it seemed more like molecules. You remember in chemistry – two hydrogens and one oxygen?"

"H2O. Water."

"Correct. When the molecules bond and create water, they become stronger than they were alone. It is also harder to separate them, although it can be done in science. When these vampires paired it changed them. They could hear each other's thoughts across great distances. They knew when the other was in danger."

I spoke slowly, trying to understand what this strange vampire bonding had to do with me. "It sounds like a useful ability, although if it took so long to cultivate, I guess I understand why it's so rare."

Alexei was watching me closely. "When we sent out our warnings, it was impossible to tell exactly who was sending the message. When they first began the process of bonding, it was recognizing the – voice – in their head. They only ever knew the one voice of their, I guess, partner. At first it was still impossible to understand more than the emotion. Only with time did the voice become words." He waited for me to understand, but I just didn't get it. What was Alexei trying to tell me?

He stood up and began pacing the room, the frustrated pacing that I had seen in the tunnels. The air in the room was turning stale and suffocating. I could see Alexei's frustration growing, and it seemed that as it grew, the room shrank and the air became more stifling. I felt my own panic rising, an indefinable fear that came from nowhere.

It pressed in at me until I couldn't sit on my bed any longer. I stood up and grabbed Alexei's arm so he would have to stop pacing and look at me. When his eyes met mine, it was like the inside workings of a lock clicking into place. I saw the deep guilt in his eyes, and I felt it echoing inside my mind.

"I am sorry. I was so certain you were in danger, and, once again, it seems that I am the biggest threat to you."

"Stop it. I can't take this guilt. It's like it's choking me." I put my hand up to touch his face, but he caught it before I got close. "Just tell me what's happening to me."

He caressed my hand and brought it to his lips for a kiss. "I do not know how or why this is happening. I told you how rare it is for two of my kind to become bonded. It has never happened between us and a human, not even one of your family. I did not think we could, but I cannot think of any other explanation for what has happened, except that somehow we have begun the process of bonding."

"Make it stop. I like you, Alexei, but I don't want you inside my head."

"If I had any certain way to stop it without risking you, I would."

My eyes narrowed. "What do you mean certain way and without risking me? Is there a way that is risky?"

He shook his head. "In both cases, after the pairs had bonded, when one of them was killed, the other also died. If I thought I could break this by killing myself without killing you also, I would do it."

Anger flared up in me. "Sacrificing yourself for me is not an option!"

"In this case it is less of an option than you think. The bonding is still early, but from everything I have been told, we are at the stage now that the others only achieved after six hundred years together."

The bubble of anger popped as quickly as it had blown up. "But we haven't even known each other for a month. How is this possible?"

"I am afraid it is my fault. I may have triggered something by entering your dreams before you were aware of your powers."

"You're guessing." I wasn't positive, but he seemed to be reaching.

"For over four hundred years I have moved through my existence sure of myself and in control of my actions. Less than a month of knowing you, and I am racked with guilt and have no clear sense of what path I should follow."

I felt a small smile tugging at my lips. "So now you're saying it's all my fault."

He finally smiled, with only a shade of the sadness and sarcasm that his smiles usually held. "You are the wild card. I do not understand how much impact your mother has had on your genetic makeup, not to mention the odd lines of inheritance. I always believed the rituals your family used in naming the heir and crowning the prince were purely symbolic, but now I am not certain."

"What does it mean that you've bonded to a human instead of your own kind?"

Alexei must have heard the worry in my voice. Or maybe he felt some tinge of it in his mind. "I do not know. It has never happened; I believed it never could. I will try to find out more, but I may not get answers. Just remember that your family's abilities make you more than the average human. We now know that, despite everything else, there can be no doubt of your bloodline and heritage."

I grimaced. "Because that's exactly what I was hoping for."

"Poor Elisabeth. I wish I knew more about you abilities, but for now you need to stay as calm as you can."

"Tell me how you knew about this."

I was sure he was going to ignore me, but he seemed to think twice and walked us back over to my bed. Instead of sitting on the edge, this time he sat with his back against the headboard and pulled me into the crook of his arm, leaning against him.

"When I saw the weather today, I headed into the mountains to hunt."

I interrupted him at once. "What were you hunting?"

Alexei sighed pointedly. "If you keep interrupting me . . . ."

"I just really want to know about this. Please." I didn't care that I was begging as long as he answered my question.

"I was hunting for whatever animal I could find in abundance. If I found a large deer or bear, I could take what I needed without feeding from several smaller animals."

"You didn't want to kill anything."

"I made vows and a treaty with your father."

"Who did you make the vows to?" My curiosity was rampant.

"To God."

I found that I was surprised and yet not surprised to hear Alexei talk of God.

"You believe in God," I said.

He nodded. "I know that when He created the monster, or demon, that ended my human life, He left me with a new choice. I try to respect the life that He has created in all its forms."

"But sometimes it has to be okay to take life. I eat meat." I didn't want him to be too hard on himself.

"I acknowledge that it is sometimes unavoidable to end another life to sustain my own, but there is a huge difference in biting into a sheep while its heart is still beating and buying lamb chops at the grocery."

I wrinkled my face in disgust. "I guess there is. Okay, so you were hunting in your less-than-lethal, appealing-to-God kind of way."

He rolled his eyes at me. "I was hunting, and I felt you in my head. I could feel the fear, and I knew it came from you, but I could not understand what the danger was. I just automatically assumed someone had tried to hurt you. It never occurred to me that you would be outside. I raced straight back to Kirkwynd and began searching for you. I felt it when the fear left your mind. It was so sharp and sudden that I was afraid you had been knocked unconscious."

"How did you know that wasn't it?"

"I could still sense your heart racing. It was like my own heartbeat was echoing yours."

"I don't get it." How could he have felt my heart racing when he was so far away?

Alexei pushed his free hand through his dark hair. "I told you my kind can control their heartbeats and body temperatures. I guess because you are human, my heartbeat started to mimic yours."

"Like calling out and listening for the echo to come back."

"Exactly," Alexei replied.

"So how did you know to wait for me in the secret staircase?"

Alexei laughed gently. "I was lucky. I had been looking for you everywhere, and I decided to listen to your friends to see if they knew where you were. That is when you appeared."

"So what happens now? Will we start hearing each other's thoughts, or will it be emotions for a while?"

"I do not know, Elisabeth."

"I meant what I said before, Alexei. I really do like you. You're my best friend. But I can't be expected to go through my teen years with you in my head."

"I understand. There was a while today when I was afraid I had let you get hurt, in spite of all of the promises I made to your father and to you."

"I guess you were as caught off guard by this thing as I am. What if it had been the other way around? That could have been horribly embarrassing."

"It could have been far more than just embarrassing. If it had gone from me to you, it might have done some real damage. A normal human brain is incapable of processing some of the memories and images I have in my mind. It might have been dangerous enough to put you into a coma."

"Then we've got to figure out how this is happening, and what we can do to control it." I smiled at him to let him know that I believed we could work it out.

He shook his head at me. "You are either the most optimistic person I have ever met or you are really in deep denial."

I laughed a little. "Why can't it be both?"

"I should go now. Your friends will be wanting a play-by-play of all the afternoon's activities."

I grabbed his arm, remembering the question he had never answered. "You said you were a fool - 'a fool for a million reasons' - but you never told me why. You told me about bonding instead, and that was important, but I want to know what makes you a fool."

Alexei looked at me hard and asked his question without blinking. "Are you sure you want to open that door, Elisabeth? Because once you do, you cannot change your mind."

I tried to stop the shiver that ran down my spine, but he noticed anyway. I had always been told that I was determined and perseverant; those were just pretty words for stubborn. "Tell me why you're a fool."

Alexei was off the bed and across the room before I realized he was moving. He stood at the window, his face a fuzzy reflection in the thick old glass. "I was a fool, an idiot, because I remembered the time before you were born, and I allowed myself to be caught up in the memories of your father so much that I ignored the warning signs right in front of me."

"Warning signs of what? The bonding?"

"No, not that. Do you remember those two dreams, before you knew what I am and that they were real?"

I breathed heavily, almost a snort. "I'm not likely to forget that. It was so embarrassing."

He spun around to face me but didn't move closer. "Why? Why was it embarrassing?"

"Because of the way I was dressed," I mumbled. "And because of the way I threw myself at you." My voice became more forceful again. "I never would have acted like that if I'd known the truth."

"I know that. I told you I knew that then. If you had known what kind of creature I am, you would never have flirted with me."

"That's not what I meant!" The words flew out of my mouth before I could stop them. Even if I could have stopped them to save myself more embarrassment, I probably would have chosen to say them anyway to stop Alexei from believing that he was a monster. "I only meant that if I had known the dream was real, I wouldn't have thrown myself at you. I'm not usually so aggressive, especially when I know the man in question thinks of me as hardly more than a baby."

"We are forever misunderstanding one another. The dream, the fact that in the dream you appeared older, was a reflection of your true self. It is only after practice that you can choose to make yourself appear as you wish others to see you. Your true self is more mature than I credited you with being. My underestimating you was my first bit of foolishness."

"Why didn't you tell me that then? I thought you meant that I would be able to control my appearance so it reflected who I really am."

"I did mean that as well. Your age was different, but your clothing had to do with your thoughts and emotions. You were dressed in a nightgown because you were feeling unprotected and vulnerable, but, as I now realize, you were also feeling the beginnings of romantic interest. I rejected you in the dream because I thought you would hate me when you found out the truth about what I am."

"I don't understand why you keep trying to make me believe you're a monster. You're not."

He smiled at my outrage. "Having you believe in me is the most amazing gift. I treated your romantic ideas as if you were any other silly school girl. That was also very foolish of me. And because of my foolishness, in not accepting what you so sweetly offered in your dreams, I allowed some boy to be the first to kiss you. And I have allowed you to believe that my only interest in you is because of your father and your family. As I said, I am an idiot. In a million ways."

"You're interested in more than just my family? You're a fool because you let Chase kiss me first?" The words came out of my mouth, but they made no more sense in my brain than if I was speaking Swahili or Chinese or some other language I didn't know.

Alexei smiled at my obvious confusion. He moved back across the small space to kneel beside my bed in front of me. "If I had known that you would not be repulsed by the thought that I am not human, then I would have very much enjoyed kissing you, Elisabeth. But I waited, and now you have Chase, and with the strange bonding taking place between us, I believe it is too late. Perhaps I should have taken my chance when I had it."

He kissed my forehead as he had before and then was gone. I heard the mechanism of the trapdoor click, but I never saw it move.

CHAPTER EIGHTEEN

I sat on my bed stunned. Was I hallucinating? Had Alexei really just said that he wished he had kissed me? What did he mean that it was too late because of the bonding? I wished I understood all of that better. Why would he be able to bond with me when no one outside of his family had ever bonded with a human before and it only happened twice within the family?

I was pretty sure he was still hiding things from me. Things about my family and the connection between his vampire family and my family. Things that Julian hadn't wanted to tell me either. How did they ever expect me to learn anything?

I was feeling especially frustrated and lost. My thoughts turned to the one person who I could have trusted to tell me the truth. My father. I stood on unsteady legs and retrieved Julian's box from my wardrobe then sat back down. Before I opened the battered envelope, I sent Charly a text that Alexei was gone. I unfolded the letter and the now familiar handwriting greeted me.

January 25

Jules,

The absolute worst part of the holidays is that now I miss you even more than I did before. Christmas was perfect. I loved going to Rome and attending the Christmas mass in the Vatican. The buildings are beautiful, and the artwork took my breath away. I wonder if my father ever got to see the dome of St. Peter's Basilica. He would have appreciated it in a completely different way. Do you remember his lectures on our place in the cosmos and the flaw of creation? I'm not sure I'll ever truly understand his viewpoint, but I just cannot believe in a God who doomed His creation to hell. If there is no chance for redemption, then why do we exist? Was His Son not a Savior for us as well? Does His Word not say that it is His will for all to repent? If that is true, then my father's belief – a belief that can only be described as predestination – cannot be correct. Perhaps I am still railing against my own destiny, but I cannot believe in a God who rejects His own creation without ever giving them a chance at redemption. I know you believe our community has a purpose, but I don't feel ready to lead the family. I don't want to let go of my chance to see the world and experience normal life.

I know that horrible woman is sinking her claws deeper and deeper into what our laws say is mine, but I don't want the responsibility of guiding the family. At least, not yet. I suppose the good news is that I have three and a half more years until I graduate from college and the responsibility becomes mine. Perhaps I will be ready to marry? Honestly, Jules, if am forced to choose a bride, you know I'll choose you. It's just another of those barbaric traditions that seem so wrong to me. Perhaps I will have that chance to change things. I just hope I never have to go through the agony my father faced. I think if he had been able to believe in a more benevolent God, he would have been more comforted. Or perhaps it was my mother's death that caused him to see God as uncaring toward us. Dark thoughts for a dark night. I suppose I'd better get back to my studies. Write soon.

Love,
Nick

I was glad I was sitting on my bed. That letter showed me a side of my father I'd never considered. He was apparently a very religious man. Something about the way he wrote about his beliefs reminded me of Alexei. I wondered if they had spent time wandering in the tunnels and talking about theology. What would my father, who had known Alexei and been his friend, think about the strange bonding between the two of us? Even more, I wondered what my father would have thought of the idea of Alexei kissing me.

No matter what I did, I couldn't keep my mind from the thought of Alexei kissing me. Had he really wanted to kiss me or was he just saying that to keep me away from Chase? Did I want Alexei to keep me away from Chase? Why would anyone pick a vampire to kiss her over a normal boy close to her own age? Was I interested in Chase or Alexei?

The only answer that I could honestly come up with was, of course, both. I had been flirting with Alexei in my dream. Yes, it was definitely more than I would have done if I had known the dream was real, but the flirtation had to have come from somewhere. I thought from the first moment I met him that Alexei was the most beautiful guy I'd ever seen. Being a vampire didn't change the fact that I found him attractive. It did change the way I looked at him though.

When I found out Alexei was a vampire, I automatically assumed he was off-limits. Partly because I didn't think you could simply date a vampire. Just thinking it sounds absurd. Even a long-term relationship would seem short for him. There was something too serious in the knowledge that Alexei was a vampire. It wasn't the kind of thing you play around with.

As for Chase, he was a regular guy. Human, like me. It was natural to be attracted to him. He's very good-looking, and he had flirted with me. Maybe I was too eager to flirt back. I remember how embarrassed I'd been about my dream.

Somehow it was all jumbled together. Chase and Alexei. Light and dark. Moonlight and sunshine.

I thought about my initial division – how I thought of Alexei as sunshine because of his bright eyes and Chase the moonlight because of his pale hair and shadowy eyes. Even then I had thought it was ridiculous because I'd known Alexei had secrets, but now, knowing that one of those secrets was that he's a vampire, it seemed even more off. Alexei, the vampire who can't go out in sunlight, still reminded me more of the sun than Chase, the normal guy. What made Chase seem so much more dangerous than Alexei? Maybe it was just that I knew Alexei would never hurt me. That he would do everything in his power to protect me. And Chase had no guarantee.

Was it wrong for me to compare them? It had to be unfair to both Alexei and Chase, but I think it was most unfair to me. They were completely different, and I was crushing on both of them. Maybe my grandfather was right to believe that God was cruel. Otherwise why would I ever be in such a situation?

The door to the room opened, and Charly walked in with Emma and Lila Grace. Charly sat down on my bed while the other two girls stayed in their own areas, busily straightening books, clothes, or anything else they could pretend needed it.

Charly didn't fool around. "What happened to you? Why did you come back drenched, and why did Alexei look like he was about to have a stroke?"

I grinned at her, as big as any of her grins ever was. It was exactly the kind of thing I expected her to say, and somehow it made me feel like I could handle the questions I'd been asking myself.

"What?" she demanded. "Why are you smiling at me like that?"

"Sorry. I was just glad that somebody was finally acting the way I thought they would."

She tossed the pillow at my head and laughed.

"I was taking a walk before the storm hit, and I got caught too far away. I found shelter in the art building for a little while, but it was still raining when I decided to come back here. Like we talked about before, I didn't want to go through the study hall while I was drenched."

"What about Alexei?" Charly asked. "He was getting really antsy waiting for you to get out of the shower."

"I know. He had mistakenly got some information that made him think I was in danger, and then he couldn't find me anywhere. It all turned out to be a false alarm."

"So, he thought you were in trouble, and then you came in looking like a drowned rat-"

"I knew it!" I interrupted. "I knew I looked awful."

"Not awful," Charly corrected. "Just wet. Anyway, I guess I can see why he was so worried. He really cares about you a lot."

"More than I knew," I said softly.

Charly seemed to realize that I wasn't able to really discuss anything more. "I guess you're wiped out after your day. How about if I go get you something to eat and bring it back up here?"

I nodded gratefully. Charly left the room. Emma and Lila Grace were still very careful not to make eye contact with me.

After a few minutes of silence that grew more and more strained, I spoke. "What's going on?"

Emma turned to me with a slight blush on her cheeks. "We didn't want to intrude, Elisabeth, honestly. But I heard someone say that they saw you going into the art building with Chase Elliot. And then Alexei was so upset. This is the second time Alexei has acted jealous of Chase. What's really going on?"

"I don't know. Who said they saw me and Chase? There's no way anyone could have seen anything from the campus; we went in through a back door on the other side of the building."

Lila Grace's eyes grew wider. "So you were with Chase?"

"I was out like I said. When the rain started, I ran to the wisteria arbor. Chase was already there. The rain started coming in sideways so we tried the building and found a way in." I made sure there was no hint of anything else in my voice because I was not ready to talk about that kiss. Or rather, those kisses.

Emma understood. "I guess we'll find out who saw what tomorrow, but you'd better be prepared. If this gets out the wrong way, your reputation could be in shreds."

I shuddered, remembering the way some of the boys at the group home had talked about girls at school. I'd worked hard to get good grades and not become like some of the other girls around. Now that I was finally in a good school and finally knew who I was, would one stormy day ruin my name? It was just another thing to add to the list of things I would worry about later.

Charly came back with some food, and the rest of the evening passed in meaningless gossip. No one brought up the topic of my afternoon activities.

CHAPTER NINETEEN

The next morning when the sun rose, all traces of the storm were gone. Light shimmered through the clear sky, burnishing the campus with a golden luster. I knew Alexei would have to go through the tunnels to get to class, so I left my room early that morning. I didn't want the other girls to know what I was doing, so I went out the normal way and down to the study hall before using the janitor's closet to go down into the tunnels.

I had no idea which way Alexei would go to get to the Langford classroom building, other than a vague idea of south, so I waited at the sort of crossroads area directly beneath the Kirkwynd study hall. It wasn't long before I heard footsteps on the stone floor. I turned toward the sound and saw Alexei round the corner and freeze.

The look on his face made me laugh. "I guess the bonding doesn't work well enough to keep me from surprising you."

He smiled back at me. "I was not expecting to see you here. But it is, as always, a pleasant surprise."

"You might not say that when you know why I'm here," I warned him.

The smile faded slowly. "Am I in trouble?"

"Should you be?" Years of hearing the other kids in foster care and group homes evade adult questions prompted the response. I shook my head. "You aren't in trouble with me, and as far as I know the end of the world hasn't happened. I just had some questions, and I figured you have to be getting sick of my perpetual questioning."

The smile came back in full force. "I never get tired of your questions, Elisabeth. They are insightful, and you have every right to demand answers. You have been far more patient that I ever could have been."

As much as I was flattered by his praise, I was also worried by it. He made me sound like some kind of saint with all his talk of insight and patience. The truth was I didn't push for questions because the answers I already had scared me. I was just too chicken to push for more.

"I have to warn you. Emma and Lila Grace heard someone say that they saw me go into the arts building with Chase during the storm yesterday. Unless whoever said it was out in the storm too, there was no way for them to see anything."

"Would you like me to check into the rumor?"

Something in his voice made me pause. I knew he was only offering to stop the gossip, not do damage to whoever was spreading it, but . . . I had the feeling that he would have been ready to inflict some pain if I asked him to.

"Just keep your ears open. I'd rather not be talked about, but I didn't do anything wrong."

"So, what did you want to ask me about?" He moved to stand close enough that I could have touched him.

I looked up in his eyes that were as blue as the sky outside. "I want to know what you meant that it was too late to kiss me because of the bonding." I said it all in one breath so I wouldn't have time to change my mind.

Alexei sighed. "Do we really have to talk about this?"

"I'd like to know. Why don't you want to tell me? Is it that bad?"

He was instantly contrite. "It is not bad. I just have no answers. I wish I had kissed you when I had the chance, although even then it could have made this situation worse."

I must have looked like I didn't believe what he was saying. He ran his hand though his dark hair.

"This will not be a short conversation. I am not putting you off, but if we get caught skipping class together . . . ."

I followed his train of thought. "After the apparent rumors that are already circulating about me and Chase yesterday. Maybe this is one time when you should use your compulsion on the teachers."

"Since you are the daughter of the man I negotiated with, your approval is all I need." He looked at me for a moment before continuing. "In all earnestness, I would not do this if it was not important. We do have many things to discuss, but there may be a problem."

"What kind of problem?"

"Charly. She is in our classes this morning and has shown considerable resistance to my compulsion."

"What should we do? We can't tell her to pretend to go along with it. She'll realize something's wrong when no one notices we're missing."

"I think that if it was just idle curiosity it would make no difference, like when she does not notice how quickly I get from one place to another and how she never sees me outside. But because this involves you, and because of last night-"

I nodded. "She saw how worried you were. She was concerned enough that she was willing to send you away in spite of how much she likes to be where you are."

Alexei frowned slightly. "Perhaps it is your influence. We cannot underestimate the effect you might be having on the people around you. This may be a really bad idea in light of the bonding, but what if we worked together to use my compulsion and your influence to make her not notice we are missing."

"How do we do that? And why is it dangerous?"

"The how is simple. I will guide you. The danger comes because I will enter your mind the way I did when you were dreaming."

"You can do that?" I heard the awe in my voice.

Alexei laughed. "Only if you let me. But I will help you, and it will be easy. I am just not sure if this is a good idea. The danger caused by our bonding might make it more practical to just go to class and meet later to talk."

I was shaking my head before he finished speaking. "I want to know now. What makes this more dangerous?"

"Since we have begun to bond our minds together, if you let me enter your mind, I might never be able to leave it."

I hissed out a breath. "Okay, that is dangerous. Just how remote a chance is it?"

"I honestly do not know. Do you want to take the chance? Or do you want to wait?"

He looked in my eyes, waiting. I wasn't sure what to do. I knew that if I would just wait until after class Alexei would tell me everything I wanted to know. But it was beginning to feel like my whole life was about waiting for later. If we did try to link our minds to keep Charly from noticing and we got stuck like that . . . I shuddered just thinking about the idea, but somehow waiting felt wrong. I needed to make a choice for myself and have an active decision in what happened in my life. I couldn't wait any longer to start being the real me, the real Elisabeth Julian Sinclair. The one who was the granddaughter of the last prince crowned of the Malhairer and the only child and heir of Nicholas Augustin Merrick Sinclair. I was the Elisabeth Sinclair whose closest friend in the world was a vampire. I was the Elisabeth Sinclair who would not run from what scared her. Not ever again.

Alexei waited for my answer, but I don't think he ever considered the possibility that I would choose not to wait.

"Let's do this now. I can't keep putting my life on hold." The words felt right as I said them, as if something else – God, the cosmos, whatever – approved of what I was doing.

"Are you sure? It would be safer to wait." Alexei might have argued longer, but I pointed to my watch.

"It's now or never. What do we need to do?"

It took a moment before he could answer me. "First, we have to be closer. We need to know for certain that Charly is in class before we try to convince her that she saw us there too."

"Can we make it there in time?" I asked.

Alexei just smiled. "We can if you let me carry you. You have seen how fast I can move."

"Fast enough that I can't even see you. Okay, what should I-"

I never had the chance to finish my sentence. He picked me up and held me cradled in his arms, against his chest, like I was a baby. Then he moved. I felt a brush of wind and then nothing. I blinked several times just to make sure I was seeing what was really there.

In less than twenty seconds, Alexei had moved us from the crossroads beneath Kirkwynd Hall to the tunnel underneath the Langford Building. I stared at him in disbelief.

"If I set you down, are you steady enough to stand?" he asked.

"That was amazing! How did you get us here that fast?"

"Elisabeth, it was not that far with only two turns." He began to put me down, and I was surprised to find my legs felt rubbery. If he hadn't been holding on, I would have fallen. "It is only a touch of vertigo. Your body recognized the speed at which you were moved even if your mind could not comprehend it."

I was finally able to stand on my own, and I started to ask another question, but Alexei shushed me. He was listening to something that I couldn't hear.

"Most of the class has arrived as well as Mr. Callahan. Charly is there, and she is already wondering where we are." He looked at me again, giving me one final chance to call off the experiment and go to class.

I spoke softly but firmly. "Then we'd better do whatever it is we have to do."

Alexei smiled a little, but he still looked worried. "I am not sure this will work. If you are too scared of what might happen, then you might put up subconscious barriers that we will not be able to cross in the short time we have."

"Tell me what to do." I smiled what I hoped was an encouraging smile.

"Sit here with me." He sat down on the stone floor and held his arms out to me. He turned me around so that I was sitting with my back to him, cross-legged between his kneeling legs, but with several inches of space between our bodies. He stretched out his arms and rested his hands on my shoulders. It was just a slight pressure. The only feeling of connection.

He spoke softly in a soothing tone. "Close your eyes and relax. Let your mind open itself as if to a daydream. Picture me the way I appeared in your dreams, and let me inside your mind."

I saw the inside of my dorm room in my head and imagined Alexei standing on the secret stair, waiting for me to open the door. In my head I pressed the switch to let him in, and he was there, in the same magnificent tuxedo as before. Knowing his history better this time, I realized it was from the early nineteenth century. He looked as handsome as he ever had, and he was smiling. When he spoke, I heard his rich baritone inside my head, rather than from the tunnel around me.

"You are amazing, Elisabeth." He took my hands and spun me around in a little dance. "Now, think about Charly. Picture her spirit, the indefinable thing that makes her uniquely Charly."

I saw her in my mind's eye – all her fiery red-gold hair and her bright turquoise eyes and the grin that was wider than the Mississippi River was long.

"That is right, Elisabeth," Alexei continued. "Now think about Charly and focus on a picture of us in class. I will do the rest."

I was never completely sure how it worked, but somehow the picture in my mind became a mist or fog around Charly's head. I knew it was just the Charly in my mind, but I suppose it was some kind of symbol. Some mental image to wrap around Charly so that she would not notice we were missing class. I wasn't entirely comfortable with the idea of forcing this picture onto my friend's mind, but I knew I had made my choice and I had to follow it through. I suppose I was only just realizing the more negative impacts of what my choice meant.

Alexei was still in my head. "Do not be so hard on yourself, Elisabeth. You do not use your gift frivolously or randomly. The others in the classroom have the same picture of us, but it was easier, less invasive. It is truly more of a testament to Charly's strength and honesty that we had to work so hard to get her mind to see what is not there. People lie to themselves all the time for far less important matters."

"I guess it's time for the real test now, isn't it?"

Alexei smiled and walked to the door of the dorm room. "Maybe it was never as dangerous as I had imagined it could be."

The door was open, waiting for him to walk out – out of the dorm room, but more accurately, out of my mind. Fear shot through me, and I called out. He turned back to me almost before I shouted.

"It will be alright. You were the brave one, letting me in when there was a chance I might not get out. Now I get to be brave and walk out, trusting that I will find my way back to where I am supposed to go."

I tried not to think it, but I couldn't stop the image flooding my brain. I saw Alexei walk out the door and fall away into nothing. Eternal nothing for his eternal life of youth and darkness.

The tuxedo-clad Alexei walked out the door and, for a moment, seemed to fall, but then I felt pressure on my shoulders from his fingertips. I let the images in my mind fade away and concentrated on the darkness of my closed eyelids.

"Elisabeth, are you alright?" Alexei's voice no longer came from inside my head, but from right behind me.

"Is it over?" I sounded small and afraid even to my own ears.

Alexei moved closer so that his chest was touching my back and hugged me. "It is over. I am so sorry you were frightened."

I opened my eyes and covered his arms with my own. "Frightened? Alexei, I wasn't frightened; I was scared to death. I thought you were going to be lost forever."

"It worked out alright. We took the chance and nothing bad happened. Actually, something important happened, and we should be very relieved. I am grateful that you had the courage to choose this path."

"What are you talking about? I'm completely lost." I turned in his arms so I could look at his eyes. In the shadowy light, they looked green again, that pale sage of spring leaves.

Alexei smiled at me. "You are confused now, but soon you will understand everything. I promise." He stood and helped me to my feet.

"Why soon? Why not now?" I demanded.

Alexei shrugged and motioned around us. "This is not the most comfortable place for a long talk, and it is not very private. I would rather go somewhere else first, if that meets with your approval, of course."

He was right. There was no place to sit but the cold, stone floor, and there were gratings nearby letting in weak shafts of daylight. It would be impossible not to have our voices carry. And I knew that deep down I wanted to be some place where I was guaranteed enough light to see his eyes when he told me whatever it was he would say. I nodded to let him know I agreed.

"I know we are not in as much of a hurry this time, but," he paused just for a second. "May I carry you?"

There was some emotion in his voice that I didn't understand, but the look on his face told me that this was somehow important to him.

"Yes."

He picked me up as gently as before, and I found myself cradled against his chest once more. I closed my eyes to keep from seeing anything and felt the wind rush over me. When I opened them, I was at an open door leading to a stone staircase that winded up away from us. It was only slightly different from the one that led to my room.

"Would you like to see my room?" Alexei asked.

I thought about the rules of girls and boys dorms, and I remembered the intensity of my feelings in my dreams when I had wanted Alexei to kiss me. I knew the rules were in place for everyone's safety, but Alexei was sworn to my protection. His kindness and his habit of putting my comfort and security above his own needs were more than enough evidence for me to trust him.

I nodded, and he carried me up the stairs, walking human slow. He pressed a catch that was almost identical to the one in my hidden staircase, and the door in the wall swung open.

"Welcome to my home, Elisabeth."

It was only in that instant, as the trap door swung closed behind me, that I remembered what he had told me before. This was the same room that he had occupied the first time he had attended the Academy, as Sasha Beloi. It was the room he had shared with my father.

CHAPTER TWENTY

Alexei set me on my feet, and I looked around the room, staring as if I could find a piece of my father that had been waiting there all those years until I arrived. I went to the window, one that was identical to the one my bed sat under. As I ran fingers over the frame, I remembered the carving on the window in the landing outside my door. My father had carved his and Julian's initials in it.

And just as I was wondering if he had left a permanent mark on this room as well, I felt the unevenness of the rough carving. I leaned to look closer and saw the "N" and "S" that I was expecting.

"I am sorry. I should have realized." Alexei's voice was low and gentle, right behind me.

I straightened and turned to him, blinking back the tears in my eyes. "It's okay. I like knowing that he was here. When I can stand in the places he stood and touch the things he touched, it makes me feel more connected to him. That's a good thing for me." I smiled at Alexei, and he smiled back at me.

"We can talk here without anyone overhearing or interrupting us, but we only have the two class periods before someone starts looking for us. I suppose you still want those answers."

"More than ever. Will you please tell me why the idea of kissing me since we are bonded is not so good?"

He smiled at my demand. He pointed to a cushioned club chair before he sat on the end of his bed. I sank into the chair, fingering the lush material. I suppose I must have given him a curious look because he answered my unspoken question.

"I brought it in special. I decided to allow myself a few comforts that I did not have the first time I was here, when I was playing roommate for your father." He became more solemn. "I am not sure how to explain all this to you without breaking confidences that are not mine to break, so if I seem to be leaving things out or searching for a way to say something, please be patient with me."

"Let's start with something that you and only you can answer. Why did you wait to kiss me, if that's what you wanted to do?"

Alexei frowned. "I told you those reasons already. I did not want to kiss you under false pretenses. I wanted you to know who and what I am. I just never believed that if you knew you would have wanted me to kiss you."

"If that's all there was to it, then why didn't you kiss me that day in the tunnel when you told me the truth? I knew then, and I told you that you're not a monster. That I could never see you as a monster."

"I thought it would be too much at once. Hitting you with all that truth and then telling you that I wanted to kiss you seemed like it would be putting too much pressure on you. You needed time to think about what you had learned before I did anything else. I will not pretend that I was not tempted. Especially when we were back in your room and I – I lost my temper. I know there can be no excuse for my behavior, but I beg you to understand. You were so accepting of me, and I did not believe that you truly understood the danger you were in. I wanted to make you see how fragile you are, how easily harmed, but I lost control. As powerful as the hunger in me was in that instance, when I held your hands behind your back and had your throat exposed, I still had a moment when I knew I could kiss you and turn that fear pounding through your veins into something else. I could have kissed you and pushed you past your natural reactions and damaged you in your innocence."

I spoke slowly but with absolute certainty. "You would never have done that. You would never hurt me. Never."

He shook his head and stood up. "That is what I cannot make you understand, Elisabeth. I have hurt you. This bonding between us hurts you. The damage my mind can do to yours is immense, and I cannot stop it."

"I guess you're right. I don't understand this at all. What is it about the bonding that you are so afraid of?"

He sat back down and looked at my face, searching for something. "Were you raised to be religious?"

"What kind of question is that?"

He sighed. "Please. I am trying to explain in a way that might make sense for you."

"I was taught the basics, I guess. Most of my foster families sent me to Sunday school. I don't see myself as deeply religious, but I believe in God." I waited to see where he was going with all this.

"Do you know the story of the garden of Eden and the Tree of the Knowledge of Good and Evil?"

"Sure. Adam and Eve were in the garden, and the snake told them to eat the apple, and when they did, they were kicked out, and all mankind has suffered ever since. That's the easy stuff."

"Have you actually read the Biblical account?" I shook my head no, and he went on. "The serpent that spoke to Eve told her that if she ate of the Tree then she would become as God. Eve misquoted what God had told her to do and allowed herself to be seduced by the serpent's words. And when she gave the fruit to her husband, Adam ate even though he understood that it was wrong. The first thing they realized was that they were naked, so they made coverings out of fig leaves."

"I remember this part. God didn't like the leaf clothes and made them clothes from animal skins."

"The point that God was showing them was that the animal had to die, blood had to be shed, to cover their nakedness. There had to be a price paid, and that price was blood, death."

"I don't think I understand the connection between the story and our situation." I watched Alexei closely. He had definite opinions on his status as a monster that seemed at odds with his knowledge of the Bible.

He gave me a little half-smile of encouragement. "I am getting there. Before Adam and Eve sinned, they were innocent. They did not know that they were naked. In part it is about physical nudity, but it is also about intellectual innocence. They did not have the knowledge of what their nudity meant. After they gained knowledge, they were banished from the garden and spent the remainder of their lives in hard labor and sadness. They became separated from God and could no longer walk with Him."

"I get that this is a warning about the consequences of too much knowledge, but why this story? Why bring God into all this?"

"Because He is a part of this. Your father and I spent long hours debating God and His reasons for allowing vampires to continue. If we exist at all, then God must have created us at some point. We had some interesting conversations about our own theologies."

"And about my grandfather's." I was thinking of the bitterness in my father's letter to Julian.

Alexei was surprised. "How did you know that?"

"I read about some of my grandfather's beliefs in one of my father's letters. He was so hopeless."

"That is true. Nicholas and I discussed your grandfather's views often. Nick completely disagreed with Prince Augustin."

"But why does all of that matter? I mean, what does that mean about the bonding?"

"It was one of the questions we debated. The abilities of a vampire to affect the minds of humans was apparently a way to make hunting and killing them easier. If vampires are demons, as most theologies teach, then the powers that they possess must be demonic in nature as well. But your family has different, although closely related, powers. If ours are demonic, then what are yours? And what happens when they are mixed? This bonding is completely unprecedented, but it raises questions that we have no answers for."

"I must be stupid because I'm lost."

Alexei moved close to me and took my hands. "You are not stupid. The fears I have about the bonding are the same fears that I had about kissing you. I do not know what would happen if we became too closely connected. I have feelings for you, strong feelings that frighten me. I have lived among vampires. We lived by a different code of morality than your family taught, but we were not the murderers or hedonists that the other vampires were. My family chose mates amongst themselves and lived together for hundreds of years in something closer than any human marriage can attain over your short mortal lifespan. I was Russian. My people were deeply religious. It was not like today, where religion is a thing brought out on Sundays. We were peasants and uneducated, but we knew the Holy Scriptures and lived what we were taught by the priests."

"You believe that you are a demon." I couldn't believe I was saying it, but it was the thing Alexei was trying not to say.

He dropped my hands as if I had burned him and lowered his eyes. I stood up and put one hand on his shoulder. I put my other hand under his chin, and he allowed me to lift his head and see his eyes. Silent tears fell from the endless blue depths.

"I don't believe you're a demon. I don't believe you're a monster." I thought of my father's words to Julian. "And any God that I believe in wouldn't damn His own creation without offering a chance for redemption."

I could feel the tension in Alexei's body. He held himself so still, but it was as if every muscle in his body was tightened or coiled, like an animal ready for its flight or fight response to take effect.

"I am damned. Perhaps I could gain redemption, but I know there is always a price. I will not let you pay that price for me. The longer we are connected, the more likely you are to share in my damnation."

"That's what you're afraid of?" Understanding finally came to my mind. "You're worried that this bonding, because you think it's some kind of demon power, will curse my soul? And the kiss, before and now? Explain that."

His deep voice was a harsh whisper, barely audible in the silent room. "I was afraid that if I kissed you I would not be able to let you go."

"You were afraid you would bite me? To try to turn me?"

He looked as if his heart was breaking. "Even if you were a normal human I would not risk your eternal soul, but with your family – who knows what would happen."

"Because my family has its own strange abilities to deal with," I finished. "I think I am finally beginning to understand you, Alexei."

He was still so tense. I wondered what I could do to pull him back from whatever emotional ledge he was on.

"Then you finally understand why it is too dangerous for us to even be friends, and yet I cannot leave you when you may be in danger from your family."

I sighed. "Alexei, you are not a danger to me." He tried to interrupt, but I put a finger across his lips to hush him. "You did nothing to cause this bonding, however it happened. You have already said that if you knew how to stop it you would, and I believe you. And you are not a threat to me. You would never hurt me. No matter what else you might believe about yourself – even if you have to think about yourself as a soulless monster or demon – please believe that you could not hurt me. If you can't believe it in yourself, believe me. I know you are not capable of harming me. I know it."

His blue eyes watched me for endless seconds as he tried to find something in my face. I don't know if he was looking for doubt or just trying to see the truth that I believed. Maybe he was searching for a way past my blind faith so he could convince me he was right and I was wrong.

"Elisabeth, I know what I am capable of far better than you."

I realized that I could argue with him until the last beat of my heart, and he still wouldn't believe me. So I did the only thing I could think of to prove to him that I was right. I leaned forward and pressed my lips against his.

When I made contact, it sent a strange feeling through my body. I'd read about kisses that were like electric shocks, but this was not scary or violent. If I could have compared it to anything, it was more like the feeling of relaxation when you sink into a warm bath or you are cocooned in luxurious blankets. But as I felt myself relax, I felt Alexei tense up even more than before, and I hadn't thought that was possible. For a moment, I was afraid he would just run. He could have been across the room before I even opened my eyes.

But he didn't. He moved his mouth against mine, and then his arms were around me, holding me gently yet protectively. He stood, and I was no longer bending over him but arched back as he leaned over me. I slid my arms around his neck. His hands met at the small of my back. He didn't pull me closer, but he began to kiss me with more interest.

The gentle warmth I had felt at the beginning of the kiss was gone. With Alexei kissing me back, it was like a million different sensations all wrapped up into one something that went beyond my description. I felt as if the stars had gone supernova inside my head, and the universe had been recreated to only include the two of us and the space inside our arms.

Alexei pulled back just enough to end the kiss, but he didn't let go of me. His eyes were dazzling, flickering with both blue and green, yet full of something I'd never seen in them before. It took me a moment to realize it was happiness.

He smiled at me and then laughed. I smiled back and waited for him to speak. I wasn't sure I had remembered how to breathe yet.

"You do take chances, Elisabeth, but I have to admit – I like the result."

"So are you finally willing to admit that I'm right about you?"

His smile faded a little. "I still believe I am a danger to you, but I suppose you were right about some things."

"The only danger is outside of your control. The things that you can control were never a danger to me."

He sighed. "You make me want to lose my control. If I could, I would keep you with me in this room forever. But that is not possible for either of us."

"It's not practical, but it sounds nice to me." I leaned over and rested my head against his chest.

"It sounds nice now, but you are only fifteen years old. I want you to see what the world has to offer for you and experience life, the way your father was so eager to."

"You sound like you're saying you still can't be my friend, just in a different way from before."

"I suppose I am. We cannot date the way the children here at the Academy do. I am far too old to pretend that I feel things that I do not feel."

I moved away so I could look in his eyes. "So you're saying you aren't interested in dating me."

"I am saying that dating has no place in my life. I am a vampire. Why do you seem to forget that so easily?"

"I don't forget, but I don't understand the rules. You don't date. Do you just have relationships that last for hundreds of years?" A thought I had never considered before popped into my head. "Did you have a – a – someone who was killed with the rest of your family?"

His lips turned up into that bitter look that pretended to be a smile. "A mate? Is that the word you were choking on? No, I have never known anyone I wanted to spend my eternity with." The unspoken words 'until now' hung there as I waited, both hoping and fearing he would say them. "You are too young to be thinking these kinds of thoughts. And you have not yet learned who you are."

I bit my bottom lip, thinking hard about everything he was saying and not saying. He was right that I didn't know myself yet, in large part because there was so much of my life and my family that I didn't know anything about. If I didn't know myself, then how could I know what I wanted?

He smiled as if he was reading my mind, the way he had seemed to when we first met. He rubbed his finger across my lip to make me stop biting it. "I will not disappear on you, Elisabeth. I will be here to help you and to guard you. But you need to find some truths for yourself."

"I think I know what you mean," I said slowly. "I'm glad you aren't leaving me. I'm not sure I could take it if one more person I care about left."

He sat down on his bed, pulling me beside him. He put one arm around me and held me close to his side. "I will never leave you alone."

CHAPTER TWENTY-ONE

I had no idea how long we sat like that in Alexei's room, but eventually he spoke again.

"We have to go to the study hall, or Charly and the others will notice we have been gone too long. Are you alright?"

"I'm fine. I just didn't want to leave." I looked at him, and he smiled at me.

"You can come back anytime. Consider this your sanctuary when you need a moment of peace."

We got up, and he opened the hidden door. As I followed him down the stairs, I thought about everything that had happened since Julian had enrolled me in the Academy. It seemed that no matter where I turned, I encountered my father's ghost. Shadows from his time with Julian and 'Sasha.' Echoes of their hopes and plans. I wasn't trying to feel sorry for myself; I was trying to acknowledge the small place I held in the larger pattern. I pictured myself as a tiny cog in the giant mechanism of my family and the world. It wasn't quite as bleak as I'd first imagined it to be. If I was a cog, then I would be surrounded by all kinds of other parts. I would never have to feel alone again because I would have a place and a purpose. A destiny.

I wondered if my destiny would require me to wear some kind of crown or tiara. Would I need lessons on how to behave like a princess? I wondered if the makeover Julian had provided was just the first step toward those 'princess lessons' that would teach me how to walk and talk and be patient. The thought of learning to be proper and stuffy was too depressing for words. I must have sighed.

"What is wrong, Elisabeth?" Alexei stood at the bottom of the stairs. Because I was still a couple of steps from the bottom, I could look directly in his eyes without craning my neck.

"I know you're not going to tell me any of my family's secrets about who I am and all that, because you've already said they aren't your secrets to share."

"I know that sounds cruel-"

I interrupted him. "I'm not asking for an apology. I get it. But I can still ask you general questions about them, right?"

He seemed amused, waiting for whatever strange topic my mind had jumped to now. "You may ask me anything you like, and I will always do my best to answer you as honestly as I can."

"You said once that you had thought most of the rituals, like my father's ceremony to be named the blood heir, were just for show."

"I am no longer certain that is true."

"I don't care about whether or not it's true. I want to know if there are lots of ceremonial things and – what do they call it – protocol for me to learn."

He actually laughed. I had to fight the impulse to kick him in the shin.

"Elisabeth, you constantly surprise me. Are you more afraid of protocol and the pomp of royalty than you are of vampires?"

"With you I can be myself. What if who I am isn't good enough to fit what I'm supposed to be as a princess?"

The smile never left his face, but it became warmer and reassuring. "The only true requirement as the princess of the Malhairer is to be the first-born child of direct descent. As the only child of Nicholas, you are the princess. You do not have to act like anything other than yourself."

"But I don't know how to act in a royal court or anything like that."

His eyes turned serious. "Julian will help you with any traditional requirements, but as for actually ruling the Malhairer . . . . Your word will become their law. Your will is the will of the people. They are tied to you through their blood and through the vows your father and grandfather took. You only need to be honest and just. As long as your people believe you are trying to be fair and that you are looking out for their best interests, then they will follow you with respect and honor as a reflection of your own respect and honor for the legacy you hold."

"But how will I know what is the best thing? How will I know if I am doing what is right and fair?"

"No one is expecting you to step into this overnight. You are still underage and will require a regent for some time. Julian will guide you and teach you, as will others."

"If the people follow the will of their ruler, then have they turned to my father's stepmother for their justice? Has she been a good leader? Do the people suspect her hand in the death of my father?"

He sighed. "Those questions come very close to the things I have promised not to say. They do not understand the truth about your father's death. He had left the sanctuary of the Malhairer. Aside from the royal family and court, no one leaves their sanctuary for very long. Your people have some of the gifts that your family possesses."

"You said that if the bloodlines were examined that Julian would be my cousin. I thought you meant that because she was a part of the court, but that wasn't what you were saying at all."

Alexei shook his head. "Julian was not technically part of the court. All of the Malhairer are descended from one common ancestor, although it goes back too far for me to know much about it. They are all related to you, though so distantly that it is more like a common heritage."

"Like Jewish people who claim Abraham as their patriarch?"

"I suppose so. You are a monarchy, a principality of a homogeneous group. The bloodlines are not watched as closely in the people as they are in the monarchy. Your family was the purest, most concentrated flow of the original ancestor."

"'Was?' Before my father married my mother?"

"He brought in a human with no known trace of your common ancestor in her blood, yet your abilities have manifested in very similar ways to your father. There has been no apparent dilution of your bloodline. It is beyond the hypotheses of your grandfather's research."

"So all I really need to be qualified to be the princess is to exhibit the same abilities that my father and grandfather showed?"

Alexei shrugged.

"Do you know how insane that is? What would have happened to the people if I hadn't been born?"

"The line has grown thin over the past few generations. Much blame must rest upon your grandfather. Prince Augustin deliberately flaunted the laws to keep from producing more heirs after your grandmother's death. If your father had returned to the throne without going on to college, it is possible that he would have lived a much longer life, but such thoughts are only torment." Alexei touched my cheek. "And then we would not have you."

Alexei cocked his head slightly. "I wonder what Prince Augustin would have thought of the new Princess Elisabeth. You look like her, his princess, from the painting at court. I think that alone would have been enough to give you his heart with a bow. If he had lived long enough to know you, I believe he would have let go of much of that anger."

"I am not the princess. Not yet, and perhaps not ever if my father's step-family can arrange it."

"Please, Elisabeth. Do not ask me any more about them. You must speak with Julian in this matter."

My eyes narrowed, but I believed Alexei. "Is it really more complicated than explaining vampires?"

Alexei laughed, but it was that bitter laugh that I hated to hear. He dropped his hand from me, the way he had refused to touch me when he had told me the truth about his family. "My vampire family is simple and easy compared to the tangled history of the Malhairer. I would like to tell you, but I do not know enough about them to be able to answer the questions that I am sure you would have. Some are the same questions that I have been trying to find the answers to for thirty years."

"Tell me about her rule as regent. I know that she tricked your family into a massacre. Does she know you are alive?"

The blue eyes were filled with pain, and I felt guilty because I had put it there. "If she knows, she does not care. I am alone and of little consequence to her."

"Then she is careless and overconfident. She underestimates your importance and your worth." I put my hands on the sides of his face so he wouldn't turn away from me.

"I am of no worth. I have no family to bargain for."

"You're wrong, Alexei. You are my friend. You were my father's friend and his roommate. You knew him, and you know me. You have information that she doesn't. If she did try to hurt me, the way she probably did my parents, you would be there to stop her. You have worth and purpose. She thinks you are alone, but you aren't. And because of you, I am not alone either."

CHAPTER TWENTY-TWO

I left the tunnels through the janitor's closet exit. We both realized it would be better if we entered the study hall separately and from different directions. I would come in as if from outside while Alexei would seem to come from his room. He doubled back after helping me navigate the tunnels. I felt confident in my ability to find my way from his room back to mine or to the janitor's closet that Julian had first shown me, but I knew Alexei's primary concern was my safety, so I didn't complain.

When I walked into the study hall, Charly stood up and waved at me. She was sprawled in a chair, half sitting and half lying in her typical fashion, with her bookbag opened and spilling onto the floor.

"What took you so long getting back here?" She shook her head and continued without pausing for my answer. "Never mind, it doesn't matter anyway. Chase caught up with me as I was leaving the classroom building. He had a message for you. I thought you were right behind me, but then I remembered you had to stay after."

I didn't question how she had the idea that I had to stay in class, but I wasn't sure I wanted to hear Chase's message. I hadn't seen him since the rainstorm yesterday, but so much had happened since then. I didn't know how I felt about Chase after Alexei kissed me, but then again, Alexei told me I needed to live life and grow up before I made any choices regarding him. Somehow, I didn't think dating Chase was the kind of living Alexei had in mind. I remembered the hurt in his eyes, lurking beneath the anger at the thought of Chase hurting me.

Charly was bouncing with more than her typical energy. "Don't you want to know what Chase said?"

"I'm not sure."

Charly laughed, drawing looks our way with her vivaciousness, but she never noticed. "It's not bad news, silly. He wants us to meet him for lunch. He and Duncan have made a picnic lunch for us and want to meet in the stables."

"All four of us? I wonder if he heard rumors about yesterday."

"Maybe he did, but he said Duncan wanted to get to know me away from the noisy cafeteria and had suggested the picnic. Chase sort of implied that Duncan really just wanted to get to talk to me away from Derek." Charly's turquoise eyes were sparkling with excitement.

"When are we supposed to meet them?" I couldn't let Charly down now, especially since I was still feeling more than a little guilty over the way Alexei and I had manipulated her memories that morning.

"In fifteen minutes. I'm gonna take my backpack upstairs and maybe put on some lip gloss. You want me to take your bag?"

"Thanks. I'll wait for you here. I need to ask Emma a question about chemistry."

"Great!" Charly was halfway across the room as she said it. She had just disappeared out the door to our stairs when

Alexei came out from his. I wondered what to tell him, but then I saw the tightness of his smile, the way his eyes were dark, and I realized he had heard everything Charly had said.

"So you're having lunch with Chase." His voice was neutral, but I could hear the effort it took to keep it that way.

"Eavesdropping were you?" It came out sharper than I'd meant it to.

"Charly is hard not to hear, even for normal students. You would be safer if you would stay in the places where there are more students, Elisabeth."

"As opposed to all the time I've been alone with you in isolated, underground tunnels that most of the student body doesn't even know exist." I realized suddenly that I was angry with Alexei and trying to pick a fight or at least get a reaction. "What do you care? You told me that I was too young and needed to experience more of life, like my father had done. I guess the fact that he had experienced all the life he ever would get before he was even twenty-five only means I should try harder."

"Living your life is not the same thing as trying to get yourself killed. You take too many chances with your own safety." Alexei's eyes were flashing. I knew we were both getting louder, but I also saw how no one was paying any attention to us and figured Alexei was once again using his abilities so that it stayed that way.

"I thought you liked it when I take chances. Like when I kissed you."

He hissed out a breath before answering. "Actually what I said was that you take chances, but I liked your results. Perhaps I was hasty in my judgment because now you are acting like a spoiled child."

"But according to you, I am a child! What do you want from me?"

"I want you to be safe." His voice sounded like a roar in my head, but I knew he hadn't really yelled.

I was so tired of not knowing what to do or what to believe. I was tired of being pulled in so many directions. I knew that Alexei wished he could leave me alone to grow up without having to watch me stumble my way through teenage relationships. I knew that he truly wanted me to be safe, even if the only danger was to my heart. I knew, even as I said the words, how hurtful and cruel I was being. "Maybe you just want me to be wrapped up in a nice little world where you can keep me, like a doll on a shelf, but Chase wants me to go outside with him and sit in the sun."

My words bit into Alexei with more sting than if I had hit him. How long had it been since he had sat in the sun and enjoyed a meal? Maybe he never had that luxury as a peasant boy in Russia. How could I say such things to him? How could I hurt the one person that I knew would never hurt me? I hated myself in that moment.

Alexei never said a word, but stared at me with those endless depths of blue and green swirling together. He stood tall, towering above me, and then bowed before turning and leaving the room. I wanted to go after him, but I didn't know what to say. How could I tell him I was sorry and that I didn't mean what I said when I had to admit that there was a part of me that did mean it? I never wanted to hurt him, but I wasn't as careful with him as he was with me. I took advantage of our friendship and forced him to admit feelings for me that he knew I wasn't ready to deal with.

I was just taking my first step to go to him when Charly reappeared.

"Did you ask Emma your question?"

"No. I didn't see her. I guess I can ask her later."

Charly shrugged her shoulders. "Let's go then. Can't keep the boys waiting."

CHAPTER TWENTY-THREE

Charly and I walked over to the stables quickly. She was excited about seeing Duncan and wanted to hurry. I felt the warm sunshine as if it was branding my skin and just wanted out of it. Chase and Duncan were waiting inside the stable. Duncan was petting the horse in the first stall, soothing her. I was surprised, not at Duncan, but at the horse, Marigold. She was one of the older horses in the stable. They actually kept Marigold in the front because she was so gentle that she was the horse fearful students were first exposed to. Marigold was a calm, unflappable girl.

Except that Duncan seemed to have his hands full, trying to calm her down. I walked over to them and reached out to grab her bridle.

"What's wrong with her?" I listened for Duncan's answer even as I cooed to the horse, putting my free hand on her neck to pat her.

"I don't know. I've never seen Marigold get spooked before, but when Chase and I came in she went a little nuts."

"Maybe there was something in your picnic basket that she didn't like the smell of," Charly suggested.

"Could be." Duncan moved closer to the door of her stall. "She tried to kick the door down. I wouldn't have believed it if I hadn't seen it." He shook his head and pointed to the hoof marks. "If she hadn't already been bridled, I would never have caught her to calm her this much."

"Why was she bridled?" I asked.

"She was supposed to be out for lessons. Actually this entire barn was supposed to be empty."

"Something has definitely spooked her. Is there someplace we can turn her loose? She might calm down if she can run and smell the fresh air."

Before Duncan had the chance to answer me, Ms. LeMaster, the riding instructor, walked in.

"What's going on? What have you done to Marigold?"

Duncan answered for us all. "Nothing, I swear. I've never seen her like this, and we have no idea what's wrong. We were trying to calm her down."

The red-brown mare had quieted quite a bit since I had started touching her. I wondered if that was some manifestation of what Alexei called my powers. If I had the ability to influence people, maybe it was the same with animals.

Ms. LeMaster gave us a sharp look out of narrowed eyes, but decided it was more important to deal with the horse than with us. She stepped up, moving Duncan out of the way, and put her hand on the bridle just above mine. "I'll take her out and see how she acts. Maybe she was inside too much this morning. She usually goes to the back pasture in the morning, but we had a problem with one of the other student's Arabian. I just wish people knew how to take care of horses before they bought them as gifts for spoiled children." She was muttering under her breath by the time she finished what she was saying and I only heard her because I was standing so close. The words had faded, giving way to gentle noises that seemed to be a language only she and Marigold understood.

She opened the stall and led the mare out. I kept my hand on Marigold all the way to the door, hoping that I was helping to keep her calm and that whatever spooked her would not follow her outside.

When I turned back to the others, I didn't see Chase. Duncan was still standing near the empty stall, and Charly was standing close to the doorway, but Chase was missing. I was about to say something when Duncan spoke.

"You can come out now; she's gone."

Chase walked out of the tack room carrying the picnic basket. "I thought I'd better hide it in case it really was a smell from our lunch that upset the horse. I also figured it would be better for all of us if the faculty didn't know we were picnicking around the stables." He gave a tiny shrug and smiled.

"Quick thinking," Charly agreed.

Duncan looked at Chase and then Charly. "Maybe we could take our lunch out in the sun, just you and me?"

I saw Charly's smile widen before she turned to see if I would agree. There was no way I could tell her no when her eyes were so full of hope and when Duncan sounded so sweet asking. I gave her a quick nod, and, almost before I could blink, Duncan had taken a paper bag out of the picnic basket, grabbed Charly by the hand, and taken her out of the barn for their own private picnic. I watched the door for a long moment after they were out of sight.

"You don't seem all that happy to see me, Elisabeth. Is something wrong?" Chase left the basket on a bench just outside the tack room and moved closer to me.

"It's not you, Chase. I had an argument with . . . someone before I came out here. I guess it's still affecting my mood."

"You need to relax. Let me rub your shoulders." He stood behind me, and I felt his long fingers rubbing the tension out of my muscles. "That feels better, doesn't it? Would you like to talk about it, what you fought about? Sometimes it helps to tell someone else, so you aren't trying to do it all yourself."

I let my eyes close and leaned into him for a moment. "I'd rather not think about it at all. That feels wonderful."

He moved my hair around to one side of my neck, and then I felt his lips on the skin he had bared. He trailed little kisses along the edge of my throat in between his words. "I want you to be happy and relaxed. There's no reason to be so tense."

"I'm feeling better. What did you bring for lunch?" I moved away to open the basket.

"Are you very hungry? I think Duncan took all the sandwiches." Chase laughed a little. "He seemed very glad to have Charly all to himself."

I smiled back. "I think Charly was pretty happy too. And, no, I'm not really hungry, but I would like something to drink if you've got it."

Chase moved the basket out of my reach. "No peeking. You'll ruin my surprise. I have a couple of bottles of water, but I also have-" He broke off and looked around for a minute. "I thought maybe it would be a romantic gesture, but now that I'm really considering everything, I don't know. I mean, you're only fifteen."

I was suddenly so tired of everyone throwing my age back in my face. "I'm old enough to do whatever I want, and there isn't anybody who can tell me what to do." I knew it wasn't true, but I didn't care about teachers or dorm mothers. None of them knew about my special family with our weird abilities. None of them knew about the existence of vampires. None of them were my parents, not even Julian.

Chase looked at me cautiously. "Are you sure? I mean, it's not really bad, but I bet you've never even had a taste of alcohol."

"What did you bring?" My curiosity was running neck and neck with my anger.

Chase pulled out a bottle with a flourish. "Champagne. It's the good stuff, too." He took two flutes out of the basket, unwrapping them from the cloth napkins that had kept them from banging together.

"How did you sneak it onto school property?"

"I had my butler ship it to me. My family doesn't exactly hold with arbitrary laws like a drinking age. Would you like some?"

"Why not?" I held the glasses while he opened the bottle with what seemed to me to be practiced ease. He poured so that the fizz bubbled to the top of the glass but didn't slide over the rim.

"Just try a sip or two and see if you like it, but don't worry if you don't. My mother says champagne is an acquired taste."

I raised the glass to my lips and felt the bubbles popping against my nose. It tasted sort of bitter but not really bad. Maybe it was because I was used to sweeter drinks like juices and sodas.

Chase set his own glass aside after one drink. "I guess we should stay in here and out of sight if we're going to have the champagne. Honestly, I wasn't really crazy about the idea of a picnic in the sun. My skin burns easier since I've been sick. I think it's the medications I was taking."

"Maybe they're not all out of your system yet. It's okay if we stay in here. Charly and Duncan wanted to be alone anyway."

"I think we should move into one of the unused stalls in case somebody comes in. We'll have a chance to hide the evidence. I wouldn't want you to get in trouble." He picked up the basket with one hand and the champagne with the other.

I carried the two glasses and followed him to the back of the barn where there were some empty stalls. He closed the half-door behind us, then leaned back across to latch the gate so it wouldn't swing open. We weren't really in our own room, but it would give us a moment before someone saw us.

When Chase sat down the basket and the bottle, he pulled out a thin blanket and spread it out. Then he removed a plastic container before sitting down.

"Will you join me?"

I smiled at him before I sat down next to him.

"Are you ready for your surprise?"

I nodded, wondering if he was going to kiss me and if I would let him. He opened the plastic dish to show me a half dozen chocolate covered strawberries. It was like something out of a romance novel – the picnic in the hay, the champagne, and now strawberries. I think I giggled a little, but the look on Chase's face was so sincere. He had really gone to a lot of trouble to make this happen, and he'd done it so quickly. Was that a benefit of being rich and privileged?

We ate the strawberries and drank the champagne. Chase had laid out the blanket so we could lean against the side of the horse stall and before I realized it, I was leaning my head on his shoulder.

"Elisabeth? Tell me about your life. We hardly even know each other, and I want to know everything about you."

I smiled a little, knowing he couldn't see it. "I'm just a girl. You're the one with the fascinating life – a fencing star. What's it like to be so good at something?"

"It's hard work and hours of practice everyday. I want to know about you. You are so much more than just a girl. You're so different from all the other girls in any school I've ever been to."

I knew I'd have to tell him something, but I wanted to tell him the truth, the whole truth. "My parents died when I was a baby. I've had several different caregivers until my guardian sent me here." That was true, but so far from the truth of my life. What would Chase think if he knew I had grown up without money in foster homes, not even knowing my real name? He would be appalled. And how could anyone really explain a mysterious family where I'm supposed to be some kind of princess with abilities that I don't even understand? The less truth I shared the better off I'd be.

"I'm so sorry. It must have been awful to grow up without your parents. I hope I didn't upset you asking about them."

"No, of course not. I was too young to really remember much. But it doesn't upset me."

"No wonder you seem so different. You've experienced the kind of loss that most of these girls have never felt." Chase put his arm around me and hugged me against his side. "I really am sorry for your loss."

"Thanks. I wish I could have known them, or at least have some idea of what they were like, but even the stories people have told me have been edited."

"What do you mean?"

"They only tell me what they think I need to know. Or what they think I can handle. If someone knows something about my parents, I wish they would just tell me the entire story all at once. I hate having to learn everything in bits and pieces."

Chase nodded. "They look at you and see a child. They don't understand that everything you've had to deal with has made you grow up faster than the average girl."

"Exactly! Julian treats me like I'm five, let alone fifteen. I've taken care of myself more or less for years."

"Julian?" There was something in Chase's voice when he said the name, but I didn't know what it was.

"Julian is my guardian, my godmother. She was my father's best friend." There was a little voice in the back of my head, warning me I'd already said enough, but I don't know if it was my anger or the alcohol that kept me talking. "She just dropped me off here and left me with so many questions and no real answers."

"That's not fair, Elisabeth. She shouldn't be allowed to leave you with questions about your own father."

Somehow as we were talking Chase had moved around until he was facing me while I leaned against the wall and his outstretched arm. He moved his hand off my shoulders to cup my face. His dark eyes looked deep into mine.

"If you were mine, I would never let anyone mistreat you ever again."

I pushed the guilty thought that Julian didn't really mistreat me out of my mind and concentrated on the part about being his.

He leaned over me until our foreheads were touching. "Will you, Elisabeth? Will you be mine?"

There was a part of me that wanted to say yes to Chase, maybe so I would belong to someone, or maybe so I could feel like a normal girl. But I knew I wasn't a normal girl. And there was Alexei. Whether either of us could admit it, I knew that there was a piece of me that already belonged to him. Maybe it was just a tiny piece that would never grow into a real relationship, but it was enough that I knew I couldn't make promises to Chase. Instead of giving him any words that would be too hard to explain, I simply closed the distance between us and kissed him, hoping he wouldn't assume that my kiss was a yes.

It wasn't dark in the barn and the sun was shining outside instead of a storm raging, but the kiss was as powerful as our first. My arms circled Chase's neck, and I let myself feel instead of think. Chase broke the kiss and pulled away long enough to tug his shirt over his head.

"I want to feel your hands on my skin," he explained before he returned to kissing me. I put my arm around him so that I could run them across his shoulders and along his spine. I felt his shiver when my nails caught the nape of his neck, and it gave me a sense of my own power over him. Before I was aware of what he was doing, he had three of the buttons on my uniform shirt open and pushed the cotton back so that he could see my bra.

My brain felt like it was racing and yet moving in slow motion at the same time. I wondered if it was an effect of the champagne or just Chase. I felt a buzzing in my head. It was like during the storm when I could have sworn I heard his voice in my head, even though I knew his mouth was kissing the side of my neck, moving down towards the cleavage my bra gave me.

One of his hands slid under the edge of my bra, just sliding across the skin covered by the thin lace. His lips were covering mine, blocking any protests I might have made with rough kisses.

I knew he shouldn't be doing these things. I knew I should be stopping him, but it was so hard to form a clear thought in my mind. And I heard his voice in my head, not demanding like it had been, but soft. Almost begging me to agree, to give in. I wanted to give in to him. It would make everything better if I just gave in to Chase and let myself become his. His mouth moved down my throat and continued on to my breast. The feeling of his lips on my bare skin surprised me. When had my skin been bared? I didn't remember taking off my shirt, but I realized I was no longer wearing it or my bra. It wasn't until I felt his hand just above my knee under my skirt that I felt a moment of true panic.

The panic cleared my head for a moment. I hadn't agreed to this. I didn't want to have sex with Chase, and I definitely didn't want to lose my virginity in a horse barn laying on a blanket in the hay.

"Chase-"

He never stopped kissing and nibbling on my skin, but I heard his voice in my head clearly. *You want this, Elisabeth. You want me to make love to you so that you can be mine forever.*

I suddenly realized that I wasn't just imagining his voice. It was the same kind of feeling that I'd had when Alexei was inside my mind that morning. Chase had some kind of mental ability, and he was using it on me. I pushed him away, both with my hands and with my mind. I wasn't really sure how I was doing it other than by thinking the opposite of the welcoming thoughts I had for Alexei. I grabbed my shirt and stood up, putting it on, while Chase sat looking stunned.

"How did you do that?" His voice was no longer the sweet seduction that he had been using or even the flirty tone he had used when we first met. It was cold and hard, pitched deeper than I'd ever heard it before.

"What do you mean, how did I do that? What do you think you were doing to me?" My voice came out in a squeak, making me sound even younger than fifteen.

He looked at me carefully, and when he spoke, his voice was back to normal. "I thought we were showing each other how much we love each other. I thought you wanted to be mine." Even as he said the words out loud, I could feel him pressing at the edges of my mind.

"Stop it!" I pushed him back from my mind again.

His voice dropped back to the cold, hard thing that I didn't recognize as Chase. "You are doing it on purpose aren't you? How is that possible? You're only fifteen. No one has abilities like that at your age."

Those words scared me more than anything else that had happened. Chase was moving to stand, but before he could I shoved him down again, grabbed my bra out of the hay, and pushed past him to the door. I don't know how I got it open before he could reach me, but I was too afraid to stop running until I was back in my room in Kirkwynd Hall.

CHAPTER TWENTY-FOUR

Lila Grace and Emma were both in the room when I got back. Somehow I had managed to keep my bra waded up in my fist during my run from the stables, but my hair was tangled and full of hay. I tossed my bra on my bed and turned to face the other girls, ready for accusations. Lila Grace let out a gasp that was barely more than a whisper. Emma looked me over from top to bottom and back up again. She spoke without taking her eyes off me.

"Lila Grace, go find Alexei and tell him Elisabeth needs him. He may already be on his way so go down the secret stairway first, then try the study hall. Go to his room if you have to, but get him."

Somehow Lila Grace did exactly as Emma commanded without a single question. I kept watching her to see what she would do next.

"Elisabeth, I'm going to go to the bathroom and get a washcloth. I think you should get out of those clothes and put on something warm that you feel comfortable in. Can you do that while I'm gone?"

I nodded, afraid that if I spoke I might start screaming and not be able to stop. I did as Emma said, changing into my jeans and a soft sweater. I put on fuzzy socks. I made sure that my bra and panties were the plainest cotton ones I owned. I threw my uniform onto the floor, dumping my other bra with it, and kicked them all under my bed.

Emma came back in with a warm washcloth. She led me to the side of my bed, and when I sat down, she washed my face. It was only then that I realized I had been crying. She was brushing my hair, pulling out the hay, and braiding it when Lila Grace came back in with Alexei.

"I found him in the study hall. He was just staring outside."

Alexei looked at me. All I could do was stare back at him. I didn't know what to say. The last thing I had said was so hateful, and I had done it on purpose to hurt him.

Emma took matters into her own hands. She wrapped a band around the end of my braid and walked over to stand close to Alexei. "She needs you. I know that there is something special between the two of you. I'm not asking questions. In fact, I'm pretty sure I don't want to know your secrets. But Elisabeth needs you. I don't know what happened, but she was hurt. Maybe just emotionally, but maybe physically. I'm going to get Mrs. Bambridge to call Miss Julian. I think Elisabeth needs her now, but until she can get her, you need to take care of Elisabeth. Can you do that?" Maybe Emma saw the guilt in Alexei's expression because she continued. "Can you take care of Elisabeth's needs right now and not worry about your own feelings, guilt or anger or whatever? Can you put Elisabeth first?"

Alexei looked down at Emma, with her close cut curls and her dark blue eyes. "You have done a better job than anyone could ever have asked. I am in your debt for as long as you live." It was whispered, but it was a true vow Alexei gave her. Emma smiled at him, then took Lila Grace by the hand and left the room.

I was alone with Alexei again. The tension between us was more than I could stand. I got off my bed and flung myself into Alexei's arms, crying like I was a little girl.

"It didn't work. Why didn't it work, Alexei? I don't know why it didn't work." I kept repeating myself, but it took some time before he was able to understand what I was saying.

"What did not work, Elisabeth? I do not know what you mean."

I finally stopped crying enough to be able to talk clearly. "The bonding that we have. It didn't work. I was . . . . And you didn't come."

Alexei said something in Russian. It was quiet, but I thought he was blaming himself or maybe even God. "I do not know why it would not work. Were you very afraid?"

"Not at first. But later I was really scared."

"Can you tell me everything from the beginning?"

"I was with Charly, and we were meeting Duncan and Chase at the stables to have a picnic. Duncan wanted to be alone with Charly, so they went outside to sit in the sunshine. I stayed with Chase in the barn. He had champagne and chocolate covered strawberries. I think maybe I was a little bit drunk. I've never had any alcohol before, but I thought it would take more than that to make me drunk."

"You had not eaten lunch. Alcohol works faster on an empty stomach." Alexei stroked my hair with one hand, while he held me close with the other.

"Chase asked me some questions about my family, and he said I was different from other girls."

"What did you tell him of your family? Did you tell him your father's name?"

"No. I stuck to the basics, that my parents died when I was a baby, and that my guardian had just decided to send me here. We also talked about his family, how he is a fencing star. Then he asked me if I would be his."

I felt Alexei clench at this, even though I knew he was trying not to. His voice was brittle when he asked his next question. "What did you say?"

"What could I say? I can't belong to him. You were right when you said I don't even know who I am yet." I pulled back enough to look at Alexei's face. "And how can I promise to belong to anyone when there is already at least a part of me that belongs to you?"

"You mean the bonding? I have tied you to me so that you can never be free." I hated hearing that bitterness.

"No, that's not what I mean. I mean that no matter what else happens in the future, there will always be a place for you in my heart, a place that is only yours. I can't give you anymore than that, at least not right now, but that will never change."

"So you have forgiven me for my jealousy earlier."

"Your jealousy? Forgiven you? Alexei, I was the one who said horrible things, things that weren't even true."

"It is true that I cannot take you out into the sunlight."

"But it was awful of me to say it like that, and it's not really what I meant." I could hardly stand to face him.

"It does not matter now. You were hurt and wanted me to hurt as well. I was jealous of that mortal boy."

I looked directly into Alexei's eyes. "That's the thing. I'm not sure Chase is just some mortal boy. When I couldn't give him the words he wanted from me, I kissed him. But, Alexei, there was something else going on. I could hear his voice in my head. At first I thought it was just my imagination or maybe an alcohol-induced hallucination, but he was talking to me in my head, seducing me, trying to get me to have sex with him."

"Did he rape you?" The starkness of Alexei's question made me gasp, because I had not been able to even think that word. Alexei must have interpreted my gasp for a yes, because he became very still and was barely touching me.

"No, Alexei, no. He didn't get that far. Although he got more than I wanted. It was like my mind was all wrapped up in cotton balls or bubble wrap, and I was thinking in slow motion. He . . . he had my shirt off before I even realized what was happening. It wasn't until I felt his hand on my leg-" I shook my head. "When I realized what was happening, I sort of pushed him away with my mind and my arms. He was shocked. He knew exactly what he was doing, and he was furious that I stopped him. He kept saying that it was what I wanted, to be his forever."

"It is good that Emma went to call for Julian. We need her as soon as she can get here. It is possible that Chase is a part of the Malhairer, and only Julian can tell us for certain. Aside from vampires, the Malhairer are the only . . . ." He looked at me as he chose his label for my family.

"People? Beings? Creatures? I know what you mean. We're the only ones with the ability to manipulate people's minds."

"No. It is not meant for manipulation, but simple influence."

"Call it whatever you want, Alexei, but what he was doing was manipulation."

Alexei took both of my hands in his and looked hard into my eyes. "Call it what it truly is, Elisabeth. What he was doing was a mental rape, trying to force you against your will. It is only because of your natural gifts, your father's legacy, that you could push him away."

"That's what he said. He said that no one had those abilities at my age. He knew I would have abilities, but didn't expect them to have manifested so early. That's what you told me about Julian, that hers only started just before she graduated, around eighteen."

"Yes. It is only because you take after your father so much that you were able to protect yourself. I am sorry I was not there to protect you today, Elisabeth. I cannot imagine why the bond did not alert me to your fear."

"Maybe it was because we were so angry with each other. Angry and hurt and protecting ourselves from each other."

"Perhaps. You may be correct, or I may be wrong about the level of this bonding. It is not the same as what happened between my vampire family. They were never able to stop the communication. They could eventually choose what to send in moments of calm, but fear or excitement would strip their control. After you pushed him away, he simply let you leave?"

I shuddered. "No. I pushed him away at least twice, and maybe I was able to keep him back while I ran. I'm not sure. I was scared and the adrenaline had kicked in by that time. I just ran back here and let Emma take charge. She's kind of amazing."

"More so than I had credited to her. She knows enough about the mysteries of life to not ask questions she does not truly want answered." Alexei walked us over to my bed, and we sat down together on the side. "Are you alright, Elisabeth? Do not simply tell me the answer you think I want to hear."

"I'm okay, now. It was really scary at the time, but you're here, and now we know to watch out for Chase because he can't be trusted. He is dangerous."

"I will deal with him as soon as Julian tells me if he is a part of the Malhairer. I swore on your father's grave that not one of them would ever hurt you."

"I know, and they won't. I took reckless chances and acted like a fool. None of that is your fault."

I don't know what Alexei would have said in response because there was a knock at the door, and Emma came back in. When she looked at me, I smiled at her, and she seemed relieved but only for a moment.

"Elisabeth, are you okay?"

"Yes. I got away before anything really bad could happen."

"Was it Chase Elliot?"

"How did you know?"

"I found one of the girls from his building outside the chemistry lab this morning. She was bruised and bloodied, but she couldn't tell me anything about what happened. It was as if she had no memory of the event at all. I don't think she was raped, but I know that Chase Elliot was with her ten minutes before I found her. I saw them walking around a corner together, but she couldn't even remember that. I thought maybe he used GHB, you know the date rape drug? It causes short term memory loss, but I didn't think it was supposed to be that bad."

"Does Chase know that you saw him?" I knew Alexei was concerned, worried about what Chase might do to Emma, especially since we realized he had his own mental abilities.

"He never saw me. I'm invisible to him. But don't worry, I'll stay out of his way. I'm actually starting to worry about Charly. Nobody's seen her in a while."

"Oh my God! How could I forget Charly? If anything has happened to her, it's all my fault." I jumped up ready to rush out the door.

Alexei pulled me back to him. "Shh, Elisabeth. We will find Charly. If anything has happened to her, the blame rests solely upon Chase Elliot."

"Where did you last see her?" Emma asked.

"She was with Duncan, Duncan whatever-his-name-is, and they left me in the barn with Chase to go have a picnic in the sunshine. But Duncan is Chase's. He'll do whatever Chase tells him to. What if Chase decided to get even with me by hurting Charly? We have to find her."

"I will go to the stables through the tunnels; I can get there faster than either of you. Is Lila Grace waiting in the study room?"

Emma nodded. "Where should we look?"

Alexei thought for a moment. "Try her next classes, but stay together. I would tell you to wait here, but I know you will not. If she comes back through the tunnel entrance I will let you know. Please try not to worry. We will find her." Alexei kissed the top of my head. He paused for a moment and then kissed the top of Emma's head as well. I wondered if it was some sort of vampire protection or benediction or if he was just catching her scent. He slipped out the trapdoor and was gone.

Emma looked at me while I slipped on my shoes. "He'll probably find her first, but let's go."

I nodded, then touched Emma's arm. "Thank you. For taking care of me, for getting Alexei, and for sending word to Julian. You are a true friend."

Emma blushed and shook her head. "You would have done the same for me or Charly or Lila Grace. It's what we do."

"But still, thanks." Emma nodded once. We went down and through the study hall, pausing long enough to let Lila Grace know where we were going. We ran through the sunshine to the building where Charly's afternoon classes were held. Her class had already started, but Charly wasn't there. We were back in Kirkwynd Hall in under ten minutes, but Alexei was there first. He had found Charly.

CHAPTER TWENTY-FIVE

Lila Grace was waiting for us in the study hall, to tell us Alexei had found Charly and had taken her back to our room. The three of us raced up the stairs but entered the room quietly so we wouldn't startle Charly. She was lying on her bed so still that for a moment I didn't think it was really her. Charly was never still. Even asleep, she would toss and turn and move all over her bed.

Alexei had one washcloth across her forehead, while he used a second one to wipe gently at the corner of her mouth. He was blocking most of the view, but I saw grass stains and scrapes on her knees. I moved closer so I could see her, and she could see me. I couldn't stop the tears from running down my cheeks. Her mouth was cut in a couple of places, and she had swelling bruises puffing out her cheek and just above her right eye. Her shirt was torn, but it seemed to be more on the arm than on the front.

"Charly, you can tell us anything you need to say, and we will listen. Elisabeth, Emma, and Lila Grace are all here to help you." Alexei's voice was soothing. "Is there something we can get for you?"

"How 'bout an icepack?" The voice was a little weak and definitely slurred from the busted lip, but it was Charly. I grinned in relief.

Lila Grace, never comfortable with a disagreement let alone violence, rushed back out the door. When she was gone, Emma spoke.

"Do you remember what happened?"

Charly shot Emma a look I couldn't interpret. "Of course, I do. I tripped over some exposed tree roots and hit my head on the tree trunk."

I looked at Alexei, but he shook his head slightly.

Emma spoke first. "Charlotte Marie Deveraux! This is serious business. If I didn't know you as well as I do, I'd think you meant that. Tell us the truth before Alexei and Elisabeth panic."

Charly looked at Emma with the most serious expression I'd ever seen on her face. "Actually, that's the story that everyone else will be getting, so don't forget it. It's weird because I can almost remember that happening. It's like I have two memories, one of what did happen and one of what was supposed to have happened."

"But you can tell the difference?" I asked.

"Oh, yeah. I can remember Chase telling me that I tripped, but I can remember seeing you run out of the barn, and Chase following you to the doorway, with his shirt off. I was afraid he had really hurt you, and then he looked at me. He told Duncan to bring me to the barn. I didn't think Duncan would do it, but when I tried to leave, he just picked me up and carried me to Chase."

Charly stopped speaking. I could tell she needed a moment to herself, so I turned to Alexei. "Why didn't it work? Why does Charly remember both?"

Emma answered before Alexei could. "Maybe Chase isn't using the typical drugs. Maybe he's using some sort of hallucinogen along with something like hypnotism to get some kind of mind control. It worked on the girl I found this morning but not on Charly or you, Elisabeth. Maybe he's been giving her doses regularly since she has total memory loss, rather than a replacement memory."

"You may be correct, Emma," Alexei said. "Elisabeth, do you remember when we were talking and I said how strong Charly's mind is? I am certain that is what preserved her memories."

"You mean I'm so stubborn I won't just believe whatever it was he tried to program me with." Her voice was shaky, but she was still Charly.

I gave her what I hoped was a reassuring smile. "Alexei's too polite to say stubborn. Can you tell us the rest?"

Charly looked at me, the bright turquoise of her eyes making the bruises look even darker. Then she looked around to Emma before coming back to stare at Alexei. "I don't think I can say this more than once. If you were any other guy, I'd make you leave, but you are so different. I know Elisabeth is your highest priority, but I can already see the guilt in your eyes." She looked back at me. "Both of you. You didn't cause this. I need to tell you what happened, but I can't deal with you blaming yourselves."

Charly paused, taking a deep breath that caused her to wince. "After Duncan carried me back into the barn, Chase shut and locked the door. Duncan threw me down. It knocked the breath out of me. Chase told Duncan to punish me, and Duncan hit me right in the face. He got my eye with the first shot, then my lip and cheek. I think he kicked me in the ribs, but that may have been incidental because I was trying to get away. Chase grabbed my hands and pinned them over my head while Duncan held my legs. My lip was bleeding a lot, but Chase didn't care. He kissed me hard. It was disgusting the way I could taste my blood on his mouth. He leaned up just a little so that I could see him. Then he deliberately leaned back down with his eyes staring into mine and licked the cut on my mouth. When he did it, he closed his eyes and swallowed like he was enjoying some decadent bit of chocolate. I wanted to throw up. His voice sounded so different from anything I'd ever heard him say before, deeper and ice-cold. And he looked different, older, harder, and not so handsome. He said . . . ."

Charly gulped in air, her eyes seeing that moment, but her hand had found mine, and she squeezed it as if I was her only lifeline. We waited, giving her the space to tell us in her own time.

"He said that he liked my blood, and he was going to enjoy making me bleed. He nodded at Duncan who moved to hold my arms. I tried to get Duncan to stop, but he was a complete blank, like he couldn't even hear me. I realized my begging was like throwing gas on the fire for Chase, so I tried not to say anything else. We were too far away from everyone anyway."

I was afraid of what she would say next. I didn't want to hear any details, but I knew from other girls that I had known who had been assaulted that if she didn't tell someone it would eat her up inside. I looked at Emma, standing on the other side of Charly's bed, letting her squeeze her hand too, and knew that the tears I saw on her face matched mine. I couldn't bear to look at Alexei, but he seemed completely focused on Charly although he kept a distance as if his male presence was enough to apologize for.

"He was only interested in hurting me. It wasn't about anything other than the pleasure of seeing me hurt. He hit me and kicked me and then hit me some more. And the whole time, he went back and forth between laughing and licking the blood on my face. I screamed. I couldn't help it even though I knew he wanted me to scream. And then he was gone. I don't know if I spaced out or actually lost consciousness, but one minute he was there, and the next they were both gone. And then Alexei was there, and he brought me back here."

She looked at Alexei for a moment before realizing she was holding Emma's and my hands. I don't know what any of us would have said in that moment because Lila Grace came back in the room with two ice packs wrapped loosely in kitchen towels.

Charly let us go to take the ice packs and put one on her lip and the other across her cheek and eye, gasping when the cold hit her skin.

Emma wiped the tears from her face and said, "Just in case there was any doubt before, we now know for sure that Grace is Lila's name and definitely not Charly's." We laughed weakly, but I caught Emma's eye and gave her a slight nod. There was no reason to upset Lila Grace any more than she already had been. Emma took Lila Grace downstairs to study so Charly could rest, and I stayed to keep an eye on her in case she had a concussion. Alexei was almost unnoticeable as Emma and Lila Grace disappeared.

"Charly needs to see a doctor," I told Alexei as soon as I was sure they were out of earshot.

"No!" Charly was adamant. "No doctors. Nothing that could let Chase know I remember anything other than tripping and falling into a tree."

"But you could have serious internal injuries. And a doctor's examination will give proof, maybe even DNA under your nails-"

Alexei interrupted me. "Elisabeth, you know better than that. Chase Elliot, or whoever he may truly be, would never leave any of his DNA behind."

Charly looked from me to Alexei. "You don't think he's really Chase Elliot?"

"Stop trying to change the subject. Charly needs to see a doctor." I looked at Alexei, wishing I could get him to read my thoughts now and use his powers to make Charly want to see a doctor. He seemed to understand but shook his head slightly, reminding me that his compulsion didn't work on Charly. He moved away from us.

"Tell me what Chase did that caused you to run away from the barn, Elisabeth. Did he hurt you?"

I tried to smile. "Not like he did you. Your face is going to be as colorful as your backpack by tomorrow." I let the smile fade. "He tried to. He was really pulling out the stops with the alcohol and whatever else he was using to control me, but I stopped him. He . . . he did get my shirt off. I'm so sorry I got you into this."

"It's not right. Even if we go to the administration, Chase probably had Duncan brainwashed into not even remembering the barn, let alone betraying him. There has to be a better way to deal with him."

286

Alexei spoke from the corner of the room. "There is, and I will."

Charly and I both shivered. "Alexei, you can't do anything stupid."

"Do not worry, Elisabeth. I am not stupid. I will find a way to deal with Chase Elliot that will be just, but will not get any of us in any sort of trouble."

That was kind of what I was afraid of. Alexei could hunt and kill Chase, and it would be justice, especially if we knew how Chase had abilities. Only I was afraid that if Alexei killed Chase, he would believe that he was permanently damned and would never find redemption.

Alexei must have read my thoughts on my face because he smiled. "Do not worry. I will not do anything until after I speak with you. You and Julian."

As if he had conjured her by speaking her name, my cell phone rang. "Hello?"

"Elisabeth, are you injured? Are you hurt?" I had never heard Julian so on edge.

"I'm fine, Jules, but I have about a million questions that only you can answer. I really need to see you."

"Thank God. I was so afraid of losing you, of failing your father, your parents. Can you wait about five minutes? I'm at the front gates." I could almost taste her relief.

"Really? You're here?" I started crying again. "Oh, Jules, I've missed you so much."

"I've missed you, too, Elisabeth. If I could make this car go any faster, I would."

"Do you want me to meet you downstairs?"

Julian's voice turned hard. "No, you will not. You will go and stay in your room which I know is very safe, and you will wait until I come there."

"Charly and I are in the room now, but Jules, Charly was hurt."

"Is she in immediate danger?"

"No. I don't think so."

"Then I will take care of everything when I get there." She disconnected, but not before I heard the buzzer letting her in the gates.

CHAPTER TWENTY-SIX

"Where will you go to talk to Miss Julian?" Charly asked, but Alexei answered.

"Elisabeth and Julian can use my room to talk. My roommates will not be in there tonight."

I know I snorted a little at the thought of Alexei's 'roommates.'

Charly continued. "But Miss Julian doesn't know you or trust you. She's super-protective of Elisabeth, and she may resent your interest."

I raised an eyebrow at Alexei. How would he get around this one? Charly continued talking.

"You should introduce her to Alexei, and let him offer his room. If Miss Julian wants to, then you can go there; if she doesn't, then you can stay here, and I'll figure out something else."

"If you aren't going to see a doctor, then you are not leaving this room tonight. I guess if Alexei waits just behind the trapdoor-" The look we shared said we both knew it would be bad for Julian to come in and see him and call him "Sasha" in front of Charly.

"I suppose I will be your surprise for your godmother." I didn't miss the tone; Julian was really going to be surprised, but would it be a good one or a bad one?

Alexei took my cell phone, pretending to check the time, but he whispered to me that he heard her on the stairs. He quickly hid in the secret tunnel.

There was a knock on the door.

I was suddenly afraid. Julian was on the other side of the door, and she had all the answers for my questions, answers Alexei either didn't have or was sworn not to repeat. Would she be disappointed with me for letting Chase trick me so easily? What would she say when I showed her my father's box?

Charly called out clearly, "It's open, Miss Julian."

Julian opened the door and scowled. "Why is your door unlocked? Don't you girls understand-" She broke off when she saw Charly's face. "What happened to you?" She tossed a quick look my way and saw no matching bruises.

Charly answered. "The official story has to do with tree roots, but Elisabeth will fill you in on everything. I can't tell it again."

Julian crossed over to where I was standing. She looked me over with a critical eye. "You've changed a lot in just a few weeks, Elisabeth. It suits you, I think. Sit and tell me everything, starting with why I received such a frantic telephone call earlier."

"I can't tell you the whole story yet. Charly was attacked, and she refuses to see a doctor."

Julian turned back to look at Charly again. "How badly are you injured?"

"I'm okay. It looks worse than it is." Charly's eyes begged me not to tell Julian what had happened. I was sorry I couldn't grant her wish.

"Julian, it's actually worse than it looks. Charly was beaten."

"By someone here at the Academy? How can this kind of thing happen?" Julian shook her head. "I don't mean it like that. I know it happens everyday in all kinds of situations, but there are special safeguards that most of the students are completely unaware of."

I took Julian's hands and looked in her eyes, hoping that she would understand the meaning behind my words. "Chase is not the typical kind of boy. He hurt Charly because he couldn't get to me." Julian's frown was confused as she tried to piece together what I was saying, but Charly saved the day.

"Emma thinks Chase has been using date rape drugs to screw with people's minds. Not just to attack girls, but to control people."

I saw the light in Julian's amazing emerald eyes as the understanding came. She walked over to Charly and whispered something in her ear. Charly seemed to fall asleep, but she was murmuring to herself.

"What is going on around here, Elisabeth?" Julian looked scared and angry, but I was shocked at whatever she had done to my friend.

"What did you do to Charly? How did you do it? Could I have done that?"

Julian's emerald eyes narrowed. "Tell me everything beginning with how you met this Chase."

"Actually, I can't start there. I have to start back at the day you left. There's someone I met, and I believe you know him, too."

Julian looked wary, and then even more so as the trapdoor swung open. When Alexei stepped into the room,

291

Julian lost what little color she did have, and her emerald eyes went wide. Her voice was so faint I barely heard it, but Alexei had no trouble. "Sasha?"

"Good evening, Julian."

"You sound just like him, but you can't be. Sasha is dead." Julian shook her head over and over.

"That is not amusing, Julian. I may perhaps be called undead, but I assure you, I am here."

"No. You can't be. Sasha and his entire family were massacred shortly after Nicholas was killed."

"My family was massacred, but I was not with them. My father, seeing my grief over Nicholas, sent me to investigate the deaths and find Elisabeth. I thought you knew I was alive." Alexei frowned at her. It was as if I was invisible. They were both so wrapped up in their memories and grief, they had forgotten I was in the room.

"It really is you? Sasha?" Julian's voice cracked, and I saw tears in her eyes. "I thought I was alone. I thought I had lost Nicholas and Elisabeth and you with your family."

Alexei moved to her and hugged her the way he did me sometimes, when a touch is more important than a word. They stood like that for quite a while, before I cleared my throat.

"Oh, Elisabeth! I had no idea Sasha was here, but I'm so glad he is. You're safer here than I knew."

Alexei shook his head at Julian. "In some ways. Some things have been harder because I did not know what you had told her. I am afraid I have revealed some of your secrets. And we have encountered other difficulties, especially today. The boy who attacked Elisabeth and Charly, Chase Elliot, possesses some mental abilities. His attack on Charly was mainly physical, although he tried to alter her memories, but he used mental persuasion to try to seduce and rape Elisabeth. He has been very intent on claiming her for his own."

"Alexei said-"

Julian interrupted me. "Who is Alexei?"

He answered. "I am Alexei. It has not been long since we were students, so I could not be Sasha again."

She nodded, so I continued. "Alexei said that Chase might be part of the Malhairer."

Julian turned and roared at Alexei. "You told her about the Malhairer? She has not been prepared in any way, and we don't even know yet if she'll be able to-"

It was Alexei's turn to interrupt. "Julian, I told her the name of the Malhairer, when I was referring to her grandfather. She knows that she is to be the princess, and that your people are a homogeneous group that are interrelated. She is like Nicholas and had already begun to feel her abilities. When she was attacked today, she pushed Chase Elliot out of her mind and probably held him back physically until she could escape. She is everything that Nicholas was at this age, and perhaps more. Besides, she handled learning what I am better than most. She sounds so much like Nicholas, telling me that I am not a monster, and that she refused to believe in a God who would damn His creation without a chance at redemption."

Julian's eyebrow shot up at that, but Alexei gave a slight shake of his head. I would have missed it, if I didn't know him so well. I knew he and Julian would need to compare notes before I got more answers, but at that moment I didn't care. I was so glad to have Julian and Alexei. Even though he still looked young, like a seventeen or eighteen year old, seeing him interact with Julian as an equal made the reality of his age stronger in my mind.

"Charly was hurt, Jules. She needs a doctor. She knows that Chase tried to give her different memories for what happened, and Emma knows as well. She's seen at least one other girl that Chase messed with. She's explaining it away as drugs, maybe combined with hypnotic suggestions. But we have to get Charly to see a doctor."

Julian looked from me to Charly and then back to Alexei. "You've told her that we have certain abilities?"

I rolled my eyes. "Those were almost his exact words, and the extent of what he said."

Julian smiled at my annoyed tone. "Very well, Elisabeth. I have some talent in the healing arts. I can go inside Charly's mind and let her body tell me how badly damaged it is. I may be able to help her heal."

"You aren't afraid her mind is too strong? Charly has resisted Alexei's attempts to make her notice him less."

It was Julian's turn to roll her eyes. "If Sasha, excuse me, if Alexei, truly wanted to use his compulsion on Charly's mind, he could have taken some of her blood. There is no protection for the mind of a human when a vampire has taken their blood."

Again I was awed by the reality of Alexei's existence through Julian's casual reference.

"You know I would never take a human's blood just to make my life easier. I made a pact with Nicholas, and I will respect that."

Julian waved her hand at him to be quiet while she focused on Charly. After a moment, she smiled. "She is a very strong young woman. The damage was not as severe as you might think. Her body is healing and will continue to do so without a doctor. The more lasting trauma will be in her mind, but we will help her in every way possible. I know these crimes should be reported, but if this Chase is one of the Malhairer, then we will bring him to the justice he deserves. And now we must talk."

"But we can't talk in this room. Charly needs it, and Lila Grace and Emma will need to sleep probably long before half my questions are answered."

"I assume you already have a place in mind."

Alexei answered. "My room. I used a gentle suggestion to create the illusion of roommates. The truth is I find it difficult sometimes to share the room with the ghosts."

Julian's expression softened immediately. "You have the same room you shared with Nick."

Alexei nodded.

"And I suppose you were the reason the tunnels seemed to be in use. No daylight for Alexei."

He nodded again.

She turned to me. "And I assume you revealed the secret door to your roommates?"

"Yes, but they all promised to only use them in case of emergency. Those tunnels are an absolute labyrinth."

Julian laughed. "You aren't supposed to know that."

"Alexei took me a couple of times, so no one would be able to overhear our conversations." I tried not to sound defensive. I also tried really hard not to think about the way I had kissed Alexei and he kissed me. Julian was ready to accept Alexei as her old friend and my protector, but I didn't want her to think about anything else until we had dealt with Chase.

"Do we need to wait for Charly to wake up?"

"I gave her the suggestion to rest without dreams. She should sleep through the night, but we shouldn't leave her alone for long."

I nodded. "I'll text Emma to let her and Lila Grace know to keep an eye on Charly. Then I can meet you in the tunnels going through the janitor's closet door."

They both seemed grateful for a chance to speak alone, but I had something I needed to take care of without Julian seeing it as well. After they went through the trapdoor, I dumped my backpack out onto my bed. I very carefully placed the box that Julian had given me into the bag, along with the box that had been my father's and had been hidden in my teddy bear for so many years, and the box Alexei had given me with the firebird on it. I knew that there was some mystery that was connected to the boxes; I still hadn't been able to figure out how to open the secret compartment in my father's box. I was especially interested in seeing Julian's reaction to the box Alexei had commissioned for me when I was born.

Six minutes later, Emma and Lila Grace were in the room with Charly, and I met up with Julian and Alexei in the tunnels and followed them to his room. I wondered if it would be as hard for Julian to be in that room as it had been for me the first time.

CHAPTER TWENTY-SEVEN

I watched memories flit across Julian's face as she looked around the room that my father had shared with Alexei. She had commented on how much I had changed, but I was amazed at the changes in Julian. When I had first met her, I couldn't imagine touching her, let alone hugging her; she had seemed so cool and perfect in her red suit. The whole time we were traveling to Paris and back again, I sensed she was keeping things from me. She had held herself so tightly.

But now she was different. She was still dressed in an expensive suit, a pale jade that made her emerald eyes even more amazing, and she was still as beautiful, but the stiffness was gone. Maybe it was her relief that I was okay. Maybe it was the shock of finding out that her friend Sasha was alive and protecting me. Maybe it was knowing that she could finally tell me all the secrets she had been keeping for so long.

She wandered to the window and along the curved wall before settling into the chair that I had used on my last visit. "I like the improvements, but we need to focus on the current situation."

I spoke up before she could continue. "Is that another way of saying that I'm not going to get any answers?"

Julian smiled ruefully. "It's my way of saying that it's way past time you received your answers. I'm sorry, Elisabeth. I was trying to protect you and give you some time to get used to the idea of having a different family than the one you believed was yours. I wanted you to have what Nicholas always wanted – a normal life. Even if it was only for a little while."

My voice was softer. "It's okay, Jules. I understand why you did those things. I've read some of my father's letters to you, and after Alexei told me about the Malhairer, the things that he wrote made sense in completely different ways. I read in his own words how much my father dreaded the responsibilities of being the prince. I also read how he wanted to change his world, especially the rules and beliefs he didn't agree with." I glanced at Alexei standing just inside the door before refocusing on Julian. "I was reminded that it would have been difficult for me to believe you if you had tried to explain the mysterious abilities our people have and the strange connection to Alexei's family without seeing the reactions the students have around us and watching him move those huge wardrobes without straining a single muscle."

Julian smiled. "I was right; you have changed. You have gained confidence as well as wisdom. You are so much like Nick."

Alexei moved from the doorway to sit near me on the bed. "Elisabeth is facing dangers that Nick could never have imagined. We must find out who Chase Elliot really is before his behavior escalates. Today was not the first time he pursued Elisabeth, and now that she has shown him her abilities, he will change his tactics."

From the looks that passed between them it was obviously something they had discussed outside my hearing. I waited for Julian's reply.

"I believe he must be one of the Malhairer, but I won't know until I can see him."

"Do you just need to see a picture of him? I think Charly has a picture of Duncan on her cell phone with Chase in the background."

Julian looked at Alexei. "It really is time, isn't it?" She didn't wait for his nod, but turned to me. "No. A picture won't tell me anything other than what he looks like now. I need to be in the same room with him." She paused, gathering her thoughts. "Do you remember that first day we met? You looked out the window."

I nodded. "I saw you get out of the car and walk towards the house. Then you looked up."

"At you. What did you feel in that moment?"

I searched my memories and tried to find the right words to describe it. "I knew that you were looking at me, that you were . . . I want to say judging me, but that isn't quite it. You were checking to see if I met some measure, some quality that I couldn't understand. And then I knew that you were taking me with you."

Julian looked at Alexei. "You're right. Her abilities are more like Nicholas than I ever imagined. I was pleased that she packed her things and was ready to leave with me before I ever had to explain anything, but I had no idea she had come so close to my own thoughts."

"Are you saying that I was reading your mind? Can we do that?"

Julian laughed. "Not exactly. It's closer to say that you were feeling my emotions. I was so desperate to have you be the right one. But even before you sensed me 'measuring' you, you felt something?"

I tried to separate the feelings. "It was almost like I recognized you, even though I knew I'd never seen you before."

"And did you feel that recognition with Chase the first time you met him?"

I shook my head. "I don't remember. I was already upset that morning, and when Chase came into the student lounge where I was, I was just hoping it wasn't-" I broke off, not wanting to have to tell Julian about my dream meeting with Alexei that I had been so focused on that morning.

Alexei touched my hand. "She was upset by me. She knew I was not exactly who I seemed to be. I thought she knew more about who she was. I was putting pressure on her to tell me, but all she understood was the pressure. I made her uncomfortable."

Julian nodded. "Strong emotions can sometimes cloud our perception, especially if we aren't aware that we have any special abilities in the first place. What about Chase? Did he have any reaction to you?"

"I don't know what to tell you, Jules. He stopped in a place he normally wouldn't have, but he said it was because he had been ill. He did ask if I was the new student he'd heard about."

Julian looked thoughtful. "And how long had you been here at that point?"

I tried to remember, but Alexei answered first. "It was her third day of classes, the third morning she was here. Rumor has it that Chase Elliot was a star fencer at his old school, but his father sent him here to recover from an illness."

"Is he a vampire?" Julian and Alexei both went still when I asked. I wasn't sure who was more surprised at my question.

"What makes you ask that?" Julian began.

"The way he enjoyed licking the blood off Charly's face when she was beaten up."

"Have you ever seen him outside during the day?"

"Actually, I haven't. I saw him outside during the afternoon of the rainstorm, but I remember thinking that Alexei was probably out because there was so little sun."

Julian looked at Alexei. "Is this possible?"

"I do not know. He is not of my family, so if he is a vampire, he cannot be allowed to remain among these students. I never thought of the other vampires looking for Elisabeth. I have not met Chase. He never seems to be where I am."

"I never thought that was strange before because it seemed like you were the one who was never where the rest of the students would be." I shifted uncomfortably beneath their gazes for a moment before continuing. "Chase didn't want to go out into the sunlight to have his picnic today."

Julian's eyes narrowed. "What picnic?"

Alexei moved off the bed to kneel beside Julian's chair. "He has been pursuing Elisabeth romantically, as a normal boy would a normal girl. Until today, he was careful not to do anything that led either of us to believe he was anything other than a completely human seventeen year old."

"He used Charly to get to me. I wasn't exactly avoiding him, but I was spending a lot of time with Alexei, trying to learn more about my family and me. He had one of his mindless followers ask Charly for the four of us to have a picnic."

"Do you think this boy's interest in Charly was something Chase told him to exhibit? Was he playing on Charly's loneliness the same way he used Charly to play on yours?"

I nodded. "Duncan took Charly out of the barn to leave us alone. Chase said that the drugs he took for his illness had left his skin easier to burn, so he wanted to stay inside. I thought it was because he wanted privacy, but what if he really couldn't go outside? Charly said he stopped in the doorway when he was following me."

"He may be a vampire, but it may be something else. Tell me about this mind control he tried on you."

I felt my face flame, and couldn't stop a fast look at Alexei. Julian noticed both. "Don't worry about anything you say in front of Alexei. He may look like a teenage boy, but he's old enough to be my several times great-grandfather."

I looked at my shoelaces, wishing my hair was loose to fall down and hide my face. My life was becoming as tangled as the braid in my hair, with so many lies and omissions overlapping the next. "It started out like the day of the storm when I was caught outside. Chase was kissing me. It was all supposed to be very romantic, but I had just yelled horrible things at Alexei, and I felt so guilty."

Julian interrupted me. "You fought with Alexei? Why?"

I looked at Alexei. His eyes were swirling bright blue and pale green as he looked at me. "It was not a fight, and you did not yell. You said nothing that was not the complete truth."

All my guilt came back. "But it wasn't fair. I was trying to hurt you when I knew that you would never hurt me. I knew that I was doing to you what you would never allow to happen to me, and I didn't care. I just wanted you to hurt."

"Because despite everything I do to try and prevent it, I have hurt you myself with my half-truths and unanswered questions. Chase knew you were upset."

I nodded, but caught the way Julian's eyes had narrowed. "Chase tried to get me to talk about it, but when I refused, he tried to distract me with his picnic. He rubbed my shoulders, and he kissed me."

Alexei moved to the wall behind Julian, so I could see them both, and they both could see me, but Julian could no longer see Alexei.

She didn't say anything, but suddenly I felt her presence at the edges of my mind, the way I did Alexei's that morning when he was waiting to be let inside. She didn't push like Chase had, but, if I let her, Julian could be inside my mind and know what I was thinking.

"Don't, Julian. Please don't." I let my voice echo all my fear and exhaustion so she would understand how I felt.

Julian's emerald eyes looked directly into my own dark ones. "You felt that? That gentle a touch, and you truly felt it?" I nodded, and she continued. "Sasha said that you were as sensitive as your father had been at your age, but I just couldn't believe it. I'm sorry to keep pushing you, Elisabeth, but I need to know what Chase did."

I looked past her, at Alexei. He was leaning against the wall with his arms crossed over his chest. He seemed completely at ease until I saw the tightness in his muscles, like a tiger ready to pounce. He nodded, and I knew I had to tell her, but I didn't want Alexei to have to hear about Chase putting his hands on me again.

"Julian, Alexei has already heard this before, and I just can't . . . I just can't tell you with him here."

"Are you blaming Alexei because he is a man? Or because he didn't protect you after your argument?"

I shook my head. "Neither. None of this is Alexei's fault. I swear I know that, but we're talking about sex and seduction. I'm fifteen, Jules. I can't talk to you about this stuff with Alexei in the room."

Alexei solved the problem in a way Julian seemed reluctant to. "I will go and get the two of you some food and something to drink." His tone became self-mocking. "My room is slightly under-stocked in the area of snack foods. Tell Julian what you need to say before I return." He stepped out the doorway without giving Julian the chance to argue.

"What exactly is going on between you and Alexei?"

"Jules, please. He won't be gone long, and I don't want him to have to hear this again. I told him before Charly was attacked, and Alexei blamed himself for not protecting me. He thinks that the reason I drank Chase's champagne and let him kiss me was the fight we had, but it's not true. I stayed with Chase and let him kiss me because he's a hot, normal boy. Or at least that's what I thought."

"Okay. Nicholas always felt that Sasha was too hard on himself, taking the blame for things that he had no control over. So after the kissing, what else did Chase do to you?"

I took a shaky breath. "He took off my shirt and my bra without me realizing he had done it. It was like there was a buzzing in my head. I told Alexei it felt like my brain was wrapped in cotton balls or bubble wrap. I couldn't focus. I could hear him talking in my head, telling me to relax and that I wanted him to touch me and kiss me. He had his hand under my skirt, and it was like I just woke up. I knew that I didn't want him to touch me or have sex with me. And then I heard his voice clearly telling me to let him make love to me so I would be his. That's when I realized what he was doing and sort of pushed back with my own thoughts. Alexei thinks that I kept him from moving while I put my shirt back on and ran away."

Julian looked at me closely. "Are you sure he said that making love to you would make you his?"

I shuddered as his words rang in my memory. "He said, 'You want me to make love to you so that you can be mine forever.' It was awful, Jules."

"I don't think he is a vampire, Elisabeth. I am almost positive now that he is a part of the Malhairer." Julian paused. I was beginning to know her well enough to recognize the pause as her reluctance to tell me something she considered unpleasant but necessary.

"Go ahead and say it, Jules. What else?"

She gave me a wry twist of her lips. "He is almost certainly someone from the royal court, but most likely from your father's step-family."

"Eew." The sound flew out of my mouth before I could stop it. It wasn't exactly incest since we were not related by blood, and it wasn't like I'd ever met any of them, but the idea that Chase could be a step-anything and still wanted to have sex with me made me want to throw up. "Do you think he knows who I am?"

Julian gave me a look that said she understood how I felt. "Undoubtedly."

"Then why? I don't understand how having sex with even a step-family member could be something he would want."

"It's because we are Malhairer." Julian's shoulders slumped slightly, and I saw the fear in the tiny lines on her face. "Alexei told you that the Malhairer are ruled by our Prince. Your grandfather was our last crowned Prince, and he died years before you were born. Have you studied absolute monarchies in school?"

"Where the king receives his authority to rule from God, and no one has any rights other than what the king gives?"

"That's right. The Malhairer is an absolute monarchy in its most literal meaning. The Prince's will is the people's law. The people cannot break the law, and in truth, most have no desire to do anything other than please the Prince. Prince Augustin was an unhappy man with a harsh reign, but he was just and careful in his dealings with the outside world as well as with Sasha's vampire family. The people outside the court were protected. The court itself was a difficult place. Many of the – we call them Elder Children but in other courts they would be the nobility. The Elders were angry that Prince Augustin had violated the tradition by marrying the Mallaidh Duchess, but there was nothing that could be done. The Prince must uphold the traditions from the past, but how he fulfills them is his choice."

"Tell me about this Duchess, my grandfather's wife. Is her will law to the Malhairer? Is she a good ruler?"

Julian looked away from me for a moment. "Her name is Theresa Sinclair. It was Mallaidh before she married the Prince, and while she gained his name, he refused to have her crowned Princess. Princess Elisabeth Nicolette Sinclair was the only woman to have that title while he reigned as Prince. You look a little bit like her, maybe even more than your parents." She looked back at me and smiled.

"Alexei told me he had seen her painting." We smiled at each other before she continued.

"The Duchess only has the power of a regent. She has no ability to make the people abide by her will. She has tried to enact laws to gain more control, but the rest of the Elder Children have kept her from gaining too much power." She paused. "I won't lie to you, Elisabeth. The past fourteen years have been hard for the Malhairer. The Duchess continues to call herself the regent although most of the Elder Children have agreed that I am your legal guardian. She is trying to retain her control by pointing to the very true fact that Nicholas was only the Blood Heir when he died, not the Prince, and as a result, you have never been made the Blood Heir. That your father eloped with a woman outside the Malhairer has given her room to maneuver and manipulate, two things she excels at. Some of the Elder Children have been afraid to look to you as our next ruler because they didn't believe you would have the ability to rule by your will."

"You mean using the special abilities that I apparently have despite my mother's completely human DNA. Julian, what are the Malhairer? Alexei tried very hard to cover up the fact that he said they are not entirely human. He made it sound like a better human, but that's not really it, is it?" It was one of the questions I wasn't sure I really wanted an answer for, but I needed to know what I was as well as who.

Julian's surprise showed, but before she could say anything there was a knock at the door, and Alexei walked back in.

"Perfect timing," I mumbled.

"I heard that, Elisabeth. And I heard your question before I came in ." He looked at Julian. "I warned you that she would ask."

"Why shouldn't I ask?"

Alexei smiled at me as he put the tray of food on his desk. "I never said you should not ask. I was only trying to anticipate your questions for Julian and prepare her. It has been a question I have seen in the shadows in your eyes. You have a need to know who you are because you already feel the pull of your people. They need you in much the same way." He looked back to Julian as he crossed to the bed. "And you cannot explain how Chase is here and a part of the Malhairer without explaining exactly what you are."

"You're right, Sasha. I just didn't expect to have to do this now. She is still so young."

"But she is Nicholas's daughter and your future Princess. She has felt the differences all her life."

I looked at them, knowing the argument was already over, and Julian would tell me, but I wished she didn't feel so guilty about it. "Jules, don't feel like you're letting me down by telling me. I already know what my future holds as far as becoming the Princess. I won't be angry at you or resent you for being the one to say it. How could I? You're my godmother, my guardian, and I love you."

Julian's eyes spilled over, the tears sliding down her porcelain cheeks, enhancing rather than detracting from her stunning beauty. "You have asked Alexei how our families became aware of one another, how we have similar abilities? The Malhairer are more closely linked to vampires than you can imagine. We are hybrids."

My breath escaped my lungs, and I couldn't seem to remember how to get more air inside. My head was spinning. I felt Alexei touch my hand and then put both hands on the sides of my face so that I was looking at him. I heard his voice inside my head ordering me to breathe.

I took a deep breath and focused on him. "Am I a-"

He didn't let me finish my question. "No! No, Elisabeth, I swear to you the Malhairer are not vampires. You are not a monster."

I took another deep breath to steady myself and whispered the only words I knew to be true as I exhaled. "Neither are you." I pushed his hands away from my face so I could look at Julian. "Then what exactly?"

"A hybrid. We are human, but we have vampire-like qualities. We are born completely human, and as we age, we gain more abilities. Many of the Malhairer never develop more than added speed and some mental persuasion, but the royal court has more, like the healing abilities that I have."

"So we don't have to go through any transformation like Alexei did when he was attacked?"

Julian shuddered. "No, thank God. I'm sorry, Sasha. Nicholas told me a little of what you endured, but I had no idea you told Elisabeth."

Alexei's face was unreadable. "She asked. It was one answer I could give her."

Julian looked at me. "No transformation like that and no blood dependence beyond the ceremonial palm cutting to bind the blood of our ruler with that of the people. Don't worry about any of that. The important thing is that members of the court, including the Duchess and her son, have other abilities as well."

"What other kinds are there?" I was more than a little afraid to ask.

"The Elder Children are called that because they are older than the rest of us. The families of the royal court come from the purest bloodline from the origin of our heritage. Not even they know how we came into existence, but they are the oldest. They live longer than most of the Malhairer, and all of us live longer than a typical human."

"Then how did my grandfather die when my father was so young?"

Julian must have anticipated my question because she nodded. "Prince Augustin gave up his life. There are certain rituals that we must complete at various times during our lives. Over the centuries, a small few have found reasons to leave the Malhairer – some for love, some because their bloodline had thinned to the point that they no longer had any real abilities. They cut themselves off from the Malhairer and became completely human. No one knows how the Prince could cut himself off from his people, but somehow he did. Instead of becoming human, he simply died. I think it's what he wanted, but it was one of the worst things to ever happen to our people."

"What about the Duchess? If she is part of the court and ages slower, what other abilities does she have?"

"She can manipulate her appearance. She uses it to maintain her youth and beauty, but she could appear to be any age or change her features so she would be disguised."

"Change her features?"

Julian looked uncomfortable. "There are so many things about the Malhairer you don't understand. This is one of those abilities that is closely related to vampiric powers."

"What do you mean?"

Julian looked surprised. "Alexei didn't tell you that vampires can change their features. That was what made me suspicious in Charly's description at lunch the day I left you

310

here. She said his eyes changed between blue and green. Eyes are the hardest to control."

I jerked around to look at Alexei. "You can change your appearance? You never said anything like that."

Julian answered me. "He can't change everything. It's more subtle, he could change his bone structure in his face and his build slightly, but he can't change his mass or his height. He could change his hair color if he wanted to but I think it's always been that color."

"But he could look older? He's not stuck as a teenager forever?"

"He could look like an older version of himself or a brother or cousin. It would be difficult to look completely different."

"It would require taking more human blood than I would ever agree to, especially after my agreement with your father."

I turned back to Julian. "And the Malhairer can do the same? We can change our appearance?"

"Some can, usually only the royal court, the nobility. It is not easy to do and, for the Malhairer, it requires some specific blood rites."

I made a face that let Julian know how repulsive that sounded to me. "Are there lots of rituals that have to do with blood?"

Julian smiled gently. "There are some since we are descended from a hybrid ancestor. But we need to focus on this Chase."

"You think he is someone else, looking like a teenage student."

"I think he is the Duchess's son, Gideon."

"The one you and my father were raised with? Jules, how could he do that to me when he's practically my uncle?"

"It's about the power, Elisabeth. He really was trying to make you his forever. Some of the strongest powers in the Elder Children are the ones most closely related to vampire powers. I think that he believed if he could have sex with you, specifically if he could be the first one to have sex with you, and he could possess your body as well as your mind and blood, that you would be his puppet. If you weren't as strong as you are, it may have worked."

"Do you mean he would have tried to drink my blood?" I was disgusted by the idea.

Alexei answered. "Do you remember Charly's description of what he did to her, licking the blood off her face even as he hit her to make her bleed more? He would have loved to taste your blood and with it your power."

"Controlling you would give them real control over the Elder Children and the entire Malhairer. They will try to deny you or control you if they can, Elisabeth. Even if the sex didn't give him control over your thoughts, they might have tried to trap you into a marriage."

I shook my head in complete disbelief. "I'm only fifteen. How could they do something like that?"

Julian smiled a little. "You've forgotten that the Malhairer live in a closed off world. From the time Nicholas and I were children, everyone expected us to marry. It was practically an arranged marriage in the oldest traditions. The Blood Heir must marry and have children to ensure the line continues to the next generation. It usually isn't as desperate as your grandfather caused it to become, but they would use the upheaval of the past twenty years as an excuse to get what they want."

"Then everything that has happened since I arrived here at the Academy has been a trick or a lie. Chase, or Gideon if that's who he is, knew exactly who I was and has been trying to manipulate me this whole time."

Alexei put his arm around my shoulders in a gentle hug. "Not everything has been a trick or a lie, Elisabeth."

I leaned into him for a moment to let him know I didn't mean him. Then I stood up, walked to the window, and opened the curtain. The sun had gone down, and I could see the stars clear enough to count them. There were so many questions that made sense now and so many new questions that I hadn't even begun to really understand. How long would I live? How had my father been able to make a life with my mother, knowing her normal lifespan was far shorter than his should have been? Did he hope I would inherit his abilities, or had he wanted me to be like my mother? Why had my grandfather ended his life? There were as many questions as stars and as much chance to get answers for these new ones as actually touching a star.

"Why didn't they just kill me when they killed my parents? Why am I still alive?" I heard Julian's sharp intake of air, but I didn't turn away from the window.

Alexei moved closer to me. "The box, Elisabeth. They need what it holds."

"She has the box? Nick's box?"

I had to turn back to her. I went to my backpack and pulled out the box she had given me along with my father's box.

"How? I have looked everywhere for this."

"It was hidden inside Ju-ju, the teddy bear you sent to me. I don't know who put it there or when, but I've always had it. I know it has a secret compartment, but I don't know how to open it." I paused. "I'm sorry I didn't tell you about it before."

Julian laughed. "Elisabeth, darling. I don't care that you didn't tell me as long as it's safe. As far as opening it, I hope that's something we can figure out, but we don't need to do it tonight."

"What do we need to do tonight?" My shoulders and neck were stiff, and I could feel the beginnings of a headache. Too much had happened since Alexei and I had skipped class that morning.

"You need to rest." Julian looked from me to Alexei. Something passed between them that I couldn't understand. "I need to check on some things, but I can't leave you unprotected."

"Leave? Are you leaving the Academy?"

"No, but I am leaving Kirkwynd Hall. I need to check some of the buildings on campus. I told you that there were safeguards in place so that the kind of violence that Charly endured should not have been possible here. I need to check those areas."

"Is it Malhairer persuasion? Like setting a ward on the trapdoor in my room that would keep people from wanting to use it?"

Julian shot a look at Alexei that seemed to accuse him of talking too much. "Yes. I need to see if they have been removed or damaged."

"Would they stop Chase if he really is Malhairer?"

"No. If they are intact, then it is more proof of what he is."

"They would not have stopped me either," Alexei said. "The Malhairer persuasion works on humans and on Malhairer who are weaker in power."

"The important thing is that I will not be able to protect you tonight, Elisabeth."

"Do you think he'll come after me tonight?"

"I don't think so, but I can't take any chances with your safety. I would like Sasha, I mean Alexei, to guard you. After everything that has happened today, do you feel comfortable staying here?"

It took me a moment to realize she was asking if Chase's attacks on me and on Charly had made me feel uncomfortable staying alone with Alexei. "I told you before that I don't hold Alexei responsible for anything Chase did. I know Alexei; he would never hurt me."

Julian turned to Alexei. "Then you must keep her safe while she rests. Tomorrow we will find this Chase, and, if he is Gideon, we will take care of him permanently." As Julian said his name, the look on her face hardened, and I could see the depth of her anger and the icy rage that would demand swift and merciless justice. I felt strangely reassured to see that she could be so fierce.

"Good night, Jules. I'll meet you in my room in the morning. I want to check on Charly before we deal with Chase."

She nodded. "Don't-"

Alexei interrupted her. "I know, Julian. Do not let her out of my sight. Do not let her go into the tunnels alone." Alexei gave Julian one of his rare, true smiles. She returned it with one of her own equally rare smiles before she slipped out the secret doorway.

Alexei pointed me toward the food that had gone untouched. "You need to eat to keep your strength up if you plan to confront Chase."

315

I shook my head at him. "I don't think my stomach agrees with you right now. It was a lot to learn."

"If you refuse to eat, then you must try to rest. Would you like me to turn out the lights?"

"Can we leave the curtain open? For a while, I mean. I know it has to be closed before dawn, but I like the starlight."

"I have a difficult time denying you anything, and this is an easy thing to give you. Get up on my bed, and I will open the curtain wide enough that you can see the stars from there, then I will turn out the lights."

I did exactly as Alexei told me. It took a little while for my eyes to adjust to the dark, but I heard him moving around the room and settle into the chair Julian had been using. I knew I was only hearing him because he was purposely making enough noise for me to hear.

"Don't sit there, Alexei. I need you closer."

His voice was warm and deep in the darkness. "Are you certain? You have been through so much."

"Nothing that you caused. You held me when I cried before we found Charly, but you've barely touched me since. I need to feel you near me." I touched the bed next to me as I leaned against his headboard, knowing that he could see perfectly even if my eyes were still adjusting. This time when he moved, I didn't hear any sounds. One second he was in the chair, and the next he was beside me on the bed. He kept just enough distance between us for me to know it was on purpose.

"What are you worried about, Alexei?"

He sounded surprised. "What do you mean? Other than keeping you safe from one of the more powerful members of the Malhairer's court?"

"You know that's not what I meant. Every time I learn something new about myself or my family, you seem to pull away from me as if that new thing will be the last straw, and I'll finally reject you once and for all. It's never gonna happen." I scooted closer to him and tucked myself under his arm.

"I am sorry, Elisabeth. It is hard to change several lifetimes of experience. Even Nicholas, as close as we were, could never accept me the way you have."

I snickered.

"What?"

"I hope you and my father never acted the way we do, Alexei. It would be impossible for me to think about kissing you if I knew you had kissed my father." I dissolved into laughter. Alexei sat frozen for a moment before he smiled.

"That was definitely not what I meant, and you know it."

I grinned at him. "I know, but it was worth it a million times over to see you smile and be less serious."

"Thank you, Elisabeth. Thank you for bringing smiles back to me." The soft words echoed in the room for a moment. "Have you been thinking about that?"

There was something different in his voice, but I didn't know what he meant. "Thinking about what?"

"Thinking about our kiss."

I reached up to hold the hand resting on my shoulder. "Well, I have had kind of a busy day – cutting class with you, our trip into Charly's mind, our argument, that awful picnic and everything that happened to Charly, and then Julian and learning the truth about my family." I took a deep breath and reminded myself that Elisabeth Sinclair was bold. "I guess I've only thought about it five or six thousand times." A nervous giggle escaped.

"After what Chase did to you in the barn, I did not expect you to be thinking of kisses. I am glad you do not look at me as you do him."

I thought of all the times Alexei had tried to put distance between us. "You are nothing alike. You are my friend, and he is a monster."

Alexei gave me a one-armed hug across the shoulders, letting me know that he remembered too. "You need to rest."

I sat quietly for a few minutes. "Why did Julian leave us here? I know what she said, but she didn't have to leave us all night."

"She knew you needed time away from her to process what she had told you. She knew I will protect you with my own life. She knew we need to be able to trust each other before we confront Chase. Maybe she recognized something else, but it does not matter. Julian follows her instincts without having to question them."

I smiled. "As opposed to me. I have to have an answer for everything."

"No, you do not. You have taken much on faith because you were following your instincts, the way you did when you kissed me. You believed I was wrong, and you followed your instincts."

"I'm not sure that would be an instance that Julian would point to if she knew." I paused and twisted enough so I could see his face. "Does she know?"

"That we have kissed? I did not tell her, nor did I tell her about the bonding, which I seem to have been wrong about. Perhaps what I thought was a bonding was just a manifestation of your abilities."

"But Julian said the Malhairer couldn't read minds."

"No, but before yesterday when I felt your panic, I had been inside your mind in your dreams. Perhaps the connection was enough for your mind to see me as a place to find help, as if you were calling to me for assurance when you were frightened."

"That kind of makes sense. I have known from the beginning that you would protect me."

Alexei slid his other arm around me. "Always."

"Can you . . . I mean, do you . . ." I didn't know how to ask the question I had wondered about since finding out the truth about Alexei.

"What do you want to know? Now that Julian has told you the truth about your family, I have no promises keeping me from giving you any answer that I possess."

"I've been wondering for a while, and now with Jules here . . ." I stared at his face half-hidden in shadow, knowing he could see clearly. "What would he think?"

"Your father?"

I nodded.

"Are you asking me what your father would think about the feelings I have for you? The kiss?"

I nodded again, feeling the flush in my cheeks.

Alexei gave me a soft laugh. "You cannot hide your blushes in the dark, Elisabeth. I can smell the blood rushing to the surface of your skin. Does it bother you to imagine Nicholas's reaction?"

"Some. I just don't know enough about him to predict what he would have thought."

"And I did, but I am not certain what he would think of this. Nicholas told me that he hoped I would someday find a mate. No, that is not what he said. He was newly married to your mother, and he hoped I would find a love like they shared. I told

319

him it could never happen because my family would never turn a human, and I could never love a vampire who cared nothing for human life. He was the one to first suggest that I might meet someone within the Malhairer. Of course, if he had lived everything would be different. You would have known me all your life. This would not have happened. To answer your question, Elisabeth, I think your father would be glad to see me open myself up, but wary that it is with you. I know he would want you to have the chance to experience enough of life to know what you want for yourself."

"This morning you said I was too young to be thinking about being your – your mate and that I needed to experience more of life and know who I am. I'm finally starting to know who I am, and after today, I'm not sure how much more life experience I can take. I'm not saying I'm ready for promises that really are forever, but I also know that I care more about you than I knew. I told you earlier that I couldn't be Chase's because there is a part of me that already belongs to you. That you have and will always have a place in my heart."

His voice was filled with familiar caution and hesitation. "I remember."

"After everything Chase did and the reasons Julian said were behind it, I need you to kiss me."

I felt the tension freeze Alexei's body. "I do not understand what the one has to do with the other."

"I'm asking too much. It's not fair, I know. I'm not trying to start some kind of relationship. I guess I'm kind of using you to forget one. But this isn't about just using somebody, anybody. I need to know that you want me because of me, not because I'm in line to be Princess. Not even because I'm Nicholas's daughter. Just for me. Please."

I knew he could see the tears in my eyes and hear the shakiness of my voice, but I didn't care. He moved so that he was kneeling beside me. It left his face completely shadowed, except for some trick of the light that caught the blue of his eyes. He put his hand on my neck and pulled me to him. He kissed me so lightly that I might have imagined it. He breathed my name against my lips and kissed away the tear that had slipped down my cheek. When his mouth moved back to mine, I could taste the saltiness of my tear. Then I forgot everything except the feeling of Alexei's lips on mine and the gentle tangle of our tongues. The world again compressed to only include the space between us.

I felt something brushing at the edges of my mind. I had an instant of fear as I remembered the way Chase had pushed at me, but even as the fear registered, I realized it was Alexei, and he was already pulling his mind away from mine. I reached out, opening the door for him, the way I had that morning. But instead of him walking through a doorway, it was immediate.

His presence in my mind reassured me that he would always protect me, but also that he would always care about me, even if I had been Elisabeth Sawyer and not Elisabeth Sinclair. He had cared about my father and was worried about what would happen with the Malhairer, but none of those things mattered as much as I did.

I sighed against his lips, and he pulled back just enough to look at me. "Never doubt me, Elisabeth."

I shook my head, unable to speak. He moved again so that my back was leaning against his chest. "Sleep now, *moya lyubov'*."

I let Alexei soothe me with his quiet murmurings that I couldn't understand while his hand stroked my arm and his presence in my mind reassured me then, I fell asleep.

CHAPTER TWENTY-EIGHT

I woke up the next morning in Alexei's arms, but I knew he had moved while I was sleeping because the curtains had been closed sometime before dawn. He had left my mind while I slept, but I could sense him. It was as if my new abilities had imprinted on him.

"Hungry?" he asked just before my stomach rumbled. "Julian brought breakfast up a little while ago."

I was reluctant to leave his arms, but the smell of the food was too tempting. I sat at his desk and ate while he straightened his room.

"Does it bother you to see me eat?"

His smiled at me over his shoulder. "Not at all. Most females do not enjoy someone watching them while they eat."

"If it doesn't bother you, then come sit with me. Did you sleep? Do you sleep? I never thought to ask if you were dreaming too when you were in my dreams."

He moved one of the extra chairs from the other side of the room and sat across from me. "Vampires do require some rest, although nothing like the amounts of sleep human bodies require. I was not asleep when I entered your dreams. It would have been too difficult to control things that way. And, no, I did not sleep last night. I was guarding you."

I was half-way through the scrambled eggs and bacon. I took another drink of my orange juice. "This is good. How long ago was Julian here?"

"About ten minutes. She brought you clothes and things to shower over here if you would like."

I nodded. "What is she planning to do about Chase?"

"She has Emma looking for him. All the safeguards were still intact. We do not think he has left the Academy. Julian is more convinced than before that Chase is truly Gideon and that he will make another attempt with you. She believes that he will think you could never resist him for long, but that he may try to kidnap you, perhaps taking you to his rooms in Wycliffe Hall."

"Do you think it's a coincidence that he is in Wycliffe when that's the dorm that was damaged by fire?"

"No. It is the only place I cannot quickly get to through my tunnels. I never changed the access points after they were damaged."

"Julian told me Gideon was sent here when she and my father were. Did you meet Gideon then?"

"Once. He was in Wycliffe Hall then too."

"How can he change so much that you wouldn't know him now?"

"I do not think he can completely. He can change his appearance, but not his scent. I never considered the idea that Chase could be one of the few Malhairer that I know."

I was finished with my breakfast. "So once we find him and we're sure Chase is Gideon, what is Julian planning for him?"

"We will deal with him." Alexei's voice was as hard as I had ever heard it.

"I don't want you to kill him."

"If he deserves to die, I will provide swift justice."

"No. If he deserves to die, Julian and I will deal with him. I don't want you to be the one responsible for ending his life."

"I will not feel guilty for taking his life."

"How would you kill him? Would you drain his body dry?"

Alexei shook his head. "No, not if he is one of the Malhairer. It could be dangerous for me to drink the blood of someone with such power."

"Then how? Tell me how you would kill him."

Alexei flinched slightly at the word "kill," but I saw it. "I would break his neck. The Malhairer may not be as easy to kill as normal humans, but they still die."

"You can't do it. You would blame yourself and wonder if you killed him for justice or vengeance. I will not let you be the one."

Alexei stood in front of me. "You are not yet the Princess of the Malhairer but even if you were, you would not be my ruler. If I choose to kill him, I will do so."

I stood up to face him, but being several inches shorter kept me from looking right into his eyes. "And if he is one of the Malhairer, then he is one of my people and subject to my law and the agreement you made with my father."

Alexei blew out a soft whistle, and shook his head ruefully. "You are already more of a ruler than Theresa Mallaidh could ever be." He gave me a slight bow. "I will agree to your reasoning for the moment, Princess."

I knew I had only stopped the argument, not won it. I finished my breakfast and got my shower. When I was dressed, I asked Alexei if he was ready to take me back to Julian.

He nodded, and led me through his secret door, through the staircases and tunnels back to my own hidden door. I knocked as he tripped the switch. Julian was sitting on the side of Charly's bed which wasn't littered with Lila Grace's stuffed animals. The dark bruises on Charly's face had already faded to the yellow that came after days of healing, and the tiny cuts were almost unnoticeable. They both looked at us as we walked in.

"Good morning, Elisabeth. You look rested."

"I slept well, Jules. How are you, Charly?"

Charly smiled, not quite her normal grin, but close. "Almost back to normal. It still hurts to move my mouth too much, but I feel better."

Julian smiled slightly. "She was ready to argue that she should be in class, but I was able to persuade her to stay hidden until we find Chase."

"And that took how much work?" I teased.

Charly tossed one of Lila Grace's stuffed animals at me. "That's not nice, Elisabeth!"

I dodged the pink cat, and Alexei caught it reflexively. I took it from him and put it away on Lila Grace's bed. "It may not be nice, but it's true." My smile faded with my teasing. "I'm so glad you're better today."

Charly was serious as well. "Miss Julian has helped me a lot. I know that Chase is pretty screwed up, but I'm not afraid of him. I only wish I could help take him down."

I looked at Julian who shook her head slightly. "Just leave him to us. I promise that he will get what he deserves, Charly."

She smiled at me. "I know he will." Julian stood up as Charly continued. "I'm okay. I think I'm going to read one of your books, if that's cool."

"Of course. Do you want me to bring you one so you don't have to get up?" I asked.

"Can you bring me those two Bronte books that were out of order?"

I laughed, remembering how she hadn't understood what the fuss over their order was about. "You've got it." I retrieved the books. "If you need anything-" I began.

"I have your cell number," she finished. She might be battered and bruised, but she was still Charly, and Charly refused to remain a victim. She was a survivor, and she would fight her way back from this attack. I hoped she could tell from my face how glad I was that she was my friend.

Julian motioned Alexei to the secret door. "We'll let you rest now, but we're only a phone call away."

Charly gave her a little wave as the three of us went through the doorway and down the steps. Alexei made sure the door was secure behind us.

"Where are we going?" I asked when we went through the door at the bottom of the stairs.

Julian looked at Alexei. "When did you last feed?"

Alexei winced, but I answered for him. "The day before yesterday. Alexei was hunting animals in the mountains during the storm."

Julian nodded at me but never took her eyes from Alexei. "Did you hunt well?"

He straightened his back so that his full height, well over six feet, was more noticeable. Julian was tall, but she had to tip her head back to maintain eye contact. "I fed, Julian."

There was a tension between them that I didn't understand. I knew Alexei was finished with this line of conversation, but Julian didn't let it go.

"What did you feed from, and how much did you take?"

Alexei had gone completely tense. "You do not need to know."

Julian reached out and grabbed Alexei's arm in a movement so fast I almost missed it. It was the first time I had seen her demonstrate any of the abilities of the Malhairer other than persuasion. "I don't care how tender your feelings are, or how much you still want to play human for Elisabeth. I do need to know. I will not go into battle against a fully blooded member of the royal court with an untested child and a weakened vampire. I will not allow you to put Elisabeth's life in jeopardy because you are squeamish."

I couldn't stand to hear her talk to Alexei that way. "I will not allow you to use him to kill Chase!"

Alexei roared at Julian almost overtop my own yelling. "You will not take Elisabeth into battle at all! She must be protected."

When we realized what the other had been saying, we turned on each other.

"You can't keep me out of this!"

"I am not your slave to order out of a fight!"

Julian smiled. "If you two are finished." We both glared at her. "I have no intention of putting Elisabeth in danger, but she is the only one of us that knows what this Chase Elliot looks like."

"I can go into her mind and see his image for myself," Alexei answered.

"You will not enter my mind uninvited, Alexei Mikhailovich!"

Julian cleared her throat. "As I was saying, Elisabeth knows Chase. As for using Alexei to kill, nothing is that simple when the Malhairer are involved. We are not easily killed, much like a vampire. Fire, of course, and beheadings are the two most certain methods, but if Chase is really Gideon, I need answers from him before he dies. And so, my original questions stand: what did you feed from, and how much did you take?"

Alexei was silent and still as a statue for a long moment, but he finally answered. "I fed from two deer. I took all the first could spare, but I stopped within seconds of taking the other."

Julian frowned. "Why? Was there something wrong with it?"

Alexei glanced at me. "No. Elisabeth called out."

Julian looked at me. "What were you doing in the mountains?"

"She was not in the mountains. I heard her calling in my mind. She was with Chase and became scared. Between the way he was trying to manipulate her mind and the connection we had already established, it appears that she inadvertently called to me. All I knew was that she was afraid, so I left my hunting to find her."

"Sasha, if you have-"

Alexei interrupted her. "I swear on Nicholas's soul that I have done nothing to cause this. It was accidental."

I was half afraid to call attention to myself but tired of hiding behind them. "When I found out the truth about Alexei, he told me he had sworn to protect me. Is it really so strange that with all these abilities that I barely understand, let alone control, I would reach out to him when I was afraid, even if I didn't realize I was doing it?"

"No, it's not, but it does complicate things," Julian answered.

Alexei laughed that sharp, bitter laugh that I hated to hear. "When have things surrounding Nicholas or Elisabeth ever not been complicated?"

Julian's response was the wry twist of her lips that barely qualified as a smile. The death of my father and the search for me, not to mention the loss of Alexei's entire family, had stolen so much from the two people I loved most. I wondered if there would ever be anything that could heal the pain they had endured.

"Then, you need to feed more to be at full strength." It was not a question, but I looked to see if Alexei would answer Julian.

He sighed. "If Gideon is a fully blooded member of the royal court, then yes, I do."

I looked at the light filtering through the tunnels. "But the sun is shining. How can he hunt now?"

Julian looked at me sharply. "Who mentioned hunting? Most of the members of Alexei's vampire family never hunted animals."

I remembered Alexei's explanation of the end to the fighting between our families. The Malhairer had demanded that the vampires only feed from people with fully informed consent, not using their vampire powers to alter their memories. My shock and displeasure at the thought of Alexei feeding from someone at the Academy must have shown on my face because Alexei turned away from me and Julian's smile was just a little smug.

"I am not like my family, Julian. I do not have the control they had when it comes to taking human blood." His voice was so quiet I almost didn't hear it.

All traces of a smile left Julian. "I will not let you lose yourself, Sasha. I will even keep you from breaking your word to Nicholas." She left through the tunnels, proving that she knew them better than she had admitted to me.

I stood with Alexei's back to me. I hated that he was so withdrawn. I started to move to him, but I had only taken one step when he spoke.

"Do not come close to me, Elisabeth."

I stopped moving. "Why not? I can understand you not wanting me to know the details of how you feed or what you feed on, but why can't I stand beside you now?"

"Because it is never enough for you. You will want to touch my arm or look at my face, and I cannot bear that right now."

"Why? Have I done something wrong?"

I heard that bitter laugh again and flinched. "Not you. I am the monster who must steal blood from other creatures to survive. I just cannot stand to see the disgust in your eyes at the thought of me feeding."

I did move then. I crossed to him and tugged on his arm so he would have to see me. "You're wrong, Alexei. It's not disgust in my eyes. I don't understand it, and sometimes I do have a bad reaction when I think about it, but not because of you. I've seen all the horror movies where the vampire sucks the blood out of the throat of the beautiful but stupid blonde. Sometimes it's hard to keep those dumb movie images out of my head."

He looked down at me, eyes so shadowed it was impossible to see their color. "You always find a way to make me feel better, Elisabeth, and I adore you for trying, but there is nothing that will make me feel better about taking blood from a human."

"Why? If what Julian said is true and your family did, then why is it so hard for you?"

"Because I am so much younger than they were. They were all centuries older and had more control. I can still remember the taste of the human blood that the creatures who made me fed to me when I was newly changed."

"Have you ever had human blood since you were taken in by your family?"

Some shadowed flitted across Alexei's face before he answered. "I have tasted human blood twice, but only because it was a part of a ritual and only a small amount. The taste was . . . I told you once it was more addicting than anything the human world has for comparison."

"You told me the craving never went away." I paused. "Are you afraid that you will want to kill whoever Julian brings you to feed from?"

"Julian will not allow that to happen. Even she knows better than to violate the treaty I made with Nicholas."

I touched his cheek with my palm, caressing it the way he had caressed mine before. "It will be okay. I promise."

I don't know what he would have answered because Julian appeared from around a corner. Alexei moved away from me in a heartbeat, but I knew Julian had seen my hand on his face. Then I saw the figure trailing behind her.

"Emma!" The golden curls around her head bounced as she looked at me and then Alexei. "What is she doing here?"

Julian tried to soothe me. "It's okay, Elisabeth. Emma has known who and what Alexei is for a while now."

Alexei looked at Emma in surprise. "You have?"

Emma nodded once. "I've known since the day Charly blew up the chemistry lab. You don't have to worry. I've kept your secret."

"But why did you bring her, Julian?" I was less concerned with what Emma knew than why Julian had brought her.

Julian looked at me, her emerald eyes like chips of green ice. "Alexei needs to feed, and this does not violate his treaty with Nicholas."

I shook my head. "No. You are not making Alexei feed from Emma."

"It's okay, Elisabeth. I want to help get rid of Chase, and if this is what it takes, then I'll gladly do it." Emma sounded completely herself so I knew Julian hadn't used any kind of coercion.

Julian spoke sharply. "This is not your concern, Elisabeth. Alexei must feed, and Emma is a willing participant. Or is there some other reason you have to object?"

Alexei spoke before I could. "Emma, do you truly understand what I am? Do you freely offer your blood to sustain me?"

Emma nodded. "I do, but I was only trying to help. I didn't mean to upset Elisabeth."

I looked at her wide eyes and knew that she had agreed, at least in part, because of our friendship. "I don't want you to feel obligated because of me."

She looked at me. "It's not just you. It's also about Alexei. He has always been kind to me. And it's about Charly and all the others that Chase has hurt. I'm not a fool. I knew it was more than just drugs and hypnotism, but it was the best cover I could think of for Charly and Lila Grace. They don't know anything about these dangers, but they have felt the effects."

I nodded slowly.

Alexei turned to Julian. "I want Elisabeth to wait somewhere else while I do this."

Julian shook her head even before he finished speaking. "Unacceptable. You said yourself that this Chase would change his tactics. It is not safe for Elisabeth to be away from one or both of us. And I know you aren't asking me to leave you alone to feed from Emma."

I could sense Alexei's frustration, but Julian pushed the point.

"You are still trying to play human for Elisabeth. You don't want to talk about it in front of her, let alone have her actually witness you feeding. You are not human or even a part of the Malhairer. You are a vampire. Stop pretending otherwise."

I hated hearing Julian's words, but they made me realize there was some truth in them. I spoke slowly and quietly, knowing I would have Alexei's attention. "She's right. You are a vampire. And you don't trust me."

The words I expected came from Alexei immediately. "Of course I trust you."

"No, you don't. If you trusted me, you would believe me when I said I don't believe you are a monster. You would believe me when I said that you are still my friend no matter what. But you don't trust my friendship enough to be who you truly are." I knew my words were cutting into Alexei's heart. I knew that the truth was he hated his own existence, believing he was a demon with no chance for redemption. But we needed him to be strong, even if that meant I had to watch him put his lips on Emma's neck and drink her blood.

Julian gave Emma a pat on her shoulder, and Emma went to Alexei. She stood in front of him and waited. Alexei looked over her head at Julian and at me. I could see the drop of his shoulders when he accepted the inevitable. I thought he would just lean over her there, but he didn't. He took her hand and walked to the doorway to our room. He opened the door and sat down with Emma next to him on the bottom steps. He removed the watch from her left arm and turned the sleeve up before looking at her face.

"Thank you, Emma, for your gift of life." I held my breath as his eyes met mine. He never blinked or looked away from me as he raised Emma's wrist to his lips and bit down. He let me see the pleasure of tasting her blood and the struggle to maintain control. I knew that if I tried to enter his mind, he would not be able to stop me because he was so focused on controlling his bloodlust. I also knew that the last thing I wanted was to be in his mind because then he would know how terribly jealous I was of Emma in that moment. I wished I could have been the one to offer him the life-sustaining liquid, but my blood was not safe.

After a moment that could have lasted minutes or hours as far as I knew, Emma slumped against Alexei's shoulder. He didn't break eye contact, and his mouth never left her wrist, but his free arm circled her body and held her up with her back against his chest. The jealousy spiked in me.

Julian moved over to Emma. "It is enough, Alexei." He still held eye contact with me, but I heard the low growl. Julian spoke again. "I said it is enough. Release her, Sasha."

Alexei blinked once. He looked down at Emma, who was conscious but pale, and pulled away from her wrist. I tried not to shudder as he slowly and deliberately licked her wrist where he had been feeding. He watched my face as he did it.

Julian pulled Emma away from Alexei and wrapped a white bandage around her wrist and gave her a bottle of some flavored sports drink. I suppose it was like when people donated in a blood bank; Emma would need to eat and drink to rebuild her system.

Alexei continued to watch me as he spoke to Julian. "Is she alright?"

"Of course she is. Was it enough? Will you be strong enough to fight Gideon?" Julian looked at him while she helped Emma find a place to sit and lean against a wall.

"I am ready."

I shook my head and looked at Julian. "I haven't changed my mind about using Alexei to kill Gideon."

Julian practically rolled her eyes at me. "Elisabeth, I cannot defeat Gideon by myself, but I am not asking Alexei to kill for me. We need answers first. When the time comes to deliver justice, I promise I will not have to ask Alexei to finish him for me."

Alexei stood and came towards me. He seemed different somehow. He moved in a different way. Predatory. "Enough of your concern for me, Elisabeth. I know what you fear, but I will not regret killing something that must die to ensure your safety. God will not damn me for protecting you, only for failing in that vow. It is time to find Chase."

Julian left Emma and stood between me and Alexei. "We don't have time for this nonsense between the two of you. At this moment I don't care what either of you think you're going to accomplish, but in case you've forgotten, they don't just want to kill Elisabeth. They want to control her and through her all the Malhairer. We have to find Chase now."

Emma mumbled something, but I couldn't hear her.

"Did you hear what she said?" I asked Alexei, but he just shook his head. We all moved closer so we could hear better.

Emma was obviously tired, but she looked at each of us. "Chase will be waiting in the chapel. I told him Elisabeth was going to be there around ten."

"Why did you tell him that?" I asked.

"He thought he was using his power on me, but I just went along with him. He was trying to find out what Charly said. He thinks you're confused because Charly doesn't remember you leaving the picnic."

Julian smiled. "Finally a piece of luck in our favor. Emma, I want Alexei to carry you back to your room. Lila Grace is supposed to be there to watch over Charly. You need to rest, but you also need to keep the two of them in your room until one of us tells you it's over. Can you do that?"

Emma nodded, and Alexei picked her up and carried her up the steps. Julian took advantage of our moment alone to whisper to me.

"I have no intention of letting Alexei kill Gideon, but I cannot keep him out of the fight anymore than I can you. I know you care deeply for him, but you still have so much to learn about yourself and your abilities."

"Don't worry, Jules. I'm not trying to date him. I know he would be a serious relationship, and I'm just a teenager. I wouldn't even have the first idea about what would happen with our different abilities."

"I'm glad you're being sensible, but it also concerns me that you've obviously thought about this." Julian sighed. "I guess we'll just have to talk about it later."

I laughed. "Jules, I would have to be blind and deaf not to have imagined dating Alexei, at least for a minute, but I'm not stupid. I know he isn't the dating kind."

Julian laughed too. "I suppose you're right, at least about the blind and deaf part. He always was a chick magnet. Oh, do people even say that anymore – chick magnet?"

"No, they do not, but if you choose to label me that way . . ." Alexei let the thought trail off as he walked back out the doorway. "Have I ever mentioned to either of you what amazing hearing vampires possess?" he asked.

Between Alexei's dry tone and the look of mortification on Julian's face at being overheard, I dissolved into giggles. Julian started laughing as well. Alexei shook his head, but our laughter was contagious, and he joined in as well. Perhaps it was a way to relieve the tension before we went to find Chase, but I was glad we had that moment to share before Alexei led us through the tunnels to the doorway that opened to the Academy's chapel.

CHAPTER TWENTY-NINE

Alexei stood silently and listened for sounds inside the chapel. He shook his head, and we went in. It was the first time I had been inside the church. It was simply built with rich woodwork polished to a gleaming shine. I didn't know much about church architecture, but I was pretty sure this chapel was built without all the formal parts of the medieval cathedrals. There was a simple oak pulpit in the front at the center, and the pews were lined up in two columns with the main aisle dividing them in the center. We came out a secret wall panel in the front of the church near the stairwell that led to the bell pulls for the steeple.

"It's so peaceful in here."

Alexei nodded. "It is not as ornate as the churches I saw in Russia, but it is a holy place."

I looked at Julian. She seemed to be looking for something. "If this was a Catholic church I would light a candle for Nicholas and for Carrie. I suppose God doesn't care about candles as much as the prayers in our hearts." I wished I had time to talk to Julian about what she believed about God.

"We need to be out of sight when Chase comes in. I do not want him to sense Julian and get away."

"Will he come in through the front doors?" I asked.

"No, not if he is Gideon," Julian answered. "As a fully blooded member of the royal court, he will be as limited by the sun's movements as Alexei. I will hide behind the organ. The distance should mask my presence until it is too late." I saw the large instrument on the wall opposite the panel. I looked at Alexei.

"I do not need something to hide behind. Look up, Elisabeth." I did as he told me and saw open rafters above the pulpit area that narrowed until they became the steeple housing the church bells.

"But how are you supposed to get up there?"

Alexei smiled. "I suppose there are some benefits to being a well-fed vampire." He kissed the top of my head and jumped. He went straight up into the air and grabbed a beam with one hand, swinging himself onto a higher beam. I couldn't stop looking up even after he had moved so deep into the shadows that I could no longer see him.

Julian looked at my face and muttered up toward the emptiness. "Show off." She moved to the organ and started to disappear behind it.

"What am I supposed to do?" I was standing in the middle of the aisle.

Julian motioned me to the front. "Sit on one of the pews, on my side of the building, and wait."

I heard Alexei's voice drifting down to me. "You might try praying." I wasn't sure if he was teasing or meant it. It wasn't a bad suggestion. I moved to the second pew close to Julian's hiding place. I leaned against the bench in front of me, resting my chin on my folded hands. Would God listen to my prayers now when we were trying to capture someone with every intention of killing him? Would God consider that murder or justice? Maybe He would expect us to show mercy. The memory of Charly describing her attack replayed in my mind and all thought of mercy was gone. I would put my faith in a God of justice in this case. If Chase was Gideon and a member of the Malhairer, then his crime against Charly was a violation of our rules. If I was to be the Princess, then I needed to know that I could deliver the justice that such leadership required.

I didn't wait very long before I heard the secret panel open. A part of me still hoped it wasn't Chase, that this was all a terrible mistake, but I felt him approach the way Julian had described. I wondered if my presence so close to her was helping to mask hers. I looked up at him hoping my face gave nothing away.

"Elisabeth, you're here. I have been looking everywhere for you." He seemed like the same boy I'd met in the student lounge, but I wondered what he was planning.

"Why were you looking for me, Chase?" I used his name so Alexei and Julian would know this was the right person. I saw Alexei jump straight down from the rafters, but he didn't make any sound, and Chase didn't notice. Alexei was blocking the secret panel so Chase had no way out.

"I was worried about you after our misunderstanding yesterday. You seemed so confused when you left."

I knew my face showed my reaction to 'misunderstanding' and 'confused,' but before I could say anything, Julian came out of her hiding place.

"You seem to be the one who is confused, Gideon. You don't seem to remember your own name." She moved quickly so that she was between me and him.

"Julian." He spat out her name like it tasted bad in his mouth. His voice was back to the cold, hard tone that I had heard in the stable.

"I'm so flattered you remember me. Why are you here, Gideon? Did your mother send you to kill Elisabeth?"

He laughed at her. "Why would we bother killing this pathetic imposter you're trying to pass off as Nicholas's child? She means nothing to us."

"If I'm supposed to be such an imposter, how did I stop you yesterday?" I knew Julian expected me to be quiet and let her handle him, but I was the only one who could choose how I would act. I was not going to let someone else fight all my battles.

"Obviously, it wasn't you at all. It was one of Julian's manipulations. She is trying to convince everyone that you are a dead child. I don't have time for your tricks, Julian." He turned to go back through the panel but stopped short when he saw Alexei.

"I think you should stay and talk. Try telling the truth this time," Alexei suggested in a low voice.

"What is this, a vampire in your service, Julian? You should know that breaks our laws."

"What laws, Gideon? The last time the Prince gave us a new law, he was still negotiating with their lord."

The first signs of pressure appeared in Gideon. His face was red, and he started to sweat as he screamed at Julian. "My mother outlawed all of these renegade vampires. He should be tied down outside to face the sun until he burns to ash like the rest of his family!"

I despised him in that moment, even more than yesterday when I heard how he attacked Charly. He had known about Alexei's family and gloried in their deaths. How could one man – one creature – who was supposed to be my family be so evil? I heard Julian respond to him, but it was as if I was underwater. Everything was slightly muted and distorted. It was vaguely similar to how he had tried to overwhelm my mind with his. Except this time, at the center of the feeling was the burning clarity of my hatred.

Julian was asking him how long they had known I was alive, how long they had known where I was, but I didn't care about answers like that. I had some questions of my own, and somehow I knew how to get answers from him.

"Stop." I spoke in a normal voice, but it sounded like I was speaking into an amplifier. It was ten times louder than I could have yelled and carried power through the air on its sound waves. Julian looked at me, but Gideon cringed. Alexei leaned against the wall, a small smile hovering on his lips.

"Kneel." The power in my voice would have been frightening to me if it hadn't come from a place of such fiery assurance. Gideon knelt in front of the pulpit as if he was a sinner pleading for salvation. "Did you help your mother deceive and murder Alexei's family?"

"Yes." He fought against saying it, but he could not stop himself.

"What have you been doing to the students here at the Academy?"

"I've been feeding on their blood."

"Why?" I was disgusted, but not surprised. There was a blackness in his spirit that I could sense, almost see.

"Because I want to. Because they are stupid humans." My eyes narrowed; his voice dropped to a growl. "Because I was hungry."

"Did your mother send you here to kill me?"

"No. She wants you alive."

"Why?" I walked around Julian to stand close to Gideon. She put her hands out like she wanted to stop me but never really tried.

He tried to put his hands across his mouth, but it couldn't stop the answers. "Because she needs you to control the Malhairer."

"Do you acknowledge that I am Elisabeth Julian Sinclair, the only child of Nicholas Augustin Merrick Sinclair, the Blood Heir of Augustin Ruarc Etienne Sinclair, the last Prince crowned of the Malhairer?"

He kept shaking his head even as he answered, "I do acknowledge it is so."

The burning center was wavering, threatening to break free of my control, but I had one more question I needed him to answer. The only question that truly mattered any more. "Did you help your mother kill my parents?"

His hazel eyes went wide and lightened to a pure gold. His features began to change. I wanted to look at Julian to see if she understood what was happening, but I was afraid to look away from him until I had my answer.

He threw himself on the floor of the church. "Please, God, don't make me answer this."

That alone was confirmation, but I wanted to make him say it. "It is not God you should beg for mercy." I saw fear in his eyes. "Tell me now!" My voice thundered in the small church, rattling the milky glass in the windows.

"She sent me to kill Nicholas. She didn't care about the human girl, but she wanted Nicholas and his child dead. I set the explosion on the boat. I knew the fire would destroy him."

Something shifted inside me. His guilt was confirmed; now I pronounced his sentence. "In starting that fire, you began a blaze that has burned for fourteen years, and now it will consume you." I don't know exactly what I did, but the fire burning in the core of my mind expanded or somehow jumped across the empty space. I saw it in my head a moment before I saw it in reality. The strange body that was part Chase and part whatever Gideon had once looked like was burning in a column of white fire that could have been sent from heaven. I watched him burn and felt only the cold embers of overdue justice. His death would not bring back my parents or any of Alexei's family. It would not take away the damage of his attack on Charly or any of the other students he had been abusing. It would keep him from ever harming another person. It was justice.

I don't know how long I would have stood there watching him burn if Julian hadn't grabbed my arm and pulled me away. Alexei opened the panel before we reached him. He pushed Julian in first and then picked me up to carry me. They could both move much faster than I could even when I was trying to hurry. I caught one final look at Chase/Gideon before the panel slid shut behind us. The skin had started to melt off his bones as he stayed on his knees where I had told him to kneel, but he was still alive. I wondered how long he would burn before he died.

CHAPTER THIRTY

I gradually became aware of voices calling my name, but I couldn't find a way to answer them. I felt a hand caressing my cheek. It seemed familiar, but I couldn't relax into it the way I remembered doing.

I heard a woman's voice and knew it was Julian, but her words didn't make sense. "It was too much for an untrained mind. It's been hours."

"Quiet, Julian. She has not been depleted. I can still feel the power inside her."

"This is all my fault. I should have found a way to train her."

"Elisabeth, you must answer me. Let me in."

I pictured the way I had heard Alexei calling me in my dreams. He had looked so handsome in his old-fashioned tuxedo with the tails. I wanted to see him like that again. I thought about the secret door in my own room and opened it. Alexei grinned at me, a huge smile I had never seen on his face before. He was standing at the door, dressed in the dark tuxedo. Julian was behind him, down one step. She was wearing the same red suit as the day she had found me. She was as beautiful as that day, but this time she was smiling too.

"Are you coming in?" I asked them. They both came into my room. Alexei rushed to put his arms around me and twirled me around, but Julian held back.

"What's wrong, Jules?"

"Nothing is wrong now, Elisabeth. You just look so beautiful."

I wondered what she meant for a moment before I realized how my dream appearance was always altered so that I looked older and how I was usually wearing a nightgown. I was surprised that I hadn't noticed because I had never felt entirely comfortable in that other body. I looked down at myself, already embarrassed, but I wasn't wearing the nightgown from either of my dreams. I was still wearing that more grown-up body, but this time it was just me the way Alexei said it would be. I was wearing a dress of silvery gray silk like a ball gown. It had three-quarter sleeves of soft lace.

Alexei saw the astonishment on my face. "She does not know, Julian."

Julian pointed toward the mirror. Alexei moved me in front of it, and I finally understood what he meant. On top of my dark hair was a crown. It wasn't some dainty fairy princess tiara. It was a real crown, heavy with its jewels and the responsibility of a monarch.

But it wasn't too heavy. It felt natural, like it was a part of me the same as my hair or my fingers.

I turned around and looked at Julian ready to ask a million questions. She stopped every one of them when she knelt in front of me and said, "My Princess."

Alexei bowed to me, still grinning. "I am glad you have accepted who you are, but it is time to return to the real world,

Elisabeth. This is too much like the dreamland, and we need you to focus on our reality."

"How do I do that?"

Julian stood and took my hand. "Just come back with us when we go out the door."

I nodded at her. "I can do that, but, Jules, please don't kneel in front of me anymore. It kinda freaks me out." She laughed as we walked out the secret doorway from my room. Crossing the doorway, the illusion of my mind gave way, and I saw the two of them sitting on either side of me on Alexei's bed.

Julian was still smiling even as tears ran down her face. Alexei had his palm on my cheek. I leaned into his warmth.

"Thank you for knowing how to find me."

Julian snorted a little. "She has done with an untrained mind what most of the Malhairer could never do no matter how much training they had, and she thanks us."

Alexei spoke softly. "Trained or not, powerful as she is, she needed us to help her find her way home."

"Is it over?" I didn't really mean to ask, but I couldn't stop the question.

Julian shook her head. "You know it isn't. Gideon is dead, but his mother is still the regent. You are safe for the moment, but you must begin training so that you will have control over your abilities. And we still don't know the secret your father's box holds."

Alexei pulled me closer for a moment before letting go. "When the Duchess hears of Gideon's death, she will blame you. It will cause her to hate you even more. She may not try to control you anymore and simply try to eliminate you."

"So definitely not over," I said with a sigh.

"It is over enough for a time. I will take care of the Academy's story for the fire, and continue my 'search' for your father's box. I should be able to give you time for your training as well as time to just be a teenage girl."

I smiled back at her. "I think I could handle that for a little while. What do we tell Charly and Emma? And Lila Grace?"

"Emma deserves the full truth. She has known what I am for so long and kept it secret. It would be wrong to lie to her now." Alexei looked at Julian for her agreement.

"You're right, but I still wonder how much she knows. You should have a private conversation with her at some point, Elisabeth." I nodded, glad that I would have at least one other person that I could talk to about all of this. Someone my own age.

"And Charly? What do we tell her?"

Julian was thoughtful. "The official story will be that Chase was caught in a fire that he was starting in the chapel. It is so beautifully close to the truth that even if someone from the Malhairer was checking, they would never find a lie. Lila Grace will be fine knowing that. We will tell Charly that Chase confessed to using drugs on her and the other boy. That he killed himself rather than face being caught."

"What about the other students, like Duncan and the girl that Emma saw? Can we do something to help them or will his death be enough?" I asked.

"You have a true monarch's heart, thinking of others. You're right, they will need help to recover from the manipulations of a fully blooded member of the royal court, but I will take care of it."

I frowned. "Can you explain that to me? I've heard you and Alexei say it, but I don't know what it means to be a fully blooded member of the court."

They exchanged another look over my head, and I knew I wasn't going to like the answer. Julian spoke hesitantly, as if she was searching for the right words. "I told you that the Malhairer are a hybrid, with some of the same abilities that a vampire has."

"Yes. You said we don't have to drink blood, but Gideon did. And he had to stay out of the sun the same way Alexei does."

"We are very closely connected to vampires. At some point in our existence, each of the Malhairer must choose the path before them. Some choose to age more like a human and limit the abilities they have. They continue to walk in the sunlight and live as close to normal human lives as we can. Some make their pledges to the Prince and the Blood Heir and continue the hidden existence of the Malhairer. Others choose to become blooded. They offer their lives in the service of the Prince, usually as guards or soldiers. We were at war with Alexei's family until my own childhood, Elisabeth. It was a sacrifice that limited their exposure to sunlight, but they gained amazing abilities that enabled us to stand up to any vampire, not just Alexei's family."

I turned to lean my back against Alexei's chest so I could face Julian completely. "How do they make this sacrifice?"

"They cut their wrists and allow their blood to fall into a chalice. It is primarily ceremonial, but they do drink from another chalice."

There was something she didn't want to tell me, but I couldn't find the right question. "What is in the other chalice that they drink?"

"Blood."

I frowned. "Their blood?" It reminded me of Alexei being fed his own blood back from the vampire who made him.

Julian shook her head. "No, not their own blood."

"Whose blood do they drink?"

Julian looked down. "They don't really drink, not like Alexei must. It's ceremonial, like a sip from a communion cup in a church."

"Whose blood is it, Jules?"

She sighed, and I knew I had found the question she didn't want to answer. "The blood of the Prince."

I wasn't surprised. If the Prince's will was the people's law, then there had to be deeper connections than just some mental abilities. Alexei had told me that he had wondered if the rituals were deeper than he had realized. "And the Prince drinks the chalice with their blood."

Julian looked at me with both surprise and guilt. "How did you know that?"

"It only makes sense. The Prince has to have their blood to complete the circle of the ritual. Are there many of these rituals that involve the Prince – or Princess – drinking blood?"

Julian shook her head. "There are a few, but you don't need to think about that now."

Alexei turned me so I could see his face. "It is not the same for the Malhairer as it is for me. Nicholas had already been named the Blood Heir before he came here. You will never be dependent on blood for your survival and you will never feel the cravings of bloodlust."

I smiled at him to thank him for reassurance. "But what about Gideon? You didn't call him blooded. You said he was fully blooded. What's the difference?"

"It was forbidden. I don't know when it first happened, other than it was sometime in the past when the Malhairer were at war with one of the old vampire clans-"

Alexei interrupted her. "The vampire clans were destroyed before I was born, all but the last." The final clan had been broken in Alexei's homeland, but not before he had been captured and changed. That was almost five hundred years ago.

"The Malhairer have been around that long?" I asked.

"Longer," Julian answered. "One of the warriors fighting the vampire clan was left wounded on the battlefield. Somehow he swallowed vampire blood. It changed him even more than becoming blooded had. He was stronger, he healed more quickly, and his mental abilities were incredible. But the price was too high. He began to crave blood. Except for his blood oath to the Prince, he was the same as any other vampire. He began to hate his differences and hate the Prince who represented all he had lost. He chose a warrior's death of honor before the taint in his blood could corrupt him to the point that he would no longer feel the pull of the Prince's will."

"What did he do?" I felt so sorry for the warrior.

Julian smiled slightly at my awed question. "He went with his brother away from the court. Away from all signs of civilization. They walked half the night, then found a place on the side of the mountain where they sat and talked until the sun came up."

"He killed himself while his brother watched? Why did he do that?"

Alexei answered the question before Julian could. "Because he loved his brother too much to ever risk harming him. If his blood oath could be broken by the vampire's taint, he wanted to die before he went mad. The bloodlust is difficult to fight."

I pulled Alexei's arms around me so that I could hug his arms, but Julian was not finished.

"Someone had to witness his death for it to be believed by the Malhairer. And when it came to his brother, Prince Augustin would not relinquish the duty to anyone else."

"Prince Augustin? The warrior was the Prince's brother?"

"One of your ancestors. It was then that the Prince first called us the Malhairer. Before that we were the people of Saint Clare, the Sinclairs."

"Why did he change it?"

"Malhairer means ill-fated. The Prince believed we were doomed for all our existence. It was one of your grandfather's most quoted stories. He believed he was suffering from the doom of all his ancestors. In the years since his death and since Nicholas was killed, there had been no Prince and no newly blooded warriors. The rise of powers within the court led me to believe that the practice of becoming fully blooded on vampire blood had begun again. I was right, but I don't know how far it has gone."

"If the taint of the vampire blood broke the blood oath with the Prince, what holds the new fully blooded members of the court in check? None of them have a blood oath with the Prince because there is no Prince. And how was I able to stop Gideon?"

Julian smiled and looked at Alexei before answering me. "It seems our Princess notices everything." She looked back at me. "Truthfully, Elisabeth, I don't know what keeps them in check or how you stopped Gideon. You should not have been able to do what you did. Call it luck."

Alexei interrupted. "Call it divine intervention."

"Whatever you call it," Julian continued, "it was something in you. Your grandfather lost only his wife. You have lost your parents, your home, your identity, and your inheritance. If anyone had cause to feel ill-fated it would be you. Yet you found something inside yourself that allowed you to enforce blood oaths that you have never received from a traitor whose oaths would have been broken by the vampire taint."

I shook my head and took her hand. "I know who I am now, and through the two of you I am finding my parents. We will reclaim my inheritance together. As far as my home-" I paused to join their hands between mine. "A home isn't a building; it's a shelter from the rest of the world. My home is with you."

"Then you have given me a home as well." Alexei kissed the top of my head and Julian smiled. Even though they didn't say it this time, I could see the same thought in both their faces. I was my father's daughter. In the room that had once been his, with his best friend and his roommate, I felt a peace that I had never known before. There was something in the room – the sound of my father's laughter, the lingering scent of his presence, the warm embrace of his love. It was nothing tangible that I could hold on to. It was an echo from the past connecting me to my future.

ABOUT THE AUTHOR

Laurel McKinley grew up in a small central Kentucky town where she spent most of her time reading, writing her own stories, and watching University of Kentucky basketball games. After graduating from Midway College with a BA in English, she attended Spalding University's Master of Fine Arts in Creative Writing Program. Capitalizing on her love of books, Laurel found a job at the public library in her hometown. *Echoes of Fire* is her debut novel and the first in the Echoes trilogy. Book two, *Echoes in Ice*, will be available in spring, 2014.

Laurel would love to hear from you. Find her at www.laurelmckinley.com.

Laurel McKinley

ACKNOWLEDGEMENTS

Writing can be a solitary process, but I could never have done this on my own. There are so many people that deserve to be thanked, but there are not enough words in the entire world to express the depths of my love and gratitude for you all.

First, I want to thank God for all of the blessings I have in my life: the ability He has given me to do this work, the supportive family and friends around me, and His divine arranging that led me to the right people at the right times.

My husband and sons have been patient and encouraging over the years, even when I stopped talking mid-sentence and disappeared into my fictional world for a while. I'm the luckiest woman on earth. Very special thanks go to my sister, Amy, who reads everything I give her and has been both carrot and stick to keep me writing. Thanks also to my extended family – you know who you are and what you do for me.

My friends and pastors, Jimmy and Melissa, you have both believed in me when I didn't believe in myself, and you always push me to be my best in everything I do.

My co-workers at the Woodford County Library, past and present, as well as the Writers Group at the library: You have been some of my earliest readers, my sounding boards, my cheering section, and my hand-holders. A special shout-out to Sylvia, Aly, Bookie, Geri, Jane, Bev, Jen, John, Kathy, Lynchie, and Karen, as well as Helen, Bryan, Ethan, John, Cindy, Jordan, James, and Jared.

The children and youth service librarian, Miss Becky, read this entire book in two different drafts. Your input, encouragement, and kindness continue to mean so very much to me.

Janice is my unofficial assistant and loudest cheerleader. Your excitement about my book gets me excited all over again. There will never be a way that I can show you what you mean to me.

Candace is my friend, lawyer, and editor. Thanks for helping this book become a reality.

I belong to a group of writers who have been an invaluable source of information and encouragement. I continue to learn so much from you, and I adore each of you. I must say a special thank you to authors Donna McDonald, Hallee Bridgeman, Kathleen Brooks, and Heather Sunseri, as well as to Bruce, Gregg, and Chris. You have all answered questions and calmed panic, sometimes without ever realizing it.

And last, but never least, I want to thank Heather Plunkett, the most amazing cover and graphic designer that I know, but even more – a true friend. You are such a talented artist and musician. I was really lucky that first May morning, standing outside the locked library, wondering where to go, that you were standing there too and we started this wild ride together. I could never have imagined everything that has happened since.